MAGIC

MAGIC

Edited by Sarah Brown
and Gil McNeil

BLOOMSBURY

First published 2002

This collection copyright © 2002 by Sarah Brown and Gil McNeil

Foreword copyright © 2002 by J.K. Rowling
Introduction copyright © 2002 by Sarah Brown

The copyright of the individual contributors
remains with the respective authors

The moral right of the authors has been asserted

Bloomsbury Publishing Plc,
38 Soho Square, London W1D 3HB

A CIP catalogue record for this book
is available from the British Library

ISBN 0 7475 5746 2

10 9 8 7 6 5 4 3 2 1

Typeset by Hewer Text Ltd, Edinburgh
Printed by Clays Ltd, St Ives plc

CONTENTS

J.K. ROWLING

Foreword

MY INVOLVEMENT with the National Council for One Parent Families came about either very simply, or very circuitously, depending on how you look at it.

The simple version involved Andy Keen Downs, the charity's Deputy Director, sitting down in my habitually untidy kitchen, pulling out a sheaf of notes from his briefcase and embarking on what I'm quite sure would have been a marvellously persuasive, well-constructed and beautifully delivered speech.

'Andy,' I interrupted, in that harassed voice by which lone parents can often be identified, 'you'd like me to be Patron, wouldn't you?'

'Well, we're calling it "Ambassador",' said Andy tentatively, cut off mid-flow.

'OK, I'll do it,' I said, 'but could we please discuss the details on the way to school, because Sports Day starts in five minutes.'

And so we discussed the National Council for One Parent Families while watching the egg-and-spoon races, a highly fitting start, I felt, for my association with a charity that is devoted to helping those parents whose lives are a constant balancing act.

The long version of how I became Ambassador

includes my personal experience of single motherhood and my anger about our stigmatisation by some sections of the media. That story starts in 1993, when my marriage ended.

I was living abroad and in full-time employment when I gave birth to my daughter. Leaving my ex-husband meant leaving my job and returning to Britain with two suitcases full of possessions. I knew perfectly well that I was walking into poverty, but I truly believed that it would be a matter of months before I was back on my feet. I had enough money saved to put down a deposit on a rented flat and buy a high chair, a cot and other essentials. When my savings were gone, I settled down to life on slightly less than seventy pounds a week.

Poverty, as I soon found out, is a lot like childbirth – you know it's going to hurt before it happens, but you'll never know how much until you've experienced it. Some of the newspaper articles written about me have come close to romanticising the time I spent on Income Support, because the well-worn cliché of the writer starving in the garret is so much more picturesque than the bitter reality of living in poverty with a child.

The endless little humiliations of life on benefits – and let us remember that six out of ten families headed by a lone parent live in poverty – receive very little media coverage unless they are followed by what seems to be, in newsprint at least, a swift and Cinderella-like reversal of fortune. I remember reaching the checkout, counting out the money in coppers, finding out I was two pence short of a tin of baked beans and feeling I had to pretend I had mislaid a ten-pound note for the benefit of the bored girl at the till. Similarly unappreciated acting skills were required for my forays into Mothercare, where I would pretend to be examining clothes I could not afford for my daughter, while edging ever closer to the baby-changing room where they offered a small supply of free nappies. I hated dressing my longed-for child from charity shops, I hated relying on the kindness of relatives when it came to her new shoes; I tried furiously hard not to feel jealous of other children's beautifully decorated, well-stocked bedrooms when we went to friends' houses to play.

I wanted to work part-time. When I asked my health visitor about the possibility of a couple of afternoons' state childcare a week she explained, very kindly, that places for babies were reserved for those who were deemed 'at risk'. Her exact words were, 'You're coping too well.' I was allowed to earn a maximum of fifteen pounds a week before my Income Support and Housing Benefit was docked. Full-time private childcare was so exorbitant I would need to find a full-time job paying well above the national average. I had to decide whether my baby would rather be handed over to somebody else for most of her waking hours, or be cared for by her mother in far from luxurious surroundings. I chose the latter option, though constantly feeling I had to justify my choice at length whenever anybody asked me that nasty question, 'So what do you do?'

The honest answer to that question was: I worry continually, I devote hours to writing a book I doubt will ever be published, I try hard to hold on to the hope that our financial situation will improve, and when I am not too exhausted to feel strong emotion I am swamped with anger at the portrayal of single mothers by certain politicians and newspapers as feckless teenagers in search of that Holy Grail, the council flat, when 97 per cent of us have long since left our teens.

The sub-text of much of the vilification of lone parents is that couple families are intrinsically superior, yet during my time as a secondary-school teacher I met a number of disruptive, damaged children whose home contained two parents. There are those who still believe head-count defines a 'real' family, who believe that marriage is the only 'right' context in which to have children, but I have never felt the remotest shame about being a single parent. I have the temerity to be rather proud of the period when I did three jobs single-handedly (the unpaid work of two parents and the salaried job of teacher – for I did eventually manage to take my PGCE, due to the generosity of a friend who lent me money for childcare). There is a wealth of evidence to suggest that it is not single-parenthood but poverty that causes some children to do less well then others. When you take poverty out of the equation, children from one parent families can do just as well as children from couple families.

My family's escape from poverty to the reverse has been only too well documented and I am fully aware, every single day, of how lucky I am; lucky because I do not have to worry about my daughter's financial security any more; because what used to be Benefit day comes around and there's still food in the fridge and the bills are paid. But I had a talent that I could exercise without financial outlay. Anyone thinking of using me as an example of how single parents can break out of the poverty trap might as well point at Oprah Winfrey and declare that there is no more racism in America. People just like me are facing the same obstacles to a full realisation of their potential every day and their children are missing opportunities alongside them. They are not asking for handouts, they are not scheming for council flats, they are simply asking for the help they need to break free of life on benefits and support their own children.

This is why I didn't need to hear Andy's well-rehearsed persuasive arguments on Sports Day. I had already made up my mind that it was time to put my money where my mouth had been ever since I experienced the reality of single-parenthood in Britain.

The National Council for One Parent Families is neither anti-marriage (nearly two-thirds of lone parents have been married, after all) nor a propagandist for 'going it alone'. It exists to help parents bringing up children alone, for example, in the aftermath of a relationship breakdown or the death of a partner, when children are faced with a new kind of family and one parent is left coping with the work of two, often on a considerably reduced income. It provides invaluable advice and practical support on a wide range of issues affecting lone parents and their children, and I am very proud to be associated with it.

The proceeds from the sale of this book will go towards the charity's Magic Million Appeal, whose funds will help maintain the broad range of services offered to lone parents who want nothing more than to pull themselves out of the poverty trap while bringing up happy, well-adjusted children. I would like to offer my very deepest thanks to the authors of the extraordinary stories that follow, and to everybody who, through buying this book, contributes to our appeal. You are offering hope to families who are too often scapegoated rather than supported – families who could do with a lot less Dursleyish stigmatism, and a little more magic in their lives.

SARAH BROWN

Introduction

T HIS BOOK is a wonderful read, full of original
stories by some of Britain's most talented and
acclaimed writers. It guarantees to immerse you in
wondrous tales of all descriptions. But the project has
a special magic thanks to the fact that the authors all sat
down for no fee to write their stories for this anthology.

The royalties they so generously donated will go to
the Magic Million Appeal for the National Council for
One Parent Families. Launched in June 2002 by the
charity's Ambassador, J.K. Rowling, the Magic Million Appeal is raising £1 million to deliver wider
advice and information services to some of the most
disadvantaged families living in poverty. £1 goes to the
Appeal for every copy of this book sold.

I became involved with the National Council for
One Parent Families in 1999 when Gordon and I
hosted a reception at 11 Downing Street to launch
their Freephone helpline. The helpline already takes
16,000 calls per year in England and Wales and thanks
to the support of the Royal Bank of Scotland and a
partnership with One Parent Families Scotland, it now
aims to double this by 2004.

For many of those families living in poverty, building a future can feel like an impossible hurdle, espe-

cially if the single parent feels there is no hope of building up the financial bridge and cultural capital to move forwards.

I remember the time my mother was raising my two brothers and me on her own. We enjoy the strongest of family bonds today with both our parents and our stepparents, but it was a tough period for us as we faced the task of rebuilding our own future.

The National Council for One Parent Families is there to provide the guidance, support and practical services that such families need. The funds from our Magic Million Appeal will go to expand its direct work and to support its partnerships with other charities and organisations. Not only can we work to provide better resources for families in need, but we can help put an end to the prejudice faced by single parents.

With the publication of any new book it is always astonishing how many people are involved – and this one is no exception.

The biggest thank you is, of course, due to all the authors for their wonderful stories – and to their agents for all their help.

The initial idea for the book came from my co-editor, Gil McNeil, whose experience before writing her own novels lies in the publishing world. Thank you to Gil for the brilliant idea and for her expertise in guiding me as a first-time editor, and to Joe McNeil for tolerating all those long phone calls that sometimes cut across his after-school quality time.

We are also grateful to Jo Rowling for lending her support to the book, as Ambassador of the National Council for One Parent Families, at an early stage, and for writing such a relevant foreword – it is not as though she does not have much else to do with her time.

The other charity Ambassadors, Kate Fawkes and Graham Taylor, and the members of the Magic Million Appeal committee, Amanda Cairns, Celia Brayfield (also one of our authors), Sue Slipman, the Duke of Devonshire, Neil Pearson, Mark Wnek and Catherine Porteous, have been great champions of the book as part of the whole Appeal. As have the whole team at the National Council for One Parent Families. All the staff are wonderful and their enthusiasm for the new work being made possible by the Appeal income makes it very worthwhile. Kate Green, the Director, and Andy Keen Downs, the Deputy Director, have been just terrific to work with on the Magic Million Appeal as have Nick Rose, Nemone Warner, Celia Joseph, Jane Ahrends, Deborah Stephens and Uche Opara.

As the National Council for One Parent Families hits its stride with new growth, a big tribute goes to Anne Spackman, the Chair of the Trustees, who has led the charity through this new exciting stage in its history, but has also been there in leaner times. She, and all the Trustees, past and present, are an inspiration to anyone considering giving time in the voluntary sector. They could write the 'How To' Guide. Thank you to Maeve Sherlock, who previously ran the National Council for One Parent Families, who has been a great ally and provided useful advice to us along the way.

Bloomsbury Publishing have been a wonderful partner in this project – providing for a generous contract to benefit the Appeal, and giving great attention to the development of the book. Thank you to everyone at Bloomsbury but especially Liz Calder, Katie Collins,

Rosemary Davidson, Minna Fry, Ruth Logan, Nigel Newton, Alexandra Pringle, Mark Rusher and Arabella Stein. Thank you also to Dotti Irving and Mark Hutchinson at Colman Getty PR for their publicity support. As professional a team of book publicists as you will ever find.

On the personal front, all books take up more time that you ever imagine and the support of family and friends lies behind any editor or author's work – not least when deadlines approach. Thank you to Richard Brophy and Angela Forrester for their administrative support, my brother Sean Macaulay, for his guiding hand over my few words, and my friend, Sue Nye. But most of all, I could not have done this without Gordon, and the support of my mother, Pauline Macaulay, and the rest of my family.

Through our experiences as parents in caring for our daughter Jennifer in her short life Gordon and I needed each other's love and support. I can't imagine how hard it would have been without Gordon there with me. I take my hat off to all parents raising their children on their own – they are all remarkable.

I hope you enjoy this book and thank you for contributing to the Magic Million Appeal as you do so.

Kate Green, the Director of the National Council for One Parent Families, gives you more information on the charity at the end of the book. Do get in contact if you want to know (or indeed give) more, or want to introduce the charity to someone you know who needs support as a single parent.

SUE TOWNSEND

Homework for Mrs Bishop

EVERYBODY THINKS that the worst day of my life was the day I come in here. But it weren't. It were the day my baby sister died. It happened when Dad was at work, and I was on my own with Mam. She said to me,

'Steven, ring Auntie Yvonne for me, her number's in the phone book under Y.' I went in the living room and picked up the phone book from off the arm of the settee where it was kept. I opened it but I didn't phone Auntie Yvonne because I didn't know which letter was Y. It was my biggest secret. Nobody knew I didn't know the alphabet. When I was in Mrs Green's class, and she taught us to sing the alphabet, I learned that all right. But when it come down to puttin' the sounds an' the shapes of the letters together, I just couldn't do it somehow.

I always thought that it would come to me in the night, and that the next day, at school, I'd be able to know which letter were which. But it never happened. Nobody seemed to notice though. When I went up to Mr Butler's class I were dead scared. He were very strict, and shouted a lot, and he made my heart beat fast whenever he looked at me. Soon after, I started to get bad pains in my stomach and I were away from school a lot. I went into hospital five times, sometimes in the middle of the night in an ambulance, but nobody could find a reason for the pains. I liked it in hospital, the sheets were clean, there were plenty of toys, I even liked the food. Mam and Auntie Yvonne came to see me every afternoon; Dad sometimes came, when he weren't working. The last time I went to hospital, I had an operation, the doctor said it was 'to explore my stomach'. Afterwards, a lot of doctors come to my bed, and one of them, the tallest one, said, 'Steven, we've taken a look inside your tummy, and everything is absolutely fine.' Mam was there and she said, 'So what's wrong with him then?' And the tall doctor's voice went quiet, and he said, 'We think the problem is inside his head.'

I never went to hospital again, an' I stopped avin' the pains.

I started gettin' into trouble at school, I were always late. I'd leave home on time, dead on half-past eight, and it were only round the corner, so I don't know what happened in that quarter of an hour. By the time I got there, the playground was empty, an' I could hear the kids and the teachers singing in the assembly hall. I'd go and sit in the cloakroom and wait until they all come out. Sometimes I felt like my legs had gone dead, like they was paralysed or something. I used to wish that Mr Butler had been in a car crash, or that his wife had died, so that he couldn't come to school that day. But he were always there in his brown suit and white shirt, and them hard, shiny shoes which made a loud click when he walked down the corridor towards me.

Don't get me wrong, I weren't stupid; if he asked a question like, 'What's the longest river in the British

Isles?' Or, 'How many days are there in a year?' or, 'What's the name of the Prime Minister?' I'd put my hand up so far, I thought I'd pull my arm from out its socket. And I'd say, 'Me, sir, me, sir,' under my breath. But he din't ask me very often.

He gave me a very bad report; it said, 'Steven will never learn anything, until he stops fooling about in class.' Dad took my bike off me for that one, and gave it to my cousin, Lee. The bastard used to ride past our house on it, and put two fingers up at me. I were glad when it got stolen from out his back garden. I even knew who took it, but I din't say ote to anybody.

Miss White should never have been a teacher. She weren't up to the job. Everybody played her up. Sometimes she used to run to the store cupboard and go inside and close the door, an' come out a bit later with her eyes all red. Also, she had a moped and a stupid blue crash helmet that everybody laughed at. I liked her nature table though, I gave her some conkers once, an' she said, 'Thank you, Steven, they're so beautiful.' She made the word 'so' last a long time.

Miss White taught our class to read with the Roger Redhat books. It was only me and Mark Foster who couldn't get the hang of them. Mark wore glasses so thick his eyes looked massive, like a photo of a fly that's been magnified a thousand times. He left at half term, and went to a special school. He's in a home for blind people now.

I was ten the day my sister died, and it was my fault. If I'd phoned Auntie Yvonne when Mam told me, my sister would have been living at home with Mam and Dad now. She would be fourteen with her whole life ahead of her. When I went back in the kitchen, on that day, Mam was sitting on the floor with her back against the washing machine, her face was screwed up and she looked ugly and scared. She said, 'Have you phoned Yvonne?' and I said, 'Yes, she's coming round.' Then she told me to go upstairs to the airing cupboard and fetch her some white towels. It was lovely and warm inside the cupboard, the towels were folded up, all neat and square. I put my head on them and stayed there for a bit; Mam started screaming so I went downstairs and gave her two towels. She put one of them between her legs and said, 'My waters have broke.' I didn't know what she was talking about then. I do now. She kept saying, 'Where's our Vonnie?' And I know it's daft, but I was waiting for Auntie Yvonne to come as well.

It got worse, Mam said, 'Phone your dad at his work.' I went out and did the same thing I'd done before, except this time I pretended to talk to the woman in the office at Dad's factory. All the time I was thinking that what I was doing was a bad thing, an' that this was going to get us all in terrible trouble. When I went back in the kitchen, Mam said, 'Is he comin'?' and I said, 'Yes, the foreman is giving him a lift.' Mam said, 'Phone Vonnie again.' While I were in the next room pretending to phone, Mam made a horrible noise, it were like an animal sort of sound. I thought that she would probably die, if she made another sound like that, so I phoned 999, and when the woman answered, I told her Mam was having a baby and she said she would send an ambulance.

It didn't take very long to come; when Mam heard the siren, she held my hand and squeezed it hard, then she told me to go upstairs to her bedroom and get the small green suitcase from under the bed. It wasn't zipped up so I opened it and looked inside, it was full of Mam's nighties and what looked like yellow doll's clothes. I zipped it up and took it downstairs, and then Mam sent me to the bathroom to get her toothbrush from out the holder, and get her dressing gown off the hook on the back of the door. I couldn't stand to see Mam's face, and the noises she was making. So I watched the second hand go round the clock on the oven instead. The ambulance men kept cracking jokes, while they put Mam in a little chair and wrapped a red blanket round her.

The neighbours came out to watch her being put into the back of the ambulance. Mam said to me, 'Stay here, Steven, Vonnie and Dad will be here soon, tell them to come down the hospital.' Then they banged the doors shut, and she'd gone. The house was so quiet; I could hear the water running in the pipes. I wanted to put the television on, but it didn't seem right. I was hungry, but it didn't seem right to eat either, so I sat on the stairs and pulled the bobbles of wool off my school jumper until it got dark, and Dad came home from work. When I told him Mam was in the hospital, having the baby, he ran upstairs in his dirty overalls, which smelt of oil and dust, and had a shower.

He came down in his best suit and the matching shirt and tie he'd got for Christmas. He smelled lovely. Then he rang for a taxi; he couldn't drive our car because he was saving up for a new engine. He kept walking up and down the hall, I think he was excited, he said, 'What do you want it to be, Steven? A boy, or a girl?' I didn't care really, but I said, 'A girl.' He said,

'Good, your Mam wants a girl. She wants to call her Lisa. Do you like it?' I said I did, and he nodded and said, 'It's what Elvis called his girl.' The taxi papped its hooter, and Dad said, 'Come with me, I'll drop you off at Grandma's.' Dad made the taxi wait for him, while he ran in Grandma's house with me. Auntie Yvonne was there, with Lee, they were eating beans on toast and watching the end of *Neighbours*. Dad said, 'Vonnie, come with me, she'll want you there.' And my auntie grabbed her handbag and her coat, and ran out of the door and got in the taxi.

It was like a speeded-up film, not like normal life. Grandma couldn't sit still; she kept wiping the surfaces in the kitchen, over and over again. Lee let me play with his Incredible Hulk doll, I took its vest off and put it back on again. But after that, I didn't know what to do with it, so I gave it back to him. Grandma said, 'Why've you got such a long face on you, Steven?' Lee said, 'He's jealous already, an' the baby's not even born yet.' They both laughed, and Grandma put her arm round me and said, 'You'll always be your mam's favourite, duck.' If I could have told anybody in the world, what I'd done, it would have been her. But I couldn't. My tongue felt as if it was trapped inside my mouth. I was surprised that any words came out at all.

When the phone rang Grandma snatched it up, like she did when a bit of coal fell out of the fire on to the rug. It was just me and her there, Lee had gone home. She mimed smoking a fag, and pointed towards the mantelpiece, where there was ten Bensons and a box of matches. I took them over to her and she lit one, and took a big drag. I waited for the smoke to come out of her mouth, but hardly any did. Her face changed, and she looked like an old woman. She took me with her to the hospital; we went up in the lift to the Maternity floor. Auntie Yvonne was standing by the coffee machine, she came over to me and slapped me hard round my head and shouted, 'You're a fucking little liar.'

Mam and Dad had a photo took of Lisa, but I have never seen it.

This is the longest thing I've ever wrote.

Dear Steven,

Well done! You have worked very hard, although occasionally your grammar lets you down. However, I am going to recommend to the governor that you be allowed to take English GCSE next year.

See you next week,

Mrs Bishop

P.S. I have left a copy of To Kill a Mockingbird *in the library – please ask for it at the desk.*

KATE ATKINSON

The Bodies Vest

VINCENT'S FATHER, Billy, died a woman's death in 1959. He had been washing the windows of their tiny Glaswegian eyrie and in an act of reckless bravado tried (and fatally failed) to reach the awkward top corner of the living-room bay. Billy was just twenty-four years old, a reluctant widower who had embraced his role as Vincent's lone parent with enthusiastic incompetence. Vincent's mother, Georgie, was already four years dead by the time her foolish husband plummeted on to the cracked concrete path in front of their tenement home on one of the long summer evenings of Vincent's childhood.

Vincent had a good view of his father's final moments, sitting as he was, one neighbouring storey lower, in the window of Mrs Anderson's flat, finishing off a supper of fried potatoes and Lorne sausage. Mrs Anderson was a homely barge of a woman, her grandmotherly bulk wrapped in a flowered Empire apron, who supplemented Vincent's rather meagre diet with a bottomless cornucopia of custard creams and bread and dripping. Mrs Anderson's small polished flat, scalloped everywhere with beige crochet mats and antimacassars and perfumed with Lifebuoy and fried mince, was a haven of domestic bliss compared to

Vincent's own home. For all Billy's efforts at housekeeping, father and son occupied a dingy set in which every available surface seemed to be crumbed with cigarette ash and desiccated fragments of pan loaf. Their clothes, washed to a uniform scummy grey, were hung to dry on the pulley above the gas cooker so that the scent of fried bacon was always on their skin.

Worst of all, perhaps, were the bed sheets, unwashed from one month to the next, pastel-striped flannelette on which no pastel stripes were now discernible and which were heavily impregnated with tangy male aromas. Vincent shared a bed with Billy even though there was a small box bed in the wall that would have done very well for him if it hadn't been occupied by an old dismembered BSA motorbike.

The windows, the cause of Vincent's orphan status at the tender age of six, had not been washed since his mother's funeral when Mrs Anderson had paid her own window cleaner to take care of them as a mark of respect. Vincent was two years old when Georgie died and had no memory of her at all so that what he felt was her absence rather than her loss. Vincent had an image of what life would have been like if his mother had lived. It involved living in a warm house and eating fruit and grilled chops, wearing clean, ironed pyjamas and sitting in front of a blazing coal fire while Georgie read out loud to him from *The Dandy*. Both Billy and Mrs Anderson implied, in their own ways, that it wouldn't necessarily be like that if Georgie was still around. 'Georgie was . . . flighty,' Mrs Anderson said, searching for an enigmatic word, so that Vincent imagined his mother as a ball of feathers wafted on a kindly wind.

Scant evidence remained of Billy and Georgie's existence as a couple, only a photograph on the sideboard in a tarnished frame which showed them on their wedding day looking far too young to make solemn vows about anything, let alone the rest of their lives. Billy was eighteen, Georgie sixteen. 'Already up the duff,' Billy explained sadly to Vincent when they occasionally contemplated this photograph together. In her knee-length, cheap bridal white, bird-boned Georgie looked as though she was attending her confirmation not her wedding, while Billy's jockey physique was ill-fitted to his borrowed suit. Even their names hinted at a childishness they would never grow out of. When Vincent himself was grown-up, he wondered if this was why they had given their unlooked-for son such a mature name – although later still Vincent suspected that he might have been named for the Vincent Rapide motorbike. As with most things to do with Billy and Georgie, it was too late to ask. Vincent supposed he was lucky he hadn't been called Norton.

Many years after their absurdly untimely deaths Billy came into possession of their wedding certificate but the 'William Stanley Petrie' and 'Georgina Rose Shaw' who were incorporated at Gretna Green in 1953 seemed to have little to do with the happy-go-luckily named Billy and Georgie of that nuptial photograph with their cheery smiles and accident-prone natures.

No one ever really discovered what happened to Georgie, of course. The way Billy told it she went out one evening and never came back – a simple narrative that explained nothing. Mrs Anderson's version of the tale was more complex – his mother had gone out for a drink with some friends, she was a 'very friendly' girl apparently, and had been found in a close the next morning by a milkman, strangled with one of her own stockings. 'No one deserved that,' Mrs Anderson sometimes said to Vincent, in a way that suggested his mother might have deserved other bad things that fell only slightly short of murder by persons unknown.

The last of the fried potatoes were cold and ketchup-sodden and Vincent's appetite had already moved on to a plate of snowballs sitting pristinely on Mrs Anderson's checked cloth when his father fell past the window like a wet sandbag. Billy's end had been presaged by the watery arc and clank of his galvanised bucket a split-second before Billy himself was pushed into space by the invisible hand of fate. Billy made no sound at all except for the muffled thud of his landing, a strangely anti-climactic noise like a shell failing to explode. Mrs Anderson, in a moment of elderly dis-traction, muttered, 'There he goes again,' as if Billy annoyed her on a regular basis with his giddy antics. Vincent had expected to look out of the window and see Billy laughing and dusting himself off and was surprised when all he saw was a crumpled heap, not immediately recognisable as his father.

Like Georgie before him, Billy was cremated, leav-ing nothing for Vincent but a few atoms dancing on the air.

Someone, somehow, traced Georgie's parents, or 'Mr and Mrs Shaw' as they seemed to prefer to be called. (It was with some difficulty that Mrs Shaw finally settled on 'Grandmother' as an acceptable epithet.) Mr and

Mrs Shaw ran a guest-house in Scarborough called (somewhat mendaciously) Sea-View. They accepted Vincent into their lives with considerable reluctance. 'You were the last thing we were expecting,' Mrs Shaw said, as if Vincent was a disappointment rather than a surprise.

A small attic room was cleared for Vincent. Georgie's old room had already been turned into a guest bedroom after Mr and Mrs Shaw decided some time ago that Georgie wasn't coming home. (They were right.) The last her parents had seen of Georgie was when she left the house one evening to go to the pictures with a girlfriend and never came back. It seemed disappearing was more of a personality trait than a consequence for Vincent's mother, although of course it later emerged that she hadn't met the girl-friend nor gone to the pictures but had run off with a fairground worker, a weasel-faced Scottish youth who had spun her round on the Waltzer before leading her astray on the beach. 'A greasy gypsy' according to Mrs Shaw. It was some time before Vincent understood that she was talking about Billy, his father. Vincent didn't think that Billy was actually a gypsy; he may have led an itinerant life but he had looked and spoken like a badly nourished Glaswegian.

Mr and Mrs Shaw had never met Billy, of course, and in their version of Georgie's life he was a swarthy ogre of a man who had carried off their not very innocent child. Even her own parents had to admit that Georgie was 'a bit of a handful'. Nonetheless, Georgie had been in possession of a school certificate, good RSA speeds (junior secretary in the planning offices of Scarborough district council!) and had

22

had a future ahead of her as the wife of some respectable East Coast burgher, instead of which she had
debunked with a microscopic Vincent in her belly and
fled to Gretna Green.

'She didn't have to do that,' Mrs Shaw told Vincent
irritably. 'We would have stood by her. Someone
would have adopted you.'

Mrs Shaw 'ran a tight ship' at the guest-house and
Mr Shaw, a man somewhat lacking in personality,
remained firmly second-in-command to his wife,
fetching and carrying breakfasts and coal scuttles
and wholesale boxes of breakfast cereals. Mealtimes
for guests were announced with a gong and were
served with commendable precision by Mr Shaw and
a squint-eyed girl called Lorna who slipped Vincent
forbidden chocolate digestives when Mrs Shaw
wasn't looking. Vincent and Lorna ate together in
the kitchen at odd hours in between the gong, dining
on toast and marmalade – a more palatable meal
they both agreed than the leftovers Mrs Shaw expected them to eat.

Sea-View was a veritable reliquary of Georgie's
effects – a scratched and muddied hockey stick in
the tool shed, her first pair of Start-Rite sandals in a
sideboard drawer. Her autograph book ('Georgie
Shaw's book – do not read on pain of death!') nestled
amongst Mr Shaw's Flanders and Swann records and
contained the mundane testimonials of her classmates
('Roses are red, violets are blue, sugar is sweet and so
are you' being the favourite token of no less than four
of her secondary-school consœurs). Vincent was particularly intrigued by the countless well-kept albums of
photographs which charted Georgie's progress from

premature birth but which stopped slightly short of her premature death.

Many of Georgie's girlish possessions had been boxed up and placed in the cellar where sea air and mildew had wreaked havoc on them. Her jewellery case, a musical box with a pert ballerina on the top, had rusted so much that the dancer now executed her pirouettes with an odd jerky intensity to the discordant music of metal grating on metal. Vincent was sad that he would never know what tune had once played on the box. ('*Au clair de la lune*'? Mr Shaw hazarded with little conviction.) Georgie's books – stories of wholesome, enterprising boarding-school girls with bemusing names like Jinty and Jax and Pippa – had become foxed and limp and smelt of earth.

Her collection of expensive dolls – sitting now on an ottoman in the Shaws' bedroom – had weathered better. Pale-faced and rosebud-lipped, they wore inscrutable expressions as they waited stoically for their owner to return. Vincent was forbidden to play with the dolls as the Shaws had developed a fear that his puny body and pale adenoidal countenance put him at risk of turning into 'a fairy' – a fate that sounded infinitely more attractive to Vincent than one where he was harried and bullied at school and largely overlooked at home, especially after Lorna left abruptly one morning on being discovered by Mrs Shaw in one of the guest bedrooms doing something unspeakable with Mr Shaw. Mr Shaw was allowed to stay on but from then on was treated by Mrs Shaw as little more than a deckhand.

From his attic perch, Vincent observed the family life he had always been denied – guests coming and going with their burdens of rubber buckets and spades, fishing nets and beach balls. The fighting, pinching, squealing children, the fretful mothers, the holidaying paterfamiliases attempting to sustain *bonhomie* – it all looked as mysterious as the adventures of Jinty. The Shaws never took Vincent to the beach, a place they held in contempt, and he was almost a teenager before it struck him that he could go there any time he wanted, although he hardly ever did as the Front was too disturbing – full of noise and sweat and stickiness. Vincent did not like the sea, he did not see a limitless grey horizon, he saw a careless edge over which anyone might fall and vanish into an infinite limbo.

Vincent's little bedroom was four storeys up so that he was able to get a good idea of how far Billy himself had fallen on his final day. Sometimes Vincent viewed it from the other way round – standing on the pavement looking up and trying to imagine what the expression on his father's face must have been when he found himself plunging to earth like a suddenly flightless bird. Vincent supposed it was one of astonishment.

Vincent had formed a theory – at the moment of death, he believed, a person would be doing the very thing that would have made him happiest in life. He hadn't known Billy well enough to be sure what that might have been but decided, in the absence of proof otherwise, that Billy flew off to his end on the seat of a 1952 Royal Enfield Bullet, a smile of bliss transforming his peaky face.

The Shaws liked Vincent best when he was quiet so he spent the rest of his childhood keeping out of the way. He became a bookish boy, introverted and obsessive, yet slightly more sanguine than might have been expected. When he was eventually accepted into a more than half-decent university to read English, Mrs Shaw remarked – by way of congratulation – that he must have got his brains from his mother, because he certainly hadn't got them from his father.

Mr and Mrs Shaw died in their separate beds many years later and long after Sea-View and its contents had gone up in flames while they were away visiting Mrs Shaw's sister in Warrington. When Vincent received the news of the fire he thought sadly of Georgie's dolls, their nylon hair incandescent, their patient plastic faces melting like candle wax. He thought, too, of Jinty and Jax and Pippa, once game for anything and now reduced to papery ash. Most of all he felt for the pert ballerina, her tiny foot stilled for ever, mid-pirouette. There was not even one photograph of Georgie left now; Vincent's mother had been successfully erased from history. Vincent did not dwell on this tragedy, however, because at the time that the last earthly relics of Georgie were being carbonised he was having round-the-clock sex with Nanci Zane and fearing that his brain might actually explode with ecstasy.

Vincent met Nanci Zane on a passenger ferry bound for Naxos when she came to his aid during a panic attack ('Hi, I'm Nanci with an i – breathe into this paper bag.') Nanci-with-an-i diagnosed agoraphobia caused by being afloat on so much sea. This was 1977 and Nanci was on a world tour after college ('Berkeley – English major') travelling alone except for a huge

26

rucksack which Vincent could barely lift. Nanci thought Vincent was cute. She mistook his timidity for reserve, his neuroses for eccentricity, his self-deprecating irony for sparkling wit – in short, he was the perfect English gentleman, particularly if you were an orthodontist's daughter from Sacramento who had never met an English gentleman before, perfect or otherwise.

Vincent was bewitched by Nanci's foreignness. For starters, she had a name beginning with a Z (or a Zee in Nanci's xenurine alphabet) and was almost unnaturally healthy – not only a vegetarian but a devotee of almost every form of exercise that Vincent had heard of and several he had not – the first person he'd ever met who did 'aerobics', something which at first Vincent thought had to do with airborne germs. She was also the first person Vincent had ever encountered with perfect teeth, teeth which 'Dad' had devoted much of his spare time to and which were indeed pearly – something Vincent had presumed was a figure of speech until he saw Nanci's small, opalescent molars and incisors. Her skin seemed to have been buffed and polished and it retained its California blush, even beneath the alien Manchester skies to which he subjected her while he finished his doctoral thesis – 'Body and Soul: the Transcendence of Death in Metaphysical Poetry'. ('Wow,' Nanci said, 'sounds cool.') Nanci 'wrote a little poetry' too but it tended towards Hallmark rather than Plath. Vincent told her it showed fantastic promise.

Nanci 're-rowted' her world tour after Naxos and went back to England with Vincent, sharing the poky redbrick terrace he rented, her wanderlust temporarily on hold while she took a course in art history and cooked complex complementary protein meals from the *Moosewood Cookbook* before demanding energetic sex. Sex with Nanci had a sporty rather than an erotic feel to it and after particularly vigorous sessions she would collapse (for a few seconds at any rate) and say, 'Wow, what a fantastic workout, Vince,' so that Vincent experienced pride for the first time in his life. Once, he asked her what the answer was that she'd worked out but she didn't understand his feeble joke.

For no obvious reason that Vincent could discern, Nanci suggested they get married, which they did with absolutely no fuss in a register office. Nanci wore a dirndl skirt, a denim shirt and a crocheted waistcoat and braided her brown hair in two thick Saxon plaits. For her bouquet, she carried a bunch of daffodils and was congratulated by a horde of friends all of whom she had accumulated with consummate ease in six months of living in Manchester. Nanci herself was the only friend of Vincent's at the wedding.

Vincent had absolutely no idea what Nanci saw in him but presuming it must be something to do with his Englishness he tried to play to his strengths – buying tweedy jackets with elbow patches, wearing spectacles he didn't really need and riding an old 1950s bicycle to and from university where he was now a junior lecturer.

Vincent and his new bride planned to abandon their damp Lancastrian abode at the end of the academic year and take a trip to California from which Vincent hoped very much that they wouldn't return. Nanci's family couldn't wait to meet Vincent apparently. The orthodontist had five daughters who all, from photographic evidence, looked just like Nanci who was the youngest. Vincent thought of them as 'the Zane Sisters', like quintuplets or a singing troupe. The whole family, even a couple of aunts, wrote letters to Vincent, welcoming him into their 'tribe'. Nanci's mother signed herself 'Mom'. Vincent couldn't wait to be absorbed into their miraculous, mysterious midst. He wondered if he could change his name to theirs – Vince Zane sounded so much more interesting (a cowboy or a gangster perhaps) than Vincent Petrie. His surname was the only thing that remained of his father now. 'And you,' Nanci said, 'you're his legacy, too, honey.'

Nanci had a rogue wisdom tooth which was the subject of endless professional-sounding conversations on the phone with her father in California during which they debated whether or not she should wait for him to fix it or put herself in the hands of a dentist to whom she was a stranger. Nanci was the favourite child of 'Dad' and consulted him about most things, tooth-related or not. In the end, the tooth became so painful that Nanci opted to have it done by an NHS dentist. Her father recommended full anaesthesia although the NHS dentist took some persuading, accustomed as he was to inflicting pain.

Vincent was giving a tutorial when the police arrived, a male and a female constable, who hovered politely on the threshold of the room as if they couldn't bring themselves to interrupt his ramblings on Henry Vaughan. They came with supportive expressions already fixed on their faces. Vincent had a surge of guilt at the sight of them although the last illegal thing he had done was to try – and fail – to smoke a joint in 1973.

They explained everything very carefully to him in the car on the way to the hospital but try as he might Vincent couldn't understand what they were saying. Even in the mortuary where he identified Nanci's body he still couldn't understand why she lay insensible and waxy with a large hospital sheet pulled up to her chin, 'Just like a corpse,' he said to the policewoman, who frowned and stared at the floor. Vincent was expecting Nanci to fling the sheet off and jump off the hospital trolley. But she didn't because she'd had a massive reaction to the anaesthetic in the dentist's chair and her heart had stopped and could not be persuaded to start again.

Nanci's family asked Vincent if he would mind if her body was shipped back to Sacramento and, seeing as there were so many more of them than there was of him, he felt it would have been churlish to refuse. The day Nanci was flown away in the cargo hold of an America-bound Boeing he spent his last minutes with her alone in the Co-operative Funeral Home. He had considered snipping off one of her plaits as a keepsake, the bright hair about the bone and so on, but in the end had decided it might look too obvious and anyway he wanted something more essential, something coralline or chalky – the bedrock of Nanci-with-an-i. To this end he came armed with bolt-cutters, purchased as furtively as a murder weapon from a local iron-monger. 'Sorry about this,' Vincent whispered to a silently decaying Nanci as he snipped off her little finger, wrapped it in a paper napkin and slipped it in his pocket.

As he stood on the observation deck at Manchester airport and silently saluted his cold, slightly incomplete wife as she rose into the sky, he clutched her finger in his hand. It wasn't the whole Nanci, but it was something. He hoped that at the moment of death she had found herself in the middle of a truly great workout and that it had given her the answers to all the questions she hadn't had time to ask.

'A relative?' a woman on the observation desk asked him as he gazed like an augur at the skies.

'My wife,' Vincent affirmed.

'She'll be back soon,' the woman said, sensing the quiver in Vincent's voice.

Vincent doubted that very much but he didn't say so.

If the Zanes noticed that a bit of Nanci was missing they never said so. They kept in touch with Vincent over the years. The sisters sent him photographs of weddings and christenings and family celebrations. He garnered formal portraits of various combinations of Zanes as well as less formal snaps of younger Zanes – in Little League livery, in Hallowe'en rig, in gowns and mortar boards. They all looked alike and Vincent had no idea who any of them were. 'Mom' sent him Christmas cards although a couple of years down the line she changed into 'Ellen' as if she had realised how absurd it was to call herself mother to a man she had never met. 'Dad' never wrote because he killed himself with a shotgun right after Nanci's death.

Vincent had thought about killing himself too but he was in thrall to such a numbing inertia that he found it difficult to do anything so decisive. For months afterwards he slept with the finger beneath his pillow and tried to dream about Nanci, but she never came. At first he had allowed the finger to mummify on the mantelpiece but it had arrived at such a disagreeable state, hard and wrinkled and so unlike Nanci's living digit, that he had rendered it – stewing it for hours in an old aluminium saucepan. This was not an act undertaken lightly and Vincent retched violently several times during the course of his unholy cuisine. He was satisfied with the result he achieved, however – the clean white bone that was freighted with a kind of magic. Of lesser things have saints been made, Vincent thought.

Vincent carried the finger bone in his pocket as other men might have carried a lucky coin or talismanic charm. Vincent hoped that if there was a Judgement Day – something he thought unlikely in the extreme – on the world's last night Nanci's soul wouldn't come looking for her body and discover it needed her stolen finger in order to be fully resurrected.

When Vincent himself died the finger bone was found and discarded by his wife as part of the meaningless jetsam of her husband's life.

Vincent died too young, everyone agreed, but in the end it was a peaceful 'crossing over' (his wife's preferred term). A virulent cancer had started in his lymph nodes and quickly metastasised first into his liver and then into his bones. At the end he was wreathed in morphine but right up until the last day was still able to recognise his wife and sons – two headstrong, angry teenagers quite cowed by his illness. He wanted to tell them that everything was all right, but he couldn't speak and besides he had no logical evidence on which to base that belief.

When Vincent entered into the world of light he was in the company of Georgie, exquisitely real and vivid in a way she never had been for him before. He was holding her hand and they were watching a flock of birds that were flying overhead. Starlings, Vincent noted, a species of bird he hadn't previously realised he liked so much.

Georgie herself, since you ask, was spinning round on the Waltzer when her soul took flight, for ever sixteen and all her life ahead of her.

JOANNE HARRIS

Class of '81

T HERE WERE twelve of us from that class of '81.
There they are on the photo, from right to left as
usual; Hannah Malkin, Claire Corrigan, Anne Wyrd,
Jane Beldame, Gloria Krone, Isabella Faye. Bottom
row; myself, looking impossibly young, then Morwenna Hagge, Judith Weisz, Carole Broome, Dizzy
McKelpie, in those coke-bottle glasses with her messy
red hair spilling over the collar of her uniform. Far left,
Paul ('Chalky') Wight, perennial top of the class and
the only boy. But that's witchcraft for you; the girls
outnumber the boys to begin with, although the high-
flying jobs always seem to go to the men in the end. I
wondered if this was the case with Paul Wight, and if
so, whether he was still single.

Already I was feeling a little nervous. We'd made the
promise twenty years ago, an unimaginable distance
away to our eighteen-year-old selves. Since then I'd
heard rumours, read a couple of pieces in the paper,
but otherwise I'd had little contact with any of my old
schoolfriends, except for the occasional greetings card
at Lammas or Yule. On the grapevine I'd heard that
Carole had joined a coven in Wales somewhere, that
Hannah had married an astral healer from Milton
Keynes, and that Isabella was some kind of consultant

in the City. It all sounded conventional enough. But second-hand accounts don't answer the real questions: who got fat, who lost their magic (or worse, dabbled with Kaos), who had a body job and lied about it afterwards.

Dizzy was the exception, of course. Who could fail to be familiar with Désirée McKelpie? She was practically a brand name – her face had looked out at us for the past fifteen years from tabloid newspapers, billboards, television screens. She worked love spells for Royals and Hollywood film stars. We knew her romances, her divorces; we sighed over her frocks and speculated over her diminishing waistline.

With a frown, I considered my own. Even at school I'd never been thin; not like Anne or Dizzy or Gloria. I'd skipped puddings in vain, and in spite of my efforts, thinness had always eluded me. Twenty years later, it still did. I wondered, rather petulantly, whose stupid idea it had been to hold our twenty-year reunion at Bella Pasta anyway.

I arrived too early. The note had said twelve-thirty and it was barely ten past. For a few minutes I lingered in the draughty doorway trying to look cool and confident, but people kept pushing past me to get in and I finally decided to take a seat at the big table at the back with the RESERVED sign and the little place-cards. Two girls sniggered as I squeezed past them, and I felt my face grow red. It wasn't my fault the aisle was so narrow. I clutched at my handbag for security and my hip brushed against a flower vase, almost knocking it over. The two girls sniggered again. It was going to be a nightmare.

I found my place (the name spelt wrong). There

were four bottles of wine already laid out, and four of mineral water. I poured a glass of red and drank it straightaway, then moved the bottle to the opposite side of the table, hoping no one would notice. Come to think of it, it was exactly the kind of thing a little sneak like Gloria Krone *would* notice, and draw attention to. I moved the bottle back.

Twenty years. Unimaginable time. I glanced at the photo again. There I was, demure in my little black uniform, holding my first broom proudly in my right hand. Of course the broom's mainly symbolic nowadays. No adult witch would ever choose to squander their *chi* on making a broom fly. Why bother, when you can get pampered in Business Class? Not that I ever have, of course. Alex says it's a waste of money. He even worked it out once; how you could buy three seats in Economy, a half-bottle of champagne, two Prêt-à-Manger sandwiches, a pashmina and a selection of toiletries *and still pay less* than you would for a Business Class ticket. Not that he ever does buy any of those those things. He thinks they're a waste of money, too. Come to think of it, the last time we flew anywhere was a budget trip to the Algarve in 1994, and he complained all the way because he said I was taking up too much space. Maybe a broom would have been better, after all.

I poured myself another glass of wine. It wasn't that I was dissatisfied with my life, I told myself. Who needs magic, when you can have security? Thirty-eight; housewife; married to a management consultant; house in Croydon; two boys, fifteen and twelve, and a familiar (for old times' sake). Deliriously happy. Well, happy, anyway. Well, some of the time.

Now the bottle looked three-quarters empty. It wasn't, of course; it's just the way bottles are made, so narrow at the top so that the moment you pour even a small glass it looks as if you've drunk half of it already. Now when the others came they'd all notice, and Gloria Krone would look at me with her long blue eyes and whisper something behind her hand to Isabella Faye – always her best friend in the old days – and the two of them would watch me like Siamese cats, purring with malice and sly speculation, 'Darling, do you think she's hitting the bottle? How *grotesque*!'

So I disposed of the evidence, and hid the bottle under a chair some distance from where I was sitting. Not a moment too soon; as I emerged from under the tablecloth I saw a woman – a witch – making her way towards me and was seized with a prickly panic. Standing up, wiping my mouth hastily with the back of my hand, I recognised Anne Wyrd.

She hadn't changed. Tall, elegant, blonde, wearing a black trouser suit over what looked suspiciously like nothing at all. I'd never liked her; she'd been part of a sporty threesome, all very well bred and jolly broomsticks. A second later, the two others arrived: Morwenna Hagge and Claire Corrigan, also in elegant black. I noticed in a moment's sly satisfaction that Morwenna had begun to colour her hair; then, with disappointment, that it suited her.

'*Darling*,' said Anne. 'You haven't changed a bit.' Her brilliant smile did not falter as she glanced down at the place-card in front of me.

I mumbled something inane about how stylish she looked, and sat down again.

'Well, one has to make an effort, sweetheart,' said

Anne, pouring herself a glass of sparkling mineral water. 'We're none of us eighteen any more, are we?'

The others were beginning to arrive now. In a burst of embraces and exclamations I saw Gloria and Isabella, more like Siamese cats than ever now, with matching blonde bobs and sleepy eyes, and Carole Broome, who I greeted with more warmth than I'd ever felt for her in the old days. 'Thank God, Carole,' I said fervently. 'I thought I was going to be the only one of us not wearing black.'

Carole had been a studious young witch in the old days, plump and lank-haired and earnest, more interested in herb lore than pyrotechnics, always the last to be picked in a game of Brooms. She was much thinner now, her hair had been braided and coiled, and she was wearing a long purple velvet skirt with an abundance of silver jewellery. I remembered the rumour that Carole had joined some kind of a radical Welsh coven, and felt suddenly uncomfortable. I hoped she wasn't going to bend my ear all lunchtime about pentacles and athames and going skyclad. I noticed, with a faint sinking feeling, that her place-setting was next to mine.

'Your aura looks terrible,' said Carole, sitting down and pouring water into her glass. 'Ugh! This water's carbonated! Waitress, please, some *natural* water, and can I talk to you about this menu?' The waitress, a harassed-looking girl with a ponytail, approached with understandable reluctance. Carole's voice was loud and flat and carrying. 'I notice there isn't a *vegetarian* option here,' she said accusingly.

Oh-oh. I flinched guiltily over the menu. I'd been thinking about getting the steak.

'Well, you could have the mushroom omelette or the fusilli' began the waitress.

'I don't eat eggs,' snapped Carole, 'and neither would you if you had any idea what it did to your karma. As for the fusilli –' She peered more closely at the menu, her eyes magnified by her glasses so that they looked like big green marbles. 'Is it *wheat* pasta? I can't possibly eat wheat pasta,' she explained to me as the waitress went off resentfully to talk to the chef. 'It's far too *yin* for my body type. Too much *yin* can cloud your aura. I think I'll be happier with just fresh, unfluorinated water and an organic green salad.'

Rather wistfully, I pushed the menu to one side. The steak and chips seemed to be receding into the distance. Fortunately I could see some other witches arriving, and I greeted them with ill-concealed relief. I'd always rather liked Hannah Malkin; and here was Jane Beldame, brisk and rather mannish now in a tweed skirt and jacket.

'Terrific to see you, old girl!' she exclaimed, engulfing me for a moment in a scent of wool and mothballs. 'Where's the booze?' She plumped down in the chair next to me (it was labelled 'Judith Weisz') and poured a hefty slug of red wine, ignoring Carole's squeak of disapproval. 'After all these years, eh? What larks we had!'

Now Jane was here I remembered them; midnight feasts in the dorm, with a glyph on the door to warn us if Matron was approaching; broom races along the Top Corridor; the time we sneaked Professor LeMage's pornographic Tarot cards and divined everyone's private fetishes . . . For the first time I began to think that maybe this reunion wasn't such a bad idea.

Judith Weisz came next, a colourless witch with bad skin who'd been less popular even than Carole, now looking much older than the rest of us, and making no protest when she found Jane occupying her place.

'Oh no, it's that creepy Weisz girl,' whispered Gloria to Isabella. 'Quick, push up so she won't sit here.'

Although Judith must have heard, she made no comment. Instead she made her way to the free place next to Hannah and sat down quietly, hands folded in her lap. I felt rather sorry for her, although we'd never been friends, and wondered why she had come.

At a quarter to one, there were still only ten of us at table. Jane had drunk three more glasses of red wine, Hannah was teaching me how to separate my astral arm from my corporeal one, Isabella was discussing body jobs with Claire Corrigan ('It's *not* black magic any more, sweetheart, absolutely *everyone* does it nowadays, there's no stigma at all'), Gloria and Morwenna were comparing love charms, Anne was interpreting the future from the dregs of Jane's wineglass, Carole was arguing with the chef ('How would *you* feel, if *you* were a tomato?') and Judith had just discovered a half-empty bottle of red wine under her chair when everyone fell silent as, fully conscious of the effect she was creating, Dizzy McKelpie made her entrance.

I remembered her as a small thing, pale and rather skinny, with quantities of red hair and ugly black-rimmed glasses. Now the glasses were gone, revealing huge eyes and lashes like moths' wings; the hair was artfully sleek, and her graceful figure was barely contained in clinging black jersey above a pair of scarlet, impossible heels. She commanded attention immediately; the other diners gaped; Dizzy pretended not to notice. Across the table I heard Gloria whisper to Isabella, 'Body job.' From the corner of my eye I saw Carole flick her fingers in the sign against evil; even Jane was watching open-mouthed. Apparently oblivious to all the attention, Dizzy walked to our table as if she were on a catwalk, and folded herself elegantly into her chair next to Judith.

'I'm so sorry I'm late,' she said sweetly. 'I had a meeting with a *very* special client who's been having the most *ghastly* trouble with the media.'

'Who?' said Gloria, wide-eyed.

'I couldn't possibly tell you. It's very sensitive,' purred Dizzy. 'I know you'll understand if I don't say any more.' She looked around the table. 'Isn't there someone missing?' she asked.

Everyone scanned the table.

'It's Paul Wight,' said Anne finally. 'I forgot about him completely.'

Easy to do, I suppose; Paul had been a brilliant student, completely devoted to his work and cautious of our female exuberance. This was generally taken to be a ploy on his part to intrigue and seduce us, but in spite of many efforts to enchant him, no one had ever managed. I now suspected that he'd been genuinely ambitious; girls had played no part in his studies. I doubted he would come today.

'Well, it's nearly one,' said Dizzy. 'If he isn't here by now, I think we should order. I've got a meeting at two-fifteen –'

Everyone agreed that no one should be expected to wait for Paul Wight, except Carole, who said that lunch, if taken at all, should never last more than half an hour, and Judith, who said nothing.

So we ordered. Carole had a special salad of karmically neutral vegetables ('Roots in general are too *yang*, and radishes have souls'); Gloria and Isabella the soup and ciabatta; Hannah the seafood tagliatelle; Claire, Morwenna and Anne the fusilli. Jane ordered the steak, very rare, and a double portion of chips – I looked at her enviously, wishing I was brave enough to do the same, though under Carole Broome's excoriating gaze I finally opted for a vegetarian pizza, which, though potentially dangerous ('Carbohydrates throw your chakras out of balance'), at least had the advantage of being karmically sound.

Only Jane had any dessert. Anne, Gloria and Isabella all seemed to be on permanent diets, Dizzy kept looking at her watch, and I suppose Carole's disapproving comments had done the rest. Instead, we talked. Someone (I thought it was Dizzy) made sure that the wine never quite ran out (much to the waitress's bewilderment), and conversation, hesitant at first, began to flow more freely. Perhaps a little too freely – now came what I had been dreading; the questions, the boastings, the lies. Dizzy led the conversation at first with anecdotes of media witchcraft, soon to be rivalled by Anne, who was a house expert specialising in cleansing and banishing rituals ('Feng Shui's just so last millennium, darling, shamanism's the thing now'); then Isabella, who worked with pyramids; Claire, who was a crystal-healer, married to an Odinist with two raven familiars and a wolf; Gloria, who had been divorced three times and was currently teaching a course on Tantric sex and meditation at the University of Warwick; even Hannah, who (to everyone's disgust but mine) had given up her job to devote herself to her husband and her little girl, already a budding witch at the age of four, and whom she obviously adored.

'You've been very quiet,' observed Carole, who had been watching me. 'How about you? Where have your studies led you?'

It was the moment I had feared. Explaining about Alex and the boys was easy enough (if uninspiring), but if she somehow discovered the real secret, the terrible, unmentionable thing . . . I said something flippant about motherhood being a full-time job, and wished Carole would choose someone else to cross-examine. But Carole was tenacious as bogwort.

'Your aura's very muddy,' she insisted. 'You haven't been letting your magic *slip*, have you?'

I muttered something about being a little out of shape.

'That doesn't sound good,' said Carole. 'Let's try a few simple exercises, shall we? How about a basic cantrip to begin with?'

'I don't think so,' I said, horrified, wishing she would lower her voice.

'Go on,' insisted Carole. 'Just a little one. No one's going to *laugh* at you, for Goddess's sake.'

Now everyone was looking at me. Gloria's eyes were narrowed and shining.

'Really, Carole,' I said feebly.

'You can manage a little one,' urged Dizzy, joining the game. 'How about a little levitation? Or a summoning?'

That was a laugh. If I could have summoned anything after all these years, it would have been a nice, deep hole to hide in.

'All right then,' she said, taking a candlestick from the table centrepiece and pushing it towards me. 'Just light this candle. Simplest trick in the world. It's like riding a broom. You never forget how to do it.'

Easy for her to say. I'd never been much good at Brooms, even when I was in practice. I began to feel sweat beading on my forehead.

'Go on,' said Dizzy. 'Show us how. Light the candle.'

'Light it. *Light* it.'

The others continued the chant, and I felt myself beginning to shake. The terrible secret – the thing no witch can ever admit – was about to be revealed. It was Alex's fault, I told myself, taking the candlestick in my hand and frowning hard at the cold wick. Being married to a non-witch is a bit like being married to a non-smoker; a daily clash of interests. Eventually someone has to give. And I was the one who gave; for the sake of our marriage and our children. Even the familiar – a black cat called Mr Tibbs – belongs principally to our boys (who don't have a spark of natural magic between them, being mostly devoted to football and cyberbabes), and spends more of his time shedding hair on the carpets and torturing mice than contemplating mysteries. All the same, I thought desperately, feeling my eyes begin to water with the effort of concentration, you'd have thought there was *something* left – some little squib – I could use now. I could hear Gloria whispering something to Isabella; from the corner of my eye I saw Dizzy watching me with that hungry, amused look, like Mr Tibbs outside a mousehole.

'Darling, I don't think she *can*.'

'She can't have —'

'She's *lost* it —'

'Shhh —'

Not even a cantrip — the smallest, most basic of spells. My face was scarlet; my armpits prickled with nervous heat. Not a glow, not a flame, not a spark. In desperation I looked up, hoping to see even one sympathetic pair of eyes, but Hannah was looking uncomfortable, Judith seemed half asleep and Jane was far too occupied with her second slice of chocolate cake to take notice of my plight. Dully I saw myself as the rest saw me; a fat, unfulfilled drone who couldn't even light a candle.

Then, suddenly, there was a flash between my fingers, followed almost instantaneously by a smell of burning. I jerked my head away just in time; flames were streaming from the candlestick; the candle itself almost consumed in blue-and-green fire. Half a second later the candle shot right out of the candlestick and exploded in a spray of coloured sparks over our heads. No one else seemed to notice at all — someone had cast a magical shield over the table.

Gloria, who had been leaning forward rapaciously, leapt back with an undignified squeal. Carole stared at the blackened candlestick in amazement.

'I thought you said you were out of shape!' she said at last.

I thought quickly and hard. Someone had helped me, that was certain; someone who didn't want to see me humiliated. I glanced up, but could see nothing more than spite, curiosity, outrage or surprise in the faces around me. Dizzy was frantically brushing sparks out of her long hair. A cinder had fallen into Isabella's glass, splashing her with wine.

'Golly!' said Jane, impressed. 'What happened there?'

I tried to smile.

'Joke,' I said weakly.

'Some joke,' grumbled Gloria. 'You nearly burnt my eyebrows off.'

'More power than I thought,' I muttered.

Relieved beyond words, I poured myself a glass of wine. For once, Carole didn't comment. I could see she was awed in spite of herself. I spent some time evading her questions; where had I done my advanced training; had I achieved spiritual illumination; who had been my mentor.

'You haven't been dabbling in anything you shouldn't, have you?' she asked suspiciously, when I modestly declined to answer.

'You mean Kaos? Don't be silly.'

I almost laughed. It takes a lot of work to become a Kaos illuminato, and I'd never even understood the principles twenty years ago. Carole continued to look at me suspiciously for a while, then, to my relief, the conversation turned to other things. Old quarrels revived, small sillinesses remembered, practical jokes relived. The noise escalated gradually; at times I could hardly hear what was being said on the far side of the table. Even I, cheered by the wine and the unexpected miracle of the rocketing candle, felt my inhibitions begin to leave me. Maybe the wine was stronger than I'd thought. Or maybe it was just the company.

But it was when Anne, Morwenna and Dizzy began a violent argument about a disparaging comment

46

Dizzy had once supposedly made to Anne about the shape of Morwenna's calves, Judith was apparently asleep, Isabella was explaining the finer points of sex-magic to Jane (with the aid of diagrams drawn on to the tablecloth in Biro), and Gloria was trying to demonstrate how to change a salt-cellar into a hamster, that I realised what had happened. This was not simply a case of good cheer gone slightly out of hand. Someone had magically spiked the mineral water.

'It's disgusting, that's what it is,' said Carole, who seemed the only one unaffected. 'Cavorting about like a gaggle of goblins. I thought this was going to be a meeting of *minds*, an opportunity to share the experiences of twenty years' travel on the Path of the Wise.'

'Oh, put a sock in it, Carrie,' said Anne, whose hair had come down in the course of the argument. 'You always were a most frightful little bleater. No wonder you ended up in a commune full of sheep.'

'Now look here –' said Carole, losing much of her smug self-satisfaction. 'Just because you were coven captain three years running –'

'Girls, girls,' said Dizzy. 'Is this any way to behave?'

'You can shut up as well,' said Carole. 'You and your media magic. And if you *really* believe that body job of yours looks anything other than *grotesque* –'

'*Body job*!' squeaked Dizzy, outraged. 'I'll have you know my body's *perfectly* natural! I take *care* of myself! I work *out*!'

'Come off it, darling,' said Morwenna sweetly. 'It's nothing to be ashamed of nowadays. Lots of witches have a little cantrip or two set by for when things begin to sag.'

'Well, it'd take a hell of a lot more than a cantrip to fix those fat calves of yours.'

I tried to intervene. I could feel a buildup of static in the air which raised the hairs on my arms and made my skin prickle. Powerful magic was building. And quickly. I wondered what exactly had been added to the drinks. A truth spell? Something worse?

'I say –' I began.

But it was too late. They were engaged. Morwenna made a grab for Dizzy's hair; Dizzy's hand shot out at Morwenna, and ropes of magic were suddenly swarming and hissing over both of them. The two witches jumped apart like doused cats, their hair standing on end.

'What did you do?' snarled Dizzy, her poise gone completely.

'Nothing!' wailed Morwenna, shaking her numbed fingers. 'What did *you* do?'

I was only happy that the shield spell over our table was still holding. Beyond it, the other diners munched on, oblivious.

'What larks,' commented Jane happily, finishing her second piece of chocolate cake. 'Just like the old days.'

'Precisely,' said Judith Weisz with a hint of sarcasm.

I'd almost forgotten about her; she had seemed half asleep during most of the meal, and as far as I knew, had hardly spoken a word. She'd been no different twenty years before; a silent, unattractive young witch who was excused from sports for some medical reason; who never seemed to get any letters from home and spent every Yuletide holiday at school. I'd had to stay myself once; my parents had had to go to an occult conference in New Zealand and I was left at school feeling thoroughly miserable, in spite of the trunkful of presents they had sent me. All my friends had gone home for the holidays, and only Judith remained. I'd already known she never went home for Yule, of course, but I'd never really thought about it before. Now I did. If she had been more approachable, and less devoted to her studies, we might have used the opportunity to become friends. But I quickly found out that Judith alone was as drab and monosyllabic as Judith in a crowd. She did not seek me out, seeming quite content to spend her days alone in the library, or in the herbarium, or the observatory. All the same, she was the only company around, except for a few masters and their familiars, and one night the two of us had shared the last of my Yule log and a bottle of elderberry wine. I'd almost forgotten about that until now; afterwards we had gone on with our studies as before, and the following year had been our last. I looked at her now.

'What did you do after school, Judith?' I asked.

She shrugged.

'Nothing much,' she said. 'I got married.'

I hoped my surprise didn't show on my face.

'He's a psychonaut,' went on Judith in her cool, quiet voice. 'He lectures in Morphic Field Theory and the Chaoetheric Paradigm.'

'Really?' I barely knew the terms; those theories had been far beyond even our most advanced courses. 'How about you?'

Judith gave a chilly smile.

'I became a metamorphosist. A shaper, if you like. Specialising in body jobs for the karmically unconcerned.'

'Goddess,' breathed Carole, who had been listening. 'You're a Kaoist.'

'Someone has to do it,' said Judith. 'And if people want to pay for my services rather than studying the arts for themselves –'

'Pay with karma taken from their next lives!'

Judith shrugged.

'Who cares?' she said. 'If Dizzy wants to spend her next life as a radish, who am I to criticise?'

Everyone was staring at us now. Dizzy's face was white.

'You always looked down on me,' said Judith in the same colourless voice. 'I was always the coven joke.'

'Judith –' I said uncomfortably.

It had occurred to me that with her resources it would be child's play now for Judith to use her powers of metamorphosis to change us all into cockroaches, if she chose to do it. Now I understood who had helped me light the candle; my throat felt suddenly rather dry.

'None of you have changed much since then,' went on Judith calmly. 'Gloria's still a little sneak; Dizzy a silly attention-grabber; Anne a snob, Carole a talentless phoney. None of you are *real* witches at all –'

(Carole gave a squeak at this, but changed it hastily into a cough.)

Judith turned to me.

'Except for you,' she told me with half a smile. 'I haven't forgotten that Yuletide when you shared your cake with me in the dorm. Fortunately, I can keep a secret,' said Judith, looking at Dizzy, though I felt maybe she was speaking to me. 'And I don't believe in revenge.'

She had stood up during this little speech, and I

noticed for the first time how tall she was. I wondered, too, why I had thought she looked old; now she looked *young*; clear-skinned; almost beautiful.

'Well,' she said in a lighter tone. 'I think that's all I wanted to say. My husband said he'd call for me about now, and I don't want to keep him waiting.'

We watched her go in silence; for once, there were no whisperings between Gloria and Isabella, and even Carole had no comment to make. Then, when we were sure she had gone, we all ran to the window. We saw them then for a moment, the *real* witches; walking away hand in hand. The man was tall and fair-haired; for a second I thought I recognised Paul Wight, though there was no way of knowing for sure. He and Judith walked slowly down the street, and I wondered how it was possible for two people to look so free and calm and so sure of themselves and the future. I watched them into the distance, as around me the other witches slunk back one by one to the table and conversation slowly returned. I thought maybe the pavement shimmered a little in their wake, but I could not be certain of that, either.

FAY WELDON

The Site

I T WAS my cleaner Susie who first told me what was happening at the site. 'Cleaner' is the word Susie uses to keep me in my place: she seems rather more like a friend and ally, but she enjoys these social distinctions. She's the policeman's wife: she comes up to my rackety household and helps out because she's bored, or so she says, and points out that I'm an artist and not a housewife by nature, as she is. Everyone should do what they're good at in this life, she maintains. She, by implication, is good at housework: I am not.

I'm a professional sculptor. The children are with their father during term time, but I still need help to keep domestic matters under control. I live in the village of Rumer in Kent, outside Canterbury, in a farmhouse. At the time I had two goats, two dogs, three cats, a pet hen, and an electric kiln in the barn. I did a lot of work in papier mâché, and it tended to creep out of the studio in shreds and scraps, and was even worse than clay for mess. If there's too much mess I can't concentrate. If there's no food in the fridge I don't stop to eat: then I'm too hungry to work. Susie keeps things in balance. I believe her to be some kind of saint. Calling her the cleaner is rather like calling Moses the jobbing gardener because he smote the rock. If I say this kind of thing to her she seems immeasurably shocked.

Susie's husband works in town and though he is always kind to me, I would not want to be the criminal who crossed him. He has managed to build the fanciest bungalow in the village, and Susie keeps a perfect garden. Rumer is a pretty, peaceful and prosperous place and has won the best-kept village in Kent competition two years running, having survived BSE, foot and mouth, the falling off of the tourist trade – it has some good Roman ruins – and kept its village store and post office. But Susie is right: as a place it can get a bit boring. My two children, in their teens, try not to show it but are always happy to get back to town at the end of the holidays.

But nothing happens and nothing happens and then all of a sudden everything happens, in places as in people's lives, and what was to happen, what was to be described in the papers as the Affair of the Rumer Site, was to take everyone by surprise.

Susie has a part-time job at the local comprehensive school, as a personal counsellor. It is her task to take alienated and troubled children under her wing, get them to school if they are truanting, sit with them in class if they are school refusers, help them with lessons they don't understand, and stay with them in the playground if they are bullied. She is not trained in any way to do it – the school can't afford anyone expensive – but there is something about her apparently stoical presence which means the pupils seem to accept her as one of their own. She is passionately on the children's side: only occasionally does she raise her eyes to heaven and shrug. Hopeless, why waste the State's money and my time. Let them go free.

One Friday afternoon in mid-July she turned up with the ironed sheets, disturbed and upset. (I have never yet ironed a sheet: Susie will not make a bed without first doing so. She has an ironing press: I have not.) The weather had been very hot: drought had set in; it was in that curious inconclusive patch of time after exams have finished and school hasn't yet shut up shop for the holidays. I'd been trying to finish the ceramic triptych I was working on before the children came down for the summer, and had managed it with a day to spare. I was exhausted and dehydrated, after days with the kiln, and still not quite back in the real world.

Now here was Susie sitting at the kitchen table actually crying. She said she had taken a group of her rejectees, as she called them, down to see the site. She'd thought the children would be really interested to see the unearthed graves and the skeletons still lying there, two thousand years on. But they had been indifferent, looked at her as if she was crazy to take them all the way in the heat to look at a few old bones, and one of the girls, Becky Horrocks, had tossed her cigarette into the open grave.

'What site? I asked. 'What graves?'

I'd quite forgotten. The row – about building the biggest shopping mall in all Europe on a site desig- nated as an area of natural beauty and scientific interest, just a mile south of Rumer – had been rumbling on for so many years I had assumed it would never be resolved. But apparently it had, the devel- opers had won, work had begun within the day and the bulldozers had been in skimming the site.

54

So much for the grebes and the greater crested warbler and the lesser toad and the marsh pippin: they would have to fend for themselves. As would the village shop, newsagent and post office. All must bow down in the face of progress: all must be sacrificed to the temple of Mammon. It was monstrous. Though as I sat there at the table with the dogs panting beside me in the heat, the thought of the chilly air around the long stretches of frozen-food cabinets filled me with delinquent delight.

'They've uncovered a Roman graveyard,' said Susie. 'Twelve graves still with the bodies in them. And what Carol says is a Druid's well but you know what she is.'

Carol was the local white witch: she had a mass of long white hair and a penchant for crystals and goddess worship. She also ran, rather successfully, the local estate agency. She was widowed and had taken on the business after her husband's death, but had changed her manner of living and dressing. Now she saw faces in the running brook, heard the Great God Pan rustling in the hedges, and suspected any stranger in the village of being an extra-terrestrial visitor from the Dog Star Sirius. But she could sell any property she set her mind to. I think she used hypnosis.

'I hope they stopped work,' I said and Susie said they had, but only just, only because there was a handful of protesters still parading the site, and they'd seen a skeleton go into the skip along with the top sward, the rare ferns, the lesser celandine and lumps of sticky yellow clay, and had called the police, who came without riot gear, and were very helpful and refrained from observing how quickly they ceased being pigs and scum when anyone actually needed them.

The police had made the JCBs pull back, and Riley's the developers keep to the letter of the law and call in the archaeologists, no matter how their lawyers protested that they were exempt, and that every day of stopped work cost them at least £100,000. And there the skeletons lay, indecently uncovered – except the one rescued in bits from the skip, now at the county morgue being dated and pigeon-holed – waiting for their fate to be decided.

There'd been nothing in the local paper, let alone the nationals. Susie reckoned Riley's had made sure of that. They didn't want sightseers holding up the work.

'That's horrible,' I said. 'The age of a body doesn't make any difference. Two thousand years ago or yesterday, it's the same thing. It deserves respect.'

Susie said what bothered her so about Becky Horrocks, the girl who'd thrown the cigarette stub, was how little she must care about herself, if she cared so little for the dead.

That evening, when the sun stopped baking and a cool breeze got up, Matt and Susie called by and took me down to the site. How parched and dry the landscape looked! I had a bad back from heaving stuff in and out of the kiln and my hands were rough and blistered, but the triptych was ready to go off. It was a commission for Canterbury Cathedral, and was part of some European-funded art and religion project. It would be touring the cathedrals of the country over the next year.

I am not a particularly religious person – not like Susie and Matt, who go dutifully to Rumer parish church every Sunday and twice on Christmas Day – but then I was not required to be: just a good artist.

The theme of the work was the coming of Christianity to the British Isles, which heaven knew was shrouded in myth and mystery anyway, and my guess was as good as anyone's.

The centre panel was the child Jesus sailing in to Glastonbury around the year 10 AD with his Uncle Joseph of Arimathea – a tin trader – and almost certainly myth. The right panel depicted Saint Pirran sailing to Cornwall from Ireland in a stone coracle – the stuff of magic, a tale drifted down from the sixth century. On the left was Saint Augustine, riding into Canterbury in 605 AD with his retinue of forty monks, sent by Pope Gregory to bring the gospel to the heathen English, for which there was a basis in history proper. The panels were in bright flower-bedecked colours, designed to glow and shine in the vaulted gloom of the cathedral: light breaking into darkness. I was really pleased with it but doing it had left me exhausted.

I thought perhaps it was exhaustion that made me react as I did. The desolation that a handful of JCBs can wreak in a couple of days is extraordinary. The whole valley was down to subsoil: a great stretch of yellow-grey earth taking up the space – perhaps half a mile across and two-thirds of a mile long – between two untouched still green and verdant hills, stretching like tautened muscles on either side of the scar. I began to cry. How could I have been so indifferent as to what was going on around me? Matt looked embarrassed.

Susie took me by the hand and led me to a square patch of stony ground, more grey than yellow, which rose above the surrounding clay. She was wearing a neat green shirtwaist dress and lace-up walking shoes.

I was in an old T-shirt, jeans and sandals. Susie always dressed up to go out: now I unexpectedly saw my lack of formality as rash. It made me too vulnerable. The living should dress up to honour the dead.

There were I suppose a dozen graves, running north to south: some were no more than oblongs let down into bare earth, others were lined with what I supposed to be lead. In the bottom of each lay a skeleton: long strong white bones; some disturbed by animals – rodents, I suppose, or whatever disturbs the dead underground, over centuries – but for the most part lying properly, feet together, finger bones fallen to one side. Scraps of leather remained in the graves: what looked like a belt here, a sandal thong there. I was distressed for them.

'They can't just be left here on their own, exposed,' I said.

'They're well dead,' said Matt. 'I don't think they'll mind.'

The wind got up a little and dust and earth swirled round the graves; already the sharpness of their edges was beginning to dull. If only rain would fall. The green surface of mother earth is so thin, so full of the defiance of the death and dust that lies beneath.

'I wonder who was here before us,' said Susie, 'laying them to rest so long ago. Young strong men: how they'll have grieved. And we don't even know their names.'

Matt was stirring the ground with his foot and turning up a few pieces of what looked to me like Roman tile.

'Reckon there's another Roman villa round here,' he said. 'That won't make the developers too happy.' But he reckoned they'd manage to get the archaeologists on site, and forget about it and build anyway. They'd go through the motions but there was too much at stake to hold up work for more than a week at the most.

Susie and I said we'd take turns grave watching. It didn't seem right to leave the graves unattended. I'd take the shift until midnight, then she'd turn up in their camper van and spend the rest of the night on site. Matt said we were crazy but went along with it. Indeed, he said he'd relieve his wife at six and stay until eight when he had to get to work. Surely by then Riley's would have got their act together and organised a watchman, and the archaeologists would turn up to do whatever they were required to do under statute.

I sat and watched the sun set and the moon rise, and the white bones began to glimmer in their graves. I thought I could hear the sound of Romans marching, but that was imagination, or a distant helicopter. I drifted off to sleep. It wasn't at all creepy, I don't know why: it should have been. There was a kind of calm ordinariness in the air. My earlier distress was quite gone. At about eleven Carol turned up with a massive flashlight and a camping chair and table and some sandwiches and coffee. She'd been through to Susie on the phone. We sat quietly together until Susie relieved us: bump, bump, bump in the camper van. Carol took me home and I slept really soundly, though in the morning my back was bad again.

I rang the Bishop's Palace to ask about re-interring the bodies. I couldn't get through to the Bishop but I explained the situation to some kind of sub-canon and he said they were well aware of it, and since the graves were lying north to south, they were not Christian burials in the first place, but pagan and nothing to do with the Church. It was up to the civil authorities to do what they decided was best. The University of Birmingham had tendered for the contract: the site was to be photographed and mapped – there had indeed been a Roman villa on the site, as well as a pottery and a graveyard – but take off a layer and the country was littered with them. The bones? They'd be placed in sealed plastic bags and taken off to the research department at Birmingham for medical or other research.

'Pagan?' I enquired. 'I thought we were all ecumenical, now.'

But no. Ecumenical did not extend to heathens. I pleaded without success but the bishopric was unmoved, nor would they put me through to anyone else. I thought about withdrawing my triptych from the cathedral in protest but couldn't bear to do that.

I went down to the site later in the day. The whole world seemed to be out and about in the hot sun, and not a scrap of shade. The graveyard area was roped off, there were security guards, the JCBs buzzed away at the far end of the site, archaeological students peered and measured. A handful of old ladies from Rumer had brought chairs and were sitting round what I saw as the master grave – it was lead-lined, decorated, and larger than the others. They were knitting. They were like Furies, or the Norns, or some kind of Greek chorus – but knitting. Well, this was Rumer. An ice-cream van plied its wares: word was beginning to get round: people were turning up in cars to stare and marvel.

Earth-moving machinery rumbled, turned, groaned and cranked in the distance, but management – you could tell them by their grey suits and pale faces, sweating in the heat – were everywhere. Carol was in urgent conversation with a grizzled man in a hat looking rather like Harrison Ford who was sitting on the end of the master grave making notes and taking photographs. A helicopter swept to and fro over the site, presumably doing the aerial survey the Canon had spoken of.

'What's with the old ladies?' I asked Carol. 'I didn't know they knitted.'

'They're from the church,' she said. 'They're making a knitted patchwork tapestry to auction for charity. They usually sit and do it in the church hall but they felt like some fresh air and all trooped around here.'

'Isn't that rather peculiar?' said I.

'No more peculiar than you and Susie sitting out here all last night,' said Carol. 'The archaeologists aren't very friendly. They're on the developers' side. Well, they're the ones who're paying. They're making a survey of the site, then they're sealing it and the shopping mall goes ahead on top of it.'

'I'll call the newspapers.' I said. 'It's a scandal.'

'The living have to exist and do their shopping,' said Carol. 'Along with the mall go sixty starter homes, a foot clinic with accommodation for six nurses, and an Internet café free for under-eighteens. Riley's put out a press release today.'

'It's still a temple to Moloch,' I said. 'And personally I have no intention of worshipping him.'

Susie came up. She had a party of A level pupils with her, the cream of the bunch, bright-eyed and bushy-tailed, making notes as to the manner born.

'They reckon the villa dates from around the first half of the first century,' said Susie. 'And the graveyard too. I reckon it's something really special but they can't afford to admit it.'

I remonstrated with the Harrison Ford look-alike: there had to be some kind of ceremony, I said. He couldn't just pack the skeletons up in plastic bags so they lay on dusty shelves for ever. He spoke Nottingham, which was rather a pity, not Hollywood. He dismissed me as a middle-class busybody. The life of the real world had to go on. It couldn't be forever caught up in its past. Fine words, I thought, for an archaeologist. A *trahison des clercs*. Even the academics had forsaken us, and bowed down before Mammon. We had quite a row, which he won. When I got to the station to meet the children I was still quite pink with anger. They had brought computer games with them. I took them down to the site: they were moderately interested, out of politeness, but not much.

'They're just old bones,' they said. 'Chill, Mum,' and went into a chorus of dem bones dem bones dem bones dry bones; I supposed they'd seen piles of bodies on TV in their time. I always looked away at the horrors. I turned on the news to find out what was going on in the world. An official drought had been declared. Hosepipe bans had been imposed in most parts of the country. That would put paid to the lettuces, already struggling, and the gooseberries would be tiny and sour.

Their father was going to marry again. That was

62

OK by me, and by them. They seemed to like her. We were all on good terms. It's always rather a shock, though. The children said I should marry again; it was easier for them if there was someone to look after me. I said I didn't need looking after and they laughed hollowly.

That night we stood around the special grave, the master grave, the grave of the tallest soldier, in the moonlight. There was Susie, Carol, Carter Wainright and I. Riley's didn't run to a night watchman. Carter was a hippie silversmith: he made the kind of jewellery Carol loved to wear: crystals set in silver – a kind of Feng Shui approach to the art of jewellery. Beads that brought you luck, ear-rings to focus the chakra required. I couldn't stand that woozy kind of thing, really, but he was a nice enough fellow. Even quite good-looking for a pagan. And not married.

'I don't see how we can be sure he wasn't a Christian,' I said. 'People travelled a lot in those days. For all we know these are the bones of the centurion John Wayne played in the film, the one who took Jesus' robe after the crucifixion and was converted. Why are people so sure such things can't be?'

'Because it's so very unlikely,' said Carter Wainright.

I bet he was christened something like Kevin Smith and changed his name when he came down here. People do. But he had a nice deep voice.

'My point is, Carter,' I said, 'If they found an early Christian cross in this grave tomorrow, they'd have to believe.'

'But they're not going to find any such thing, are they?' he said.

'They might,' I said. 'You never know. If you come back to my house tonight I can show you all sorts of early Christian references. If you add mercury to the silver mix they always assume it's old silver. Should anyone take it into their head to do any testing.'

'I know all about that,' he said. 'I had a job once faking old clock faces. "Restoring" they called it, but from what they charged, I called it faking. I came down here to Rumer to live a more honest life.'

'Two wrongs don't make a right,' said Carol primly, but she didn't sound very convinced.

'I don't think we'd better tell Matt,' said Susie. 'He's such a stickler.'

'You can't do this,' said Carol.

'Yes, we can,' I said. 'Then they can give these bodies a decent burial and we can all get some peace and some sleep.'

I bent down and picked out of the grave what looked like a sliver of wood, or had once been wood, in a blackened kind of way. And I gave it to Carter Wainright and he put it in his pocket.

'Give it the trace of a wooden frame,' I said, 'just to confuse the issue.'

I noticed my blistered fingers were getting better. Touch had been quite painful and cooking the children's chicken dinner had been hell. Carter Wainright came back with me for the books and a certain amount of canoodling did take place, I must say, before he took his leave. I didn't want to be a burden to my children: a silversmith and a sculptor could live fairly amicably together. And he swore his name was truly Carter Wainright and I believed him.

In the morning my back was better and my fingers

64

unblistered and smooth. This is what a little sex can do for you, I concluded. And amazingly, it started to rain. You could practically see the lettuces breathe the moisture in, and their hearts swell and curl and firm. All the animals went out into the wet, which was rather unusual for them, and skittered about in pleasure. The ground was parched, how it drank in the rain.

I went down to the site with the children. Now that there were news-teams and cameras and journalists with notebooks, they took more interest. Apparently a Christian cross, a Chi-Rho, made of silver and wood, had been found in the grave of one of the centurions. They reckoned the sudden rain had loosened the earth, which was why they hadn't seen it before. No one had expected rain; it certainly hadn't been forecast, and it was local only.

Harrison Ford from Nottingham was in a foul mood. This was the last thing he had wanted. Carol reckoned he was on some sort of performance bonus. He was in conference with his friend from Riley management, Marcus Dubiddy; I saw the Chi-Rho lying on a piece of plastic by the grave while they argued. Both men looked thoroughly cross.

The rain had stopped pelting and now drifted in a kind of warm gentle misty shroud over the site. Those of us in jeans and T-shirts were at an advantage over the suits, whose ties began to look flabby very quickly. My son Joel even consented to join the dustpan-and-brush brigade, volunteers rounded up locally to help the Birmingham students sieve the ribboned-off sections of the site. They had five minutes' training before setting to. At least there was stuff to find: oyster shells, and bits of metal and broken Samian ware, all of which were being catalogued, plastic-bagged, and logged. Faster, faster, urged the overseers. They must cover more ground, more quickly. I felt protective of him, as if he were being whipped to build a pyramid.

Joel eavesdropped on Dubiddy's conversation – I had been marked out as a troublemaker. The Chi-Rho was to be sent by courier to the British Museum and they'd date it as a matter of urgency, and value it.

I must admit we panicked, Carter, Carol, Susie and I. We were to be discovered. The silver would be traced back to Carter: my involvement would be suspected. We had forged an early Christian cross. They would think it was some elaborate plan to make money out of the tourist trade. They would not believe our motives. Who nowadays would put themselves out to get a few old dry bones a Christian burial?

We drank too much Chilean red that night, round at my place, to quell our nerves and celebrate the removal of the triptych to Canterbury Cathedral. The carriers had come that day. The more we thought about it the more delinquent our forgery seemed, and indeed impertinent. The Roman legions came from all over the world: the centurion could have belonged to any of a dozen faiths. Many worshipped Mithras, the Sun God. Susie said she didn't think he was a Mithraic, see, it was still gently raining; surely Mithras would have honoured his own? It was fine enough over the rest of the country: only our graves dwelt in this gentle, moist, life-giving Christian mist.

Matt, usually so wary of Carol, for his sort and her sort do not usually agree, came up and drank with us, and they told each other jokes. Susie became quite pink and giggled: Carter decided he had fallen in love with me; the children persuaded me to take in a stray cat who kept trying to live with us, while I tried to let her know, tactfully and firmly, that it was not to be. That night there was a terrific thunderstorm and lightning struck the village shop. The postmistress said it was the spirits of the unburied dead up there on the site bringing bad luck.

The British Museum sent an e-mail to Harrison's laptop the next day. The Chi-Ro was genuine. Two thousand years old, give or take a decade. Riley's put out a press release. Carter was beside himself with pleasure. Not only had he found me but he was one of the greatest forgers alive.

The next day the press turned up in force. Priceless, or at any rate in the region of three million pounds. We could say nothing, and we had won nothing. It was too late. Riley's put guards on the site and strung a barbed-wire fence around it. But still the bones were to go to Birmingham the next day. And within hours after that the skimming would continue and the vast screed would be laid, and that would be the end of our history, not to mention the nesting sites of the lesser crested bittern, et cetera.

Then a canon from Canterbury rang me to congratulate me on the triptych, and I think he meant it.

I brought up the matter of the graves.

'If they've found a Chi-Rho in a Roman soldier's grave,' I said, 'and the British Museum has validated it, then can't we just accept that the dead soldier is a Christian? Sure, he might have stolen the cross, but for that matter he could have been present at the crucifixion.'

It was amazing with what equanimity I could lie. I put it down to being in love. The Canon hummed and hawed and then all of a sudden cheered up, and said of course. He would be happy to do some kind of service of reconciliation, before the bones were bagged. He'd get through to the Rumer parish priest. I said they'd have to be quick. He said the Church could be if it had to be.

And sure enough early the next morning, while a restive Harrison Ford and his team stood back, and the JCBs stood silhouetted against the skyline with the young sun behind them – the storm had cleared the air – the knitting women set up a trestle table with a white cloth and a pot of wild flowers on it; and the Canon, an eagle of a man, turned up in his little Volkswagen, even bringing with him a bishop from a neighbouring diocese – he had his crook with him and his gold embroidered over-vests, or whatever they're called, in the back seat – and all those concerned and interested turned up, and a few journalists as well.

And the priests performed a service of reconciliation: and we sang a few quavery hymns, lost on the breeze – 'Oh God our help in ages past' – then the table was folded, and the altar cloths, and we all drifted off, and peace descended on the valley. All of a sudden it was a place like anywhere else.

Then Harrison and his team darted in like a team of vultures to take their pickings away, and their vans moved off. The JCBs surged down the hill to get to the part of the site they'd been denied, and a hundred cement mixers queued up on the new roads waiting to get in. Goodbye, marsh warbler, goodbye. The future knocks on the door, and if you don't let it in, it simply batters it down.

But peace and prosperity have descended upon Rumer as if it were blessed: visitors come from all over the world to see the knitted patchwork tapestry, which won an international art prize and now hangs behind the altar, instead of being auctioned. To our relief the mall traffic was rerouted away from the village: a free bus service runs three times a week there and back for those without cars. Our flowers win at Chelsea: we grew a record carrot and its photograph was in the *Mail*. We keep the post office and the village store and the little school was even re-opened; the young stay instead of going off to the big city – why live away from paradise?

As for the mall itself, that prospered mightily. The fruit was always fresh and the bread stayed cheap. The charity shops were given concessions. The Internet cafés sopped up the alienated young and have given them purpose and achievement. Becky Horrocks took up computer studies. Matt was promoted to crime prevention officer and could work locally, to Susie's pleasure. The mall even boasted a little museum, endowed by Riley's and the University of Birmingham, where you could see photographs of the site, and the outline of the villa and the graveyard, and a replica of the Rumer Cross. I could not find out what happened to the original. It was probably bought by Bill Gates or Steven Spielberg to enrich their collections.

I married Carter Wainright (in church, of course). My hands stay smooth and strong the better to continue to work. So do his. We are both employed these days doing restoration work, mostly for cathedrals.

Carter replaces stolen silver plate (there's a lot of that to do) and I forge, fashion and bake metal, stone and clay, making good whatever the weather undoes.

We don't say it to each other, but we can both see in retrospect that what was going on at the site was miraculous, outside the normal order of things. It would not surprise me if it were indeed a sliver of the true cross I picked up that day and which Carter worked with: and that it leaves its blessed traces behind. I think we will be forgiven for our deceit: we were meant to do what we did.

JOHN O'FARRELL

The Man Who
Made Himself Disappear

In a remote mountain region of the Amazon rainforest lived a tribe of people that had somehow remained cut off from the rest of the world for thousands of years. They knew nothing of Western civilisation except for the occasional passing aeroplanes which they worshipped as gods. They did not have the wheel or even the most basic knowledge of smelting metal. They had never been to a craft fayre, played Cluedo and would have struggled to appreciate the irony of Rolf Harris's version of the rock classic 'Stairway to Heaven'.

One day a young hunter from the tribe was walking through the forest when he struck his foot upon something. He shrieked out in pain, noticed he had cut his toe and hopped back home as quickly as he could to get it seen to. As an irritated afterthought, he glanced back to see what it was that he'd walked into, but the undergrowth obscured the small hard object that had been lying in his path. If he had looked more carefully he would have seen a Breville sandwich maker, which had magically appeared from nowhere a few minutes before he came along. It was not something he was in the habit of looking out for. The Breville lay in the undergrowth for about an hour and then suddenly disappeared again and so the Amazonian Indians never even saw it.

It would have been useless anyway. They didn't have electricity.

Ten thousands miles away in the countryside outside Oxford in England, the most brilliant physics professor of his generation was standing alone in his kitchen wondering whether he might pick up the telephone and dial the number of Janet the wonderful laboratory assistant who worked with him at the university. She lived in a nearby village and often gave him a lift home, but their long-term friendship was a source of some anxiety to him. It was still only a friendship.

Despite being a brilliant scientist who lived alone and conducted his own research, this particular professor was rather disappointingly not eccentric. There was no unkempt white hair or chaotic laboratory – he looked more like a middle-ranking accountant in a provincial insurance company. He had once worn a bow tie, but that's hardly sufficient to qualify him for genuine Eccentric status. He was of medium height, with a quiet voice and modest needs; everything about him was normal and unremarkable except his brilliant, lateral mind that was greatly admired throughout the British scientific community, even if some of his students had a problem affording him the respect he deserved. Professor Martin Presley could answer most questions about space, time and the universe, although tragically the question he was called upon to answer most frequently was, 'Any relation of Elvis?' You'd think that the nickname of Elvis for Professor Presley would have been far too obvious, and indeed the students appreciated this; so they dubbed him Elvis as a double-joke; as if the nickname was so tiresomely un-witty that it was highly amusing to go all the way back to first base again. The porters at the college called him Elvis as well, but it wasn't so clever when they did it. It was not funny and people really should have known better.

Today was Sunday and Elvis had spent most of the day in his workshop at the bottom of the garden. As the afternoon drew on he had begun to think less about his work and more about the lovely Janet, and although he only saw her during the working week when she drove him home and sometimes came in for a cup of tea and a toasted sandwich, he had come up with a plan which he felt sure would grab her attention and force her to contact him.

Janet was an attractive and radiant woman in her early fifties who had steadfastly refused to be cast as a victim when she had lost her husband a few years earlier. People would still greet her with a sympathetic mock-glum expression and say, 'How *are* you, Janet?' and if she happened to be in a cheerful mood they would insist on telling her how brave she was being. She liked Martin because he was the only person who did not talk to her like she was a spaniel that was going to be put to sleep the following morning. He treated her like he treated everyone else; namely with quiet courtesy and consideration, the effect of which was only spoiled when it became apparent that he hadn't heard a single word that had been said to him.

The doorbell rang and he looked through the hall-way window to see a rather flustered-looking Janet clutching a Breville sandwich maker. On her hands were a pair of pink washing-up gloves and she held the object as far away from her body as possible. Martin opened the door.

'Your sandwich maker, I believe.'

'Hello, Janet. Ah you recognised it! Why are you wearing washing-up gloves?'

'I thought it might be radioactive or something.'

'If it had been, I'd say pink rubber gloves would have offered fairly limited protection.'

'Martin, how did you do that? How did you make this suddenly appear in the middle of my lawn while I was pulling up the ground elder?'

'Sorry. Was it a bit of a shock?'

'Oh no, I'm quite used to apparitions of sandwich makers covered in huge red ants feeding of the old cheese run-off.'

'Ants? Really?'

'Yes, they were enormous, like something off a nature documentary.'

'How are they?'

'What?'

'The ants. Were they OK?'

'I don't know – I brushed them all off with the longest-handled broom I could find.'

'But they were alive? It's just that I've never done this with living organisms before.'

'Done what? What's going on?'

'I'm sorry, I owe you an explanation. Come on in; I'll put the kettle on.'

And Martin's mind was racing as three simultaneous thoughts fought for space in his crowded mind. Firstly the exciting news that his invention seemed to work for living creatures as well as inanimate objects;

secondly that his plan to get Janet round to see him had worked so perfectly; and thirdly that, even though it appeared safe to move living creatures, it was probably for the best that he'd got her to come round of her own volition rather than using his invention to instantaneously relocate her from her back garden in the village of Preston Crowmarsh.

They walked into the kitchen and Janet put on the kettle because she knew he would have already forgotten.

'These ants . . . they didn't appear distressed in any way?' he continued.

'Martin, you nearly give me a heart attack, and then you ask if the ants were distressed. No, the ants were not distressed. I am distressed.'

'Of course, sit down.'

'I am sitting down.'

'Oh yes. And they weren't noticeably deformed or anything? I mean they still had six legs and everything?'

'Martin. Tell me, how did you do that? Was it magic or what?'

It wasn't exactly magic. Professor Martin Presley had made a discovery as significant as any in the history of science and with it had developed an invention so powerful and revolutionary that it was difficult to imagine how any sort of status quo could be maintained for very long. He had developed a way of moving things instantaneously from one location to the other, anywhere on the surface of the earth. There was no puff of smoke or shimmering mirage; the object was just in one place at one moment and then in an instant it was somewhere else. He had been testing the machine for years, wanting to make sure that it was absolutely safe and reliable before it was revealed to the world. Thousands of people had been unwitting victims of Professor Presley's experiments, losing everyday objects and just idly blaming their own carelessness.

Socks were a particular favourite of his. He would set the computer to target a certain launderette and then see if he could relocate an individual sock hundreds of miles away. Over the years countless individuals had come out of launderettes wondering how they managed to lose yet another sock while, a few hundred miles away, a farmer might idly wonder how a muddy old sock came to be lying in a grass verge on the lane up to the farmhouse. That was Martin enjoying a private joke. Single woollen gloves would be whisked from coat pockets and placed on the railings next to bus stops. Shopping trolleys were regularly moved from one place to another; a trolley from Sainsbury's Homebase in Norwich was relocated to the PC World car-park in Swansea and nobody had even attempted to explain it. He was also in possession of thousands of miniature Polly Pocket figures, a large collection of hub-caps and the log-book of HMS *Conqueror*. He'd even managed to remove the letter E from the EEC without anyone so much as passing comment.

It had taken Professor Presley a decade to perfect this machine and now he felt the time had come to share his secret with someone else. He could have gone to the Government or the Patents Office or rung up the BBC and asked to speak to the producer of *Tomor-*

row's World, but he felt there was a far more important place to start. He knew that he was probably in love with Janet, and he wanted to show his discovery to her.

'Thank you,' he said, five minutes later, only half-aware that she had made him a cup of tea.

Janet had at first presumed that she must be the victim of some clever conjuring trick, an optical illusion or some form of hypnosis, and indeed there was still a large part of her mind which was determined to rationalise what had happened this way. But later that afternoon when Martin actually demonstrated the machine; when he instantly relocated the sundial from the middle of the overgrown rosebed at the front of his house to the neglected orchard at the bottom of the garden, she was convinced that she was witnessing a truly historic scientific breakthrough. Her amazement was unqualified, except when Martin attempted to explain to her the scientific formula which made the process possible, when she found herself nodding and staring blankly. But it didn't matter how he did it; it was miraculous and awe-inspiring and the whole world was changed for ever.

'Martin, do you realise what you have done?' Her excitement was growing so quickly she could barely get the words out. 'Can't you see what this means?'

'That the sundial won't tell the correct time any more?'

'When I was a little girl and I didn't want to eat up my broccoli, my mother would always say, "Think about all the starving children in India who would love to eat your broccoli." And I would think, Fine. They can have it, I really don't mind . . .'

'Yes, I used to think that as well.'

'Well, don't you see? Now they really can have the broccoli!'

'Except with me it was always Yorkshire pudding.'

'They can have the Yorkshire pudding as well . . .'

'Oh dear, poor things . . .'

"There's always been enough food for everyone in the world, but now you, Professor Martin Presley, have found the answer to mass starvation. This is the end of world poverty, drought, disease; everything. With this invention you can instantly move the world's food surplus to those in need, you could irrigate the deserts by instantaneously moving tonnes of polar ice, thereby averting rising sea levels, incidentally,' she added as an aside barely stopping to catch her breath, 'or you could use floodwater, of course, yes, instead of washing away homes and crops, floodwater could be strategically redirected to water crops in Ethiopia, and medicines could be moved to those who need them immediately, and, and well, you have just found the solution to all the problems of the human race. You are the saviour of all mankind.'

Martin had wanted to impress her and it seemed to be going quite well.

They spent the rest of the evening drawing up a list of ways in which the machine might be employed to solve all the problems of the world. Martin pointed out that if they were going to start with a little reservoir in the middle of the Sahara then they would have to have somewhere to put all the sand, but Janet had already thought of that.

'Wouldn't it be lovely if Brighton had a sandy beach instead of all those pebbles?'

'Ooh yes, much nicer. Ah, but where will we put all the pebbles?'

'Sea defences: Holland. Oh, minus a dozen or so big ones for my rockery,' she added.

Janet couldn't believe how many of the world's problems seemed to come down to a simple logistical problem of moving resources from one place to another. At the moment the only risk she saw to their plans was the personal safety of Martin. Excited by the news that the ants had survived a trip from the Amazon jungle he was suddenly very keen to try the machine out on himself. Every time she mentioned a distant part of the world where there was a problem, he wanted instantly to transport himself there to see for himself. She pleaded with him that it might be dangerous, arguing that if he zapped himself off into the ether he might never come back again, and then the secret of the machine would be lost for ever.

'And what's more,' she added. 'I'd miss you . . .'

'Would you really?' said Martin.

'Of course I would.'

But the next morning Martin did not turn up at the university and a slightly anxious Janet went round to his house fearing that he'd failed to heed her advice. She rang the bell, she peered through the front window, she went down to his workshop at the bottom of the garden but there was no sign of Martin or indeed his invention. This absence of the machine was some sort of comfort. Well, if he has transported himself to some distant corner of the globe, she thought, at least he had the good sense to take with him his means of getting back again. She let herself in with the key she knew was hidden in the shed and made herself a cup of tea. She wanted to wait and make sure he got back all right. During the course of the day she wiped down the surfaces by the window many more times than they needed it, and at eleven o'clock that night she finally went home again.

The British and American governments had been alerted that something strange was happening when a spy satellite photographed a small mountain of cheap umbrellas that Martin had been idly constructing in Southern Chad. During a long phone call to the White House, the President of Chad had vehemently denied that he was secretly stockpiling umbrellas but was still forced to give permission for a UN inspection team to be admitted to the site to examine them. At the same time, erratic movements of large objects were being detected by radar stations across southern England with the epicentre of the phenomenon being located at a little village outside Oxford.

Soon after Janet had departed that Sunday, Martin received a visit from several government officials. They were very nice, very polite and very, very insistent that he pack some things and come with them immediately. He asked if he should bring his machine but as he looked out of the window he saw it being lifted into the back of a secure-looking truck. There was no sense in which Martin was being arrested or physically forced to go with these gentlemen against his will and yet he could not help feeling as if he had done something wrong. He decided to be as co-operative as possible because he didn't want to see what would happen if he wasn't. He was quizzed at length about the machine and its development and he resolved to give completely honest answers.

'Who else knows about this invention?' they asked.

'No one,' said Martin. 'No one at all.'

Well, mostly honest answers.

At the end of a disorientating day, Martin found himself agreeing to go at once to the United States. They made him feel very important; they were amazed and impressed by his invention and said they believed him when he claimed it was foolproof. So he offered to use the machine to transport them all to America instantaneously and then they were slightly less enthusiastic about it. They flew overnight on a military jet which had a proper bed you could lie down and sleep in. They assured him that his university department would be notified that something urgent had required his attention and said he would be provided with everything he needed while he was away. The next morning there were cars to meet him at the airport with tinted windows and motorcycle outriders and he was made to feel important and special and called Professor Presley-sir! and he didn't even notice that a couple of the less senior military attachés kept giggling and humming 'You ain't nothing but a hound-dog!'. He was driven straight from the airport to the centre of DC and as his limousine sped along Pennsylvania Avenue it was explained to him that he was going to meet the President of the United States.

'The most important man in the world!' exclaimed Martin.

'Er, maybe . . .' said the official. 'Though something tells me that right now the most important man in the world is *you.*'

The car pulled up and they entered a building through a small door off a car-park, and he realised with a slight sense of anti-climax that this rather unimposing entrance had led him to the interior of the White House. He was going to meet the President! Professor Presley suddenly foresaw a slight problem. Because he'd spent all of his spare time working away on his experiments, he never really watched the television or read any newspapers and now he realised that he had no idea who the current President of the United States was. He was pretty sure it wasn't Ronald Reagan any more, but beyond that he was at a complete loss. He was ushered along a grand corridor where he looked in vain for clues to his identity; hoping to see a portrait with a name underneath or some mail on a little side table that might have the President's name and address on the front of the envelope, but there was nothing. Martin decided that the best policy would be to behave as confidently as possible and finally he was guided through some large double doors and into a beautifully furnished room where a tall man in a suit finally stepped forward to greet him.

'Mr President!' said Martin, boldly offering out his hand.

'I'm not the President,' said the tall man looking bemused. 'I'm from White House security. I'll be taking you from here to meet the President.' And then in a very matter-of-fact way he said, 'We are walking down the corridor now . . .'

'Yes we are,' relied Martin brightly.

'I was talking into my mouthpiece.'

'Oh I see. Sorry.'

'We're going up the stairs . . .'

Martin just managed to stop himself agreeing with this observation and resolved to say nothing more until they went into a large office when Martin's escort announced; 'Professor Presley, the President of the United States!' and Martin looked at a row of four men who stood there smiling at him. He knew enough about American politics to know it probably wasn't the black guy. But as for the other three, it could have been any of them. If he'd had his machine with him he would have just zapped himself straight back to Oxfordshire. A few very long seconds passed until the oldest of the four men stepped forward and offered his hand. This was it – he was going to speak, the President of the United States was about to introduce himself. What would the leader of the Western world say to him?

'So, Professor Presley,' he said with a half-chuckle, 'are you any relation to Elvis?'

The President turned out to be very charming. He was intelligent and personable and interested in Martin's account of how he had patiently developed this machine at his home in England. Martin understood the President's insistence that the utmost secrecy be maintained about the project. He himself had instinctively felt that the invention should not be widely publicised until the United Nations or whoever started using it for the important work that he and Janet had planned together. He gave the President their list of all the ways in which the machine could be used to alleviate the great suffering around the world and the President scanned it and looked impressed. He handed the list to an aide who read it and nodded wisely. He passed it along the line and the next aide read it and nodded wisely. By the time it got to the end it would have been difficult for the last aide to react any differently.

But there was another urgent matter about which the President and his advisers needed to talk to him: the threat of terrorism.

'Martin, imagine if this power fell into the hands of one of the rogue states around the world.'

'Or a group of international terrorists. They might even try to kidnap you and force you to construct another machine that they would use for their own ends,' said one of the aides.

'Especially with the worsening situation in Costa Rica,' added another, and there was a heavy pause, during which he felt he was supposed to agree.

'What's happening in Costa Rica?' said the professor.

'Don't you read the papers?'

'Not often, Mr President.'

'Please – Martin, we're on first-name terms here.'

'Of course. Thank you, er – Mr President.'

It was explained to the professor that with the knowledge he possessed his personal safety was a matter of utmost global security and that for the time being it would be best if he remained in a specially refurbished luxury unit on a nearby military base. This was a comfortable suite that had been especially designed so that he was 100 per cent safe from any kidnap attempt or terrorist attack. He wanted to ring Janet and tell her all about this, but found that his safety was so important that his suite was locked and he couldn't get out to use the phone. So he called one of the obliging orderlies and handed him a letter to post to her and over the following couple of weeks he became increasingly disappointed that she seemed to be taking so long to reply.

In the meantime he kept himself busy with work and reading. Any books that he requested were quickly provided, and following his embarrassing encounter with the leader of the Western world he resolved to start reading newspapers and watching the television news. He read about the President's re-election campaign and the growing crisis in Costa Rica and he saw disturbing footage of a famine developing in the Horn of Africa and wondered why, if they had his machine, no food seemed to be getting through as yet. He wrote a letter to his friend the President, in which he liberally sprinkled the President's name to demonstrate how well he knew it, asking how things were progressing with the list of humanitarian operations that he had suggested for his machine. But the note only received a rather impersonal reply from a White House aide saying that the matter had been passed to the appropriate department. After three weeks in his secure accommodation he asked an orderly to find out how much longer it would be until the international situation became stable enough for him to be allowed to return home. The orderly was very sympathetic and very concerned on his behalf and said he would make sure he found out. The following day he had been replaced by a new member of staff.

Martin now spent much of his time just watching television. One night he was watching a popular garden-improvement challenge when he thought of a way that his machine could be employed in a hit new television series: *Third World Make-over!* With the help of his invention, two teams could each be given a weekend to convert an impoverished sub-Saharan dictatorship into a prosperous post-industrial democracy. MDF and crazy paving supplied as necessary. Suddenly the transmission was interrupted by a news flash. The reporter announced that American forces had finally been forced to take military action against Costa Rica and that limited bombing of strategic installations in San José had begun. As explosions lit up the night sky behind the CNN reporter, she attempted to explain the type of strategic bombing that was taking place. She confirmed that no US aircraft had been involved but curiously neither did any missiles seem to have been tracked coming into Costa Rican airspace. The only explanation the excited reporter could offer was that these new 'super-smart bombs' had somehow just been placed in exactly the right locations at the moment that they detonated. And the reporter jumped slightly as several more explosions lit up the city behind her.

Martin switched off the television and stared at the ceiling. He wondered if Janet had any idea what had happened. When the two of them had sat down to work out all the wonderful ways in which the machine might be used, neither of them had supposed that he had invented the world's ultimate warhead delivery system. Undetectable, instantaneous, and more accurate than anything ever devised, the machine could send a bomb to any point in the world. There was no expensive tracking system, no risk of losing American pilots and no warning for whoever was on the receiving end of the attack.

He lay awake for several hours, rising at one point to test the strength of the lock on his window. He sat down and began another letter to Janet now knowing that she probably had no idea where he was or what had happened to him. 'Remember that exciting afternoon in my garden when you said that my machine had given them the ability to solve all the world's problems?' he wrote. 'Well, they always had that, didn't they? They didn't need my machine; they always could have done those things if they'd wanted.' And then instead of going through the charade of giving the orderly the letter he screwed it up and threw it in the bin.

Back in Oxfordshire, Janet was in the local police station where Martin had been formally listed as a missing person.

'But there's more too it than that . . .' she said to the desk sergeant. 'You see, he made this incredible machine that could make things disappear and re-appear somewhere else.'

The world-weary officer glanced at the next person waiting to be dealt with.

'And the thing is, you see . . .' Janet continued, 'I'm pretty certain that he used this machine to make himself disappear, but as we know he just hasn't re-appeared.'

'Sounds like this magic machine must be playing up a bit, love.'

'Well, obviously that's what happened. I told him this was always a danger if he started dabbling with the laws of nature. He must be stuck in the fourth dimension or something.'

'OK, well, I'll radio whoever we've got patrolling the fourth dimension this evening and make sure they keep an eye out for them . . .'

On the way home an exasperated Janet stopped off to buy a newspaper. She flicked through the pages outside the newsagent's. US forces bomb San José, famine in the Horn of Africa and the American President had somehow managed to get three hole-in-ones in a charity golf match in Florida. But they still hadn't published her long letter all about the professor who had made himself disappear. All the wonderful things that his invention could have done, and now it would never be used. And all because dear Martin had accidentally made himself vanish. She'd warned him that his machine might be dangerous.

ANDREA ASHWORTH

Flamenco

J ED FRAZER has a new toy: a pair of super-zoom
binoculars meant for spying the beauty of winged
things on Sundays, when he's out in the hills with his
dad. His face is aching. The sockets cradling the boy's
blue-grey eyes are pressed, bony, eager, against the
peepholes. He's in love with the zooming-in lens.

There.

There she goes.

Winged, in a way.

He blushes at the sugary rush through his guts. The
boy blushes in the curtained dark of his bedroom, and
touches the wheel that controls the lens. Gives it slight,
trembling twists until she is conjured up, clear.

Pearly pink lips, slathered in gloss, teased into a pout.
The girl slinks along Victoria Road, her face budding a
sulky kiss. For herself. And for the world, which is
watching, every second, every minute, every hour.
Every day, Emmy senses herself, caught on film. She
can practically hear the reel whirring.

Mostly it's projected against the sky – this film – on
a great, arching screen that anyone can see. Sometimes
it's played in an echoing cave, to God, stroking his
beard, carving notes in stone. Or to her gran, squinting

through heavy-rimmed spectacles, the rest of her a dusty lilac blur.

The strap of Emmy's stiletto bites into her ankle.

'Tss!' Her blister bursts. A veil of bloodied skin peels back: a weeping, vinegary sore. Wincing on the inside, the girl keeps her cheekbones in line, haughty, high. Beneath lashes treacled with mascara, dark sea-watery eyes gaze out, greeny-blue, over her pout.

She's new around here.

She's sure no one (not God; not Gran; not even, at times, herself) can see the face behind the face she has smoothed on.

'Oi!' On the nape of Jed's craned neck, Tom lands a slap: 'Gizza loada that.'

The older boy grabs the binoculars, sticks them to his face and peers out from the bedroom above Norah's Ark, the pet shop on Victoria Road.

Up. Down. Twiddling.

Zoom in. Zoom out.

Up again. Down again.

'Nothin'!' Tom shoves his fourteen-year-old brother: 'What you looking at, then?'

Jed's eyes have a way of going glazed, so they reflect nothing, when they're full of something. His light-brown face has two reddened Panda patches, sore from spying.

Screwing the lids back over the binocular lenses, Tom gives his kid brother a sideways glance: 'Freakazoid.'

Everyone drains from the garish red foyer. Clutching Maltesers and Opal Fruits and Coke, all chatter and jubbling elbows, they giggle, dribbling popcorn, into another world.

Emmy's face sears, a mask of hot prickles, when people stare. Then again, there are so many unseeing strangers. When the blank ones brush by, she prickles differently: invisible, in spite of the sparkly stilettos and the pink gloss oozled on to keep her from dissolving in the dark.

That quiet – after the house lights sigh down, before the curtains jump up – makes the girl shiver. She snuggles in her stale velvet seat and gazes into the dark. The ceiling is domed and sprinkled with stars that wink in the musty universe. In the cluster of hushed seconds, she has a sense of her self, twinkling.

An almighty mouse squeaks as the curtains spring, their rails aching to be oiled. Then the rumble of a big-time, electrified drumroll: a divine motorbike, revving to take off. The screen swells with colour, pulses, hurls light. Upturned faces are licked by ghostly beams.

'Ssh!'

'Ssh.'

Shushes crescendo, 'Ssssssh!' before the tide of giddiness ebbs and the film oceans up.

Someone stands, unleashing a shadow, gigantic, across the screen.

Emmy Rawlins. The new girl at school: Emmy.

Whispers simmer in the back seats. From the very last rows, filthy noises rise. Up near the front, where the short-sighted and not-cool ones sit, Jed strains his neck to look across.

There she is. Crowned by the projector's rays. A halo.

Boos break out with hisses in the popcorn-exploding

middle, crammed with acne-cursed kids. Mr Dulwich, the manager, comes slicing through the mote-furred dark, his torch poised to quell snotty riots.

Suddenly, Jed blinks. The manager's beam swerves, crashes, and there the boy is: a creature struck stupid by headlights.

An awesome eye, the torch ponders him. Then it wavers, loses its glow. The manager tap-tap-taps on the glass over the dying bulb. When it flashes back to life, it's the girl's turn to be framed. Her face whacked angelic with light, she freezes in the aisle.

Above the shimmer of her lips, her greeny-blue eyes sting, watery. She glances away from the glare and her eyes alight, stunned, unfocused, on Jed.

Can she see me?

One gigantic wink, and the manager's batteries give up.

Did she see me?

The torch goes dead. Everyone falls back into the movie. Squirming laughter, creasing faces, oblivious.

Emmy's face is accidentally gorgeous. Her features look as if they've been snatched from here, there, any old where. But the way they go together, making her Emmy, gives her a sweet edge.

Going to the pictures or sidling over to Leighton Park with Julie Marriott's gang after dark, she squeezes into her stilettos and lets loose with pink gloss and mascara. The rest of the time, she lets her face go soapy clean. But that bareness lights up her loveliness all the more brightly. It makes people feel strange, though they don't know why, and neither does she.

Because of her looks, Emmy has to pay, in some small

or not-so-small way, every day at school. Because of her looks, she has been sucked up into Julie Marriott's gang.

'You're either in or you're out.'

At the end of Emmy's first week at Leighton High, Beth Marlow had asked – had ordered – her to come see Julie and The Others in their 'office': the sunless place behind the generator, on the far side of the school yard, past the vats of pig slop.

'So, you're in?' Julie Marriott's arms were clamped across her puffed-up chest.

Emmy hadn't said a word. Her eyes had spoken for her, spikes icing up in their watery blue-green. Spikes that said she was in. (Though they had frosted up out of fear, mixed with a kind of thrill.)

Mazzy C thrust a pack of Benson and Hedges at her, one cigarette jutting out further than the rest: 'Smoke.'

Emmy slid it out of the gold box. The generator growled. Her throat burned and tanged: her first cigarette. The others narrowed their eyes and pursed their lips to spew airy, eye-stinging creatures, curling smoky limbs.

Laughter bounces off the graffiti-scarred tiles, along with fluorescent beams. A glass, swiped from the dinner hall, squats upside-down on the linoleum floor. Someone flicks off the lights.

Titters dry up, giggles die, then the echoes of giggles, until they are all huddled – an eerie octopus, five-headed – in half-light and quiet.

Emmy feels, suddenly, cold. But she can't reach for her cardigan. Can't rub her goosepimply arms. Should not shiver. Hers is one of five special fingers chosen to guide the Ouija glass.

'Dead steady,' the others have warned her.

Their fingernails are shiny as cars: blood-red, silver, gold, neon-pink. (Emmy's clear, but gleaming too.) Heads bowed together, the girls' scents mingle into a purring mist of hormones and intense, love-hate effort. Perfumes, oils, creams: each one's secret worship of her body comes wafting up.

The glass begins to buzz. Something's pulsing between the girls in the dark. A sense of who is who, who likes who, who is cool. Who is sexy, who is funny, who is hard. Who is it, and who is not.

'Now . . .' Julie Marriott tells her girls to hum. They hum.

Some of them, brewing hot under their shirts, spurt hiccupy laughs.

Julie opens her eyes and glares – 'Hum!' – then closes them tight again.

Emmy's mouth is a nervous engine: 'Hmmm . . .'

She has watched the gang set up their Ouija before. She's heard them swearing, foul, bubble-gummy nothings, to get the filth out of their system. (Bad luck, Bwa, to mix the f-word with Ouija.) She's seen them stubbing cigarettes in the cracks of the tiles, laying down – ever so slowly, just so – the letters, A b C d E . . . in a scrappy circle of scribbled-on library slips.

But she has never seen what happens next.

She has only heard of the glass coming to life, because, before that hushed moment, she and everyone but Julie and the others – the precious few who are in – have always been kicked out of the school loos.

The glass vibrates.

Emmy peers through shuttered lashes.

The glass snails towards the letter d.

94

It pauses. Urges on towards E, where it hovers. Finally, it jerks, slides, slows, settles on f.

The alphabet is alive, letters beckoning the glass towards them.

F. Emmy's chest sets off, clamouring – hammering, idiotically, hard, a demented drum.

F.

F for Frazer. Jed Frazer. The boy who's always at the piano, bowed over the keys, alone, in assembly hall. During lunch hours and after classes, he plays, to echoing, high ceilings. Even first thing in the morning, he's there: hunched, burning, plinking, pounding his insides out.

Emmy, stealing behind the stage curtains, has come in touch with the room's thunder. Other kids sneer: dusty posh rubbish, leaves your ears crammed with cobwebs. But it's not like that. Emmy has crept behind the curtains and she has heard, she has felt, the hall fill up, overflow, with glorious sound. Storming through beauty to something massive. At the same time disappearing, trickling, into the hidden, hot coils of her chest.

She knows this boy, in a way. The spiralling insides of her ears, the breathing, damp creases in the backs of her knees know him. But she has never – has she ever? – glimpsed his face.

The glass screeches over the linoleum, pouncing on R.

Emmy's throat's so dry her tongue sticks to the back of her mouth. Her feelings might show up, could come babbling along her arm, tingle through her finger. Out.

'Eff . . .' Shelley Bayley broadcasts, slowly, through her long nose. 'Arr . . .'

Emmy's back is hot, her face hotter. All the nights, the muzzy, half-dream mornings, when, tangled in the bake of her duvet, she has buried her face, her eyes, her lips, even her tongue, in her pillow. Thinking of him, the boy with no face, and feeling an enormous thirst. A thirst that makes her ache for some magical water, golden cold fizzy, a kind of champagne. Or for the taste of another tongue.

'Fuc–!' Rachel chomps the curse back down her throat. 'Oh man!'

Her neon-pink nail chips as the glass veers violently: O.

Giggles snort as the glass creeps, sniggering, towards the letter G.

'Ha, ha!' Emmy acts cool. 'Very funny, you lot.'

'. . . Frog!' Shelley laughs, after everyone else, her stupendous boobs quivering.

'Duh!' Mazzy C is quick to be cruel. 'OK.' She flexes her fingers, cracks a few knuckles, bends back over the glass. 'Me.'

Now that Emmy has been used to flush out sillier spirits, the pipes are ready for serious stuff.

Fingernails congregate. The girls hum. The glass sets off.

'T . . .'

'O . . .'

Splotches of raspberry burn Mazzy's face; she knows which letter is coming next.

'M!' Rachel sputters. 'It's a fix. I could feel you pushing it, Mazzy.'

Rachel has her own sights set on Tom Frazer.

'Tom Frazer?' Emmy asks. 'The one with the brother who plays piano?'

The back of his neck, bowed. She feels her guts whipping, tightening butterfly knots.

'Yeah, the other one's Creepy-Crawly Jed Frazer.' Julie's voice drips, poisonous. 'Spiderman: fingers all the way to his elbows.'

Shelley's boobs grimace. 'Freaky Frazer.'

'But his *brother* . . .' Mazzy C pulls a face of delicious agony. 'His brother is Some Thing Else.'

The others chant: 'Tom, Tom, give me one!'

'He's not freaky, though, is he? The other brother?' Emmy skims her gaze over the scattered scraps of the alphabet, then looks up. 'The one who plays piano?'

Julie's eyes glint as she decrees: 'He is.'

They look pickled, the orbs that hover to contemplate Emmy, then skitter hither and thither, propelled by the flick of a tail or the slower sashay of fins. The girl shudders. Imagine having transparent eyelids, never being able to turn away from the world. The curse of forever seeing. Though fish are blessed with brains that forget, which is probably what keeps them afloat.

Through the door of the next room, sweating into the shop crammed with boxes and cages and tanks: a boy's growl, a girl's murmurs, 'Ahmm.'

Emmy moves away from the locked door, towards the window at the front of the shop. A green-caped parrot squawks and winks a dry, knowing eye. A percussion of passionate burps. Then, from his feathered breast, a girly, thrilled, 'Ahmm.'

She backs away from the parrot. Her ankle snags on a gang of dog leashes, crawling out of their basket, on to the floor. Untangling her clompy school lace-ups, she hurries to the window. Over a cardboard box – a snowy huddle of rabbits, newborn – she holds her breath.

Emmy feels dizzy, surrounded by so much shuffling, squawking, slithering, barking, gurgling life – all held-in, for sale. Alone in Norah's Ark at half-past six, when she ought to be home, cobbling together some toast and whatever for tea. Mazzy C, out to grab a bit of Tom Frazer before Rachel could pluck up the guts, had dragged her over as soon as Mr and Mrs Frazer had taken off, their caravan hiccuping behind them, for the weekend.

Emmy had cowered behind the old-fashioned cash register, its long-armed keys sticking up in confusion. 'How's it work?'

'Don't be soft!' Dying to melt into the living room at the back of the shop with Tom, Mazzy had insisted that Emmy watch over things: 'It's teatime; no one'll come in.'

But Emmy's sure that every person who passes by, exhausted, on their way home, will spot the velvety huddle in the box and will have to come in for a stroke. She puts out her hand. Their ears: so silky they feel almost wet. After that – that touch – how could anyone go away without a new life snoozing in his or her palm?

She goes and sits, very still, behind the ancient till.

'Ahmm-a-ah.' Mazzy's breathless, high gasps float in a different world from Tom's deep grunts. 'Oh-oh-oh.'

The shop's front door jangles. A boy ambles in, goes to the cardboard box and looks down. He sees what the girl saw, moments before. A nestle of pulsing fur, a clutch of eyes glued tight. Warm, breathing balls of long-eared dreams.

Jed gentles his hand into the box. He's been playing for two crashing hours, and his fingertips want something soft. His blue-grey eyes have gone funny. Looking up from the sleeping things, he blinks.

A girl. Behind the till, where his brother should be. 'Where's –?'

Emmy bites her lip. The back door is a loose lid, spilling groans from Tom and Mazzy C and the settee, tormented, beneath them. She has to press her finger in the groove between her nose and the crown of her lips, to keep laughter quiet. The situation doesn't feel funny. It feels awkward, dirty, deep-down exciting. The inside-out, not quite the opposite, of funny. But her mouth is itching to laugh, doesn't know what else to do.

It's her mouth – pouting, but not pearly pink – that Jed sees first. Coming up from his piano trance, it takes him a full, unfurling minute to absorb the girl's face, naked. Weirdly close-up: blond hairs downy above the pout. He has to translate the features of a bare-lipped stranger, right there in his mum and dad's shop, into the girl, the glossy girl, on whom he has been – through his binoculars upstairs in his bedroom; in the sweaty popcorn murk at the pictures; mazily in his mind – spying.

The boy flops his music books on the counter and they riffle open. The staves are alive, writhing inky tadpoles. Clues. Emmy's ears grow hot. She knows him, in a way.

' 'Sthat what you were playing this morning?'

Jed squints at the swirl of notes, fringed with his scribbled reminders: go lightly there; here, dive in; hold tight; take off. His neck flushes.

He feels spied on, feels sort of peeled. At the same time, something new: a fleeting, darting-fish feeling he might like to be seen. By her.

'Yeah.' Jed looks at the music he has tiptoed and thought and thundered through, over and over and over.

Amid the shop's shuffling animal noises, a flock of hallelujahs heaves off the staves to soar.

Emmy feels she should, somehow, plunge.

Jed coughs, contemplates his feet. At the back of his neck, dark curls wisp, slightly damp. He coughs again, blushing on a stumble of words.

'Fish need feeding.'

The boy stoops under the counter and comes up with a box of foul-whiffing flakes. Schloop: the sky-trembling music evaporates into the stinky air.

Emmy follows him to the aquarium along the back wall.

They look at the tiny, all-seeing things, swishing here, there, nowhere.

They dip their fingers into the smelly powder and sprinkle it on to the water.

Mouths, so many sucking Os, blink on the humming surface. They set the water bubbling: fish lips. A few kiss the fleshy pads of the girl's fingertips, desperately gobbling the nothingy flakes. From her fingertips to her guts, something shoots: gorgeous electricity. It spingles out in all sorts of directions, deep and delicious.

The girl lifts her eyes. They open, dark blue-green, to the boy's pale blue-grey. Greeny-blue and blue-grey. Bluey-greeny-grey-blue.

Hovering next to the gurgling aquarium.

The living-room door swings open and MTV blasts into the shop, along with Mazzy C, triumphantly rumpled.

'Come on.' She grabs Emmy.

Emmy's fingertips are sopping wet, like Jed's. Dripping, after lingering in the tank. She throws him a furious look as she leaves. Better, fiercer, than the smile she's fighting to keep off her lips.

The door jangles, and the girls are gone.

Emmy's riding high on the swing in the kiddies' corner of Leighton Park. It's dark, and the sky's freckled with stars.

Sick, she feels, from too much swinging, but she can't stop, won't stop, mustn't stop. Under the slide, girls are pulling faces, squealing 'Yeuch!', snorting about lads' inches, centimetres, milli-fackin-metres! Lads are flaunting sharp, biology-book terms, using them and slimier words to go foraging under the girls' clothes, making jokes about their most mysterious parts. Emmy's afraid that, if she stops swinging and goes over, she'll see something she doesn't want to see. She'll have to show something she doesn't want to show.

Circling a couple of grassy roll-ups between them, the gang's whispers and madding, firecracker laughs are swathed in a musky air. A few of them straggle over to Emmy, trailing wisps of the sly-sweet halo.

'You din't, did yer?' Taylor looks up (eyes snatching under her skirt) as she soars. 'You din't snog that pansy-wuss at the pet shop?'

'I told yer.' Mazzy C, a spurt of grotesque giggles, grabs after Emmy's ankle as she sails down. 'I told yer,' she sniggers, 'she snogged the lad silly.'

Emmy has kissed not a soul. Ever.

But there's no point trying to tell truths to this lot. They all have ears for their old mate Mazzy, who's as loud as she is sure.

'Absa-feckin-lootly, them two got it together, and not – lemme tell you: *not* – just with their lips.'

Mazzy believes she saw it. Right there, in their eyes, when she found them, Emmy Rawlins and Jed Frazer, next to the fish. They were facing each other, pupils fat, as if they'd just swallowed. Mazzy's convinced. She even feels jealous. Forget what everyone likes to say about that creepy-quiet, crawly-fingered Jed weirdo. Mazzy's own eyes had, at that moment, looked shallow and smudged, like an ashtray tipped up. Tom's had been just plain empty.

Emmy keeps swinging, scooting down and shooting up, down and up, down and up, up, up in an arc that smacks her with a black breeze and pulls her closer to the big starry above.

'Jed Frazer, Bwa!' Petey Brown holds on to his sides as if they might crack. 'That plink-plink piano freak?'

From Emmy's perch in the sky, Petey and Julie and the others don't seem frightening. They seem small. Small, insecty things that can be shut up with a swipe.

But then the pendulum swings. Her seat skims down, close to the ground. Julie Marriott, concrete-shouldered, is glowering behind her smoke.

'I told you.' Julie takes a deep breath. The embery end flashes, angry orange. 'The lad's a freak. Know what I mean?'

Emmy's stomach plummets on her next swing to the sky.

A thwack of loneliness gets the new girl as she jerks

back to earth. She lets her stilettos crash into the gravel. They screech like a car with bad brakes; she comes to a dizzying full stop.

Emmy stands up, shaking, others closing around her in the dark.

'I know,' she says, dazed, 'I know what you mean.'

Julie nods, unspools smoke from her nose, and sticks the mossy roll-up between Emmy's lips.

She sinks into her pillow, sinks deep down, deep, into its feathery well. No embracing the softness, burying her face in it, imagining.

Just a lonely, backwards falling.

Her forehead cracks and her brain comes loose from its bony mooring to float up, up, up and away.

It's like watching a movie of yourself, sitting on the bench across from the washers, while the dirties whiz around and around. Emmy's facing her reflection, stretched strange in the machine's porthole.

It's her self, at the spinning core of the universe.

Then again, it's just herself, wishy-washy, insignificant, watching the peel of her days – her knickers and socks and school shirts, her one, single, pink-pale bra – dancing around in the suds at the back of Bernadette's Launderette.

Suddenly, everything shakes. The clothes, fresh from first rinse, start to surge and spin, feverish, finally whizzing at screeching speed. Emmy feels something revolving, furious, inside her.

Why? She watches the clothes zoom into a blur. Why?

Why didn't Jed Frazer just go on and kiss her? When

he had the chance – the perfect, stark-staring, obvious chance?

Huh. Jed Pansy Wuss Piano Freak Frazer.

Her foot kicks forward, then back. Forward, back, forward, back, forward, back, until her toes snag and she kicks herself.

Why? Why didn't she just go on and kiss *him*, when she had the perfect, stark-staring, obvious chance?

Huh. Cringing: what Julie Marriott and that lot would say, what they'd do, if ever she came close to Jed Frazer.

Jed Pansy Wuss Piano Freak Frazer.

Emmy's reflection peers at her, goggle-eyed, from the quaking porthole.

Jed Pansy Piano Freak Frazer.

The clothes splash and slap. Who's in, who's out, who is who, who likes who.

Jed Piano Freak Frazer.

The machine shudders, winding up for its *grand finale* rinse. Emmy's foot glides forward, then, slowly, back.

Jed Frazer.

Blue-green eyes and grey-blue.

Jed . . . Frazer.

Bluey-greeny-grey-blue.

The spinner is screaming, wringing the last of the grime away.

Jed.

A series of forlorn hiccups, and the machine finally shudders, stop. After a long, silent, still moment, the porthole pops open.

Cranking the lid off a can, Emmy hums.

She spoons the tomatoey mess around in the saucepan, then slops it into a bowl, over a few cardboardy triangles of toast. What she eats when her mum is out working nights: same old Alphabetti spaghetti. Usually, she catches herself sighing over the dish. Afterwards she feels jumbled and dull, shuffling through her homework.

But tonight the girl's insides are fiery. She pokes her fork into the bowl. Glistening promise, a glorious swirl of noodly letters. Her own private Ouija: they all seem to be Es and Js.

Emmy's no longer allowed in the school loos when Julie Marriott and the others are smoking and doing their thing. She's no longer keen to hang out in, even step into the loos at all. She's no longer in. She has dared to step out and, at least for a while, they'll make her pay, every day, in some small or not-so-small way.

The phone rings. She leaps up.

Could be that funny girl with a lisp, Charlotte; could be Laura, or Jen Derby, from swim class. Could be him.

'Yeah.' Emmy cradles the phone under her chin, like a violin. Smiling, 'Hmm.'

She reaches for the stinky-sweet box behind the stereo. The speakers vibrate, working up to something big, as the girl sprinkles flakes from her fingertips.

On the table, opposite the Alphabetti spaghetti, squats a shiny-bellied glass bowl. Its sides play with the world's reflection, and in it swishes, flamenco, unblinking, a pearly pink fish.

ARABELLA WEIR

The Stuff Dreams Are Made Of

Tits. jugs. Stack. Bazookas. Mammaries. Baps. Titties. Balcony. Charlies. Blubber bags. Boobies. Hooters. Knockers. Melons. Racks. Whatever term used to describe breasts, be it abusive, childish, coy, clinical, embarrassingly oblique – it didn't matter. Sandra Heggarty knew them all. And not one of them fazed her. In fact, nothing rattled her much, well, that is to say, nothing in the breast department. She'd heard every conceivable means to describe the two bits of flesh every woman in the world carries before them. Moreover, she was completely comfortable with every one of the wide variety of euphemisms. Because she knew breasts.

Sandra was more familiar with breasts than a guy whose job it is to pick out a particularly eye-catching pair for a glossy lads' magazine. In fact, so at home with breasts was she that she made her living out of them. To Sandra, breasts were things of profound, deep and personal interest. To her they were all the same. She didn't care if they hung down to a person's knees like a pair of socks with two tangerines dropped in the bottom. Neither did she care if they defied gravity with spectacular aplomb, standing up to attention like a keen cadet's salute. It was of no matter to her if an unclothed woman's chest revealed nothing more than a sight similar to two deflated rum babas lying limply on a pudding trolley. To her kind and caring mind, they all presented one thing. A terrible and pressing problem.

In Sandra's quietly expert opinion most of the world's ills involving a woman could be accounted for by a badly fitting bra. She was absolutely confident Mrs Thatcher would never have embarked on the Falklands War had she been the owner of a properly fitted bra. Too tight a strap, a mildly chafing under-wire, a baggy cup – any apparently minor (to the untrained eye) snag could lead to long-term misery for the unhappy wearer. And the worst of it, in Sandra's view, was that the sufferer would not even be able to pinpoint the source of their distress.

Most, well at least half, of the nation, it appeared to her, went around unaware that they were wearing the wrong brassière. Ever since she'd started working it had been Sandra's mission to change that. Her belief was that virtually no woman she ever came across had a properly cared-for chest. That said, not for one minute did her interest in them ever veer towards the sexual. Sandra's interest was completely altruistic and unsalacious. It lay solely in a determination to improve the nation's breasts' lot and therefore that of their owner.

Sandra Heggarty was a caretaker of breasts, a breast-worker, a breast angel, a breast missionary. If she could, she was going to see to it that every British woman's chest was housed correctly and comfortably. Sandra owned a lingerie shop. Women came from far and wide to be counselled by her. She was a trained bra fitter and she was the best.

Even though she could barely remember her, Sandra had inherited her unusual skill from her mother. Her parents, Jack and Mandy Heggarty, had owned a haberdasher's. The kind of old-fashioned shop that sold things nobody bought, or indeed needed, until they got really old. At which point, a vital need for many of the extraordinary array of items available at Heggarty's belched into existence. Girdles the colour of an artificial limb; enormous pants (for both genders) that looked and felt like a sack and could easily accommodate not only the wearer but a large bag of baking potatoes; a seemingly unending quantity of satin ribbons – available in every ghastly pastel imaginable; nighties made of material that crackled and sparked in the night and made your hair stand up on end. The establishment catered almost exclusively for the un-stylish, belt-and-braces, bus-pass set. From an early age, all Sandra had been interested in were the bras they stocked. The ones her parents' shop sold were ungainly and so restrictive they could have doubled up as strait-jackets. However, she was fascinated by them and the possibilities they offered.

Sandra was an only child. The family had lived upstairs from the shop, which was the bottom of a converted house in a small village in the Midlands. Mandy Heggarty had done a bunk when Sandra was eleven years old. The timing couldn't have been worse. Within what felt like a few short minutes (it was actually five months and twelve days) of her mother's unexplained, and never discussed thereafter, departure, Sandra's body had decided to explode into adolescent action. She was a bright girl. She had absorbed the scant sex education handed out with brusque embarrassment by the teachers at school. She knew about puberty and the ensuing changes it brought. All the same, she hadn't been prepared for parts of her body to erupt almost overnight. Of course she knew that grown-up women had bosoms. Aside from her mother (whom she dimly remembered as having a pair) she also knew about them because ladies came into their shop to buy the things made expressly for putting them in.

Although Heggarty's was the only shop of its kind for miles, once Mandy had left, Jack had feared he would lose his customer base, which was largely female. Even so, he chose never to equip himself with any of the deluge of manufacturers' information regarding 'intimate fittings' as he described them. As it was he could only just about face ordering the things. It caused him enormous embarrassment just looking at them in a buyer's catalogue and when the oily, ladies-man salesman came round encouraging him to feel the quality of the material the new, soft-look cups were made of, Jack nearly fainted. Consequently he stuck, with religious zeal, to the same orders made by his departed wife, thus avoiding any uncomfortable head-on confrontation with brassières.

It never occurred to him that fashions in that area, as with others, changed, nor that his clientele might wish to purchase more up-to-date items of support. He was lucky. The shop's patrons had indeed appreciated Mandy's expert eye and sorely missed it once she'd gone. But their matronly concern for the lone Jack and his daughter outweighed their need for modish change. And over time they grew to appreciate the gentlemanly refinement with which he averted his eye when wrapping up their wares. They settled for the same style of undergarments they'd worn for years and, amazingly, managed to pass on this trend to their daughters. Accordingly most of the local women sported a somewhat old-fashioned-looking bosom. Girls not much older than Sandra sported rock-hard, sticky-out chests not seen since the days when their mothers had begun emulating the formidable women rarely seen outside post-war public-information films.

So, in spite of the extensive, albeit vicarious, coal-face knowledge Sandra had of breasts, she was none-theless taken aback when faced with her own. She'd assumed they would grow very, very slowly like her dad's prize marrows – some of which didn't come to fruition at all depending on the weather. She'd thought it would be like that with her body's development. She'd expected her bust, for which she was as fully prepared mentally as any young, unsophisticated, motherless girl can be, would develop in a considered, modest manner. She'd imagined that it wouldn't reach noticeable proportions until she was older – at least not until she'd left school and maybe got a job – where surely other people would have breasts too.

But what had actually happened completely knocked her for six. Within the space of one, life-changing, week, just after turning twelve years old, the space between the young Sandra's armpits had transmogrified from an almost dead-flat, bony surface into an undulating mountain range, the crowning glories of which were, what seemed to her, a pair of unwieldy orbs.

Although aware, peripherally, of the change, Jack had characteristically ignored it. Seeing as he practi-cally broke into a cold sweat when merely unwrapping the bra-delivery boxes he could hardly be expected to sit down and have a frank and open discussion with his newly endowed daughter. Instead he elected to do something much more true to form. A few days after Sandra's surprise development, once supper was over, Jack suggested that she go down to the shop to check that everything was locked up properly. For a moment she was surprised, her father never asked her to do things like that, so meticulous was he about all that side of things. However, she was an unquestioningly obedient child and did as she was told.

The moment she switched the light on inside the shop she realised that it had been a ploy. Her attention was immediately drawn to the set of behind-the-counter drawers where the bras were found. Each drawer was pulled out ever so slightly in an attempt, Sandra immediately guessed, to invite search. This had been his clumsy way of seeing to it that she equipped herself with some appropriate underwear. Her heart sank. She did not want to wear one of the dreadful contraptions sold by her father. She did *not* want to go about looking as if she was hiding a couple of hardback books horizontally under her sweater.

However, knowing that she had no choice, Sandra eventually selected a couple of the least offensive bras she could find. She closed the drawers and winced at the thought of the excruciating discomfort her father must have felt as he deliberately left the drawers open. She knew that applying himself even this delicately to her feminine needs would have cost him dearly. All the same she dreaded donning the scratchy devices of constraint she now held unwillingly in her hand.

* * *

The years went by and still Sandra, now fifteen, had grown no more accustomed to the apparel she'd been forced to wear for three miserable years. She begrudgingly admitted that wearing something was better than nothing but only because she'd discovered, to her cost, that she'd drawn too much attention the one time she had ventured out bra-less. She'd elicited many disapproving looks, worse even, she remembered, than the time her granny had gone out without a hat. Consequently, Sandra had become unhappy and withdrawn and had begun to fall behind at school. She stopped being able to see how she was ever going to make something of her life as long as she was held back by the ghastly garments. She was aware of their presence every single minute of the day and they dominated her every waking thought.

But one day everything changed. Sandra was attending her regular check-up at the dentist's and in the waiting room she happened upon a dog-eared copy of *Harper's Bazaar*. Living alone, as she did with her father, she rarely came across publications such as this, dedicated exclusively to beauty and glamour. As she casually flicked through the pages her heart stopped as a bewitching vision leapt out at her. She'd never seen anything like it before in her life and yet she knew it was the very thing she'd always been looking for. An exquisite, delicate bra made of lace and trimmed with satin adorned the figure of a woman who, she noted with joy, looked comfortable and really happy. And Sandra knew it was because of the bra. With an unshakeable conviction Sandra knew that anybody fortunate enough to wear a bra like the one she was looking at would always enjoy a wonderful life. Filled with excitement, Sandra decided to skip the appointment. She had a mission of much greater importance to fulfil. Committing the bra's brand name to memory (and the particular style), Sandra ran home as fast as her legs could carry her.

It wasn't until she burst through Heggarty's front door that Sandra remembered the unspoken rule that existed between herself and her father. Never once had anything of a remotely intimate nature been discussed. Nor had she ever been involved in the ordering process (in fact, she'd often wondered how her dad actually managed to purchase any of the 'intimate fittings', so deep was his reluctance to delve into that area). All the same, aware that she was breaking a taboo, Sandra was driven to share her new-found vision with her father. She *had* to make him realise that there were other bras out there and that they held the key to a whole brave new world for all the women in their village.

Predictably Sandra's zeal was met with a stony, indignant face. Jack was dumbstruck with horror that his daughter should bring up such a distasteful, to him, subject. He remained completely impervious throughout her impassioned argument and drew the conversation to a premature close forbidding her ever to discuss the matter again. Sandra was utterly crushed. She felt desperate as she contemplated a life stretching before her consigned to horrid, scratchy bras. Her desperation was made all the worse now that she'd seen that there was another, infinitely better way. The bra she'd seen had spoken to her, it had touched a core deep down inside of her. She'd been blind and now she could see. But her father's belligerent resistance to change had driven a wedge between them.

Until this moment they had rubbed along together well enough. While the relationship had excluded any form of intimacy, Sandra had not, until now, questioned what it lacked or how it might be improved. She now felt completely alone in a way that she'd never felt before. She couldn't have known that it was almost word for word the same conversation that ended her parents' marriage. Her mother had also attempted to bring about change but had also been thwarted at every turn. In the end she'd gone off to seek out a better bra on her own, leaving all that she held dear behind her.

After a few days of bitter silence Sandra too decided to do the same. Much as it pained her to leave her father, she simply could not contemplate a life without bras of the kind she'd seen. With the bold rashness that only the very young – who still believe dreams can become realities – have, she set out to find the company responsible for making the bra that had changed her life. And so, she ran away to Paris in search of them.

Nine years later one sunny spring morning in a small, elegant flat just off the Rue St Etienne in Paris's quietly fashionable 9th arrondissement, Sandra readied herself for work with the same methodical attention to detail she employed every morning of the week bar Sundays. As she prepared her customary *café au lait* the doorbell rang. It was the postman with a letter. Although he could easily have posted it through the letterbox he preferred to deliver Sandra's missives personally. He was a friendly, middle-aged man who looked out with affectionate paternal feelings for the young English girl who rarely got mail.

After a brief, pleasant conversation Sandra looked at the letter and decided to take her time opening it. It was from her father. Once settled in Paris she'd dutifully kept him up to date with her developments and had always made sure, when she moved, that he'd known her address, but they hadn't seen each other since she'd left England. Neither of them had changed their positions on lingerie. As a result, they had concluded, by tacit agreement, that meeting up would have been pointless and insincere. Therefore it was with some trepidation that Sandra eventually opened the envelope. Her father had decided to retire and in his characteristically oblique, roundabout way was writing to offer his only child the chance of taking over the shop.

Sandra's heart began to soar. All the years she'd put in at Le Balcon Blanc were finally going to pay off. Every long, after-hours, yet to her endlessly fascinating, lesson she'd sat through drinking in the words of wisdom from the undisputed mistresses of feminine support wear had led to this. Sandra was now a fountain of knowledge. She knew every possible means of creating smooth, discreet undercarriaging. She had an expert eye. In one look she could tell, not only precisely what a customer's requirements were, but also which style of support would suit her way of living while also immeasurably increasing her quality of life.

However, Sandra's flair had begun to be bridled by the other ladies at exclusive Paris outfitters. While they were a talented and efficient bunch, not one of them had ever enjoyed her particular gift. Over time Sandra had naturally become the most sought-after assistant with her personal clientele who wouldn't consider allowing anyone but her to fit them. Even so, it had not been in the company's interest to encourage Sandra to break ranks and she had started to feel more and more frustrated.

The letter's arrival was, therefore, perfect. She had never dared to hope that her father might one day invite her, what with her wildly differing views, to take over his shop. Yet here was the clarion call she'd dreamt of getting ever since leaving home. Bras had torn them apart and bras would bring them together.

Sandra was deeply disappointed after she'd completed her first quarter's stock check. If truth be told, she hadn't really needed to do the inventory at all. She'd already known that the sales had been minimal. In fact, the only things she had sold were the few remaining items from her father's reserves. Sandra couldn't understand where she was going wrong. She had embarked on the whole venture with such high hopes. She couldn't understand what was holding the women folk of her village back.

On a limited budget, using the savings she had accumulated in Paris, she had repainted the front of the shop, rejecting the ugly municipal brown it had been its entire life for a glorious pale lilac. In itself, a bold step for a small, closed community. Inside she had made only a few changes, replacing the curtains on the changing rooms and giving the place a lick of paint to brighten it up.

She'd kept the radical changes to her merchandise.

She'd bought in beautiful French and Italian lingerie, bras of every conceivable colour with matching pants, red bras with black straps, gorgeous see-through bras with lace-up fronts, bras that did up at the back, the side, the front, that didn't do up at all. Knickers made of fine lace that covered a lot and knickers made of fine lace that covered virtually nothing at all. Matching bra-and-pants sets in fine cotton, satin, silk, lace (she even had a few sets in rubber but she didn't tell anyone about them, she thought she'd wait until someone asked). Sandra had planned to cater for every possible need, every possible taste and most importantly, in an area with high unemployment, every budget. She just needed to get her hands on their breasts, as it were.

After another dismal few weeks, just when she was beginning to wonder how she could keep going, Sandra had a brainwave. Many of the customers she'd left behind in Paris had written kind letters bemoaning her departure and as a result she had all their addresses. She wrote to each one of them, describing what she had to offer, and little by little the orders came in. Her old clientele trusted her judgement to such a great degree that no one ever asked to see samples or photographs of the lingerie in advance, they simply ordered the stuff she recommended sight unseen. And they were never disappointed. Sandra remembered each client perfectly.

Within a few months she was doing lively business, so much so that she was even beginning to find it hard to keep up. However, she still rarely sold anything to anyone from the village and when she did it was invariably to a young girl evidently making the purchase furtively and unbeknownst to her mother. But it was the women of the village Sandra had come back for and she yearned to turn their heads around. She longed to introduce them to comfortable yet attractive underwear. She was sure it would change their lives, just as it had hers. And then she had another idea.

If somehow they were exposed to the goods, she reasoned, without necessarily having to try them on, they would surely be won over by their infinite superior quality and comfort. So, using the remainder of her capital, Sandra started a lingerie mail-order service. She was planning on selling some of her existing stock while slowly introducing her own designs. Initially, she was able to create three full-time jobs and after considering what might be fairest and indeed expedient, in terms of exposing the greatest number to the goods, she advertised for six part-time workers. Much to her surprise, as she'd anticipated the same initial resistance to all things connected to her, the jobs were taken up instantly. However, local jobs were in very short supply, particularly ones suitable for women, and the applicants had elected to overlook their disapproval of Sandra and focus on the much-needed extra income.

Mrs Weston, who had been a contemporary of her mother's, was first in. After her came Mrs Weston's neighbour, Mrs Simms, then Miss Cameron, the village spinster, then a young unmarried (and according to village gossip unmarriageable) girl in her late twenties, Mary Tennant; her friend Josie Wigglesworth followed them and finally Shirley Rogers, a married mother of three, whose youngest had just started school. Since her return Sandra had been on nodding acquaintance with them all but was viewed with suspicion by each and every one.

As she watched her new employees arrive for their first day at work she could tell that not one of them had ever spent one day of their adult lives out of a Heggarty's contraption. They each sported the same unforgiving, forbidding, rock-hard bosom common to the village's women folk. The generic look was similar to how one might imagine Mae West would have looked wearing combat gear. Sandra resolved to do something about that if it killed her.

She had set up a small workshop in the old store room at the back of the shop. At first the women handled the goods as if they were radioactive. It was as if they thought they could catch something terminal from the lingerie. Sandra wondered if deep down their fear was based on exactly that, a dread that they might get something deeply suspect and unfamiliar from these strange items. As much as was possible, considering they were supposed to be handling and packaging the bras and pants, the workforce kept the stuff at arm's length. They were a tight-knit, grumpy group and rarely spoke when Sandra was in the room.

Alone at night, with her dad silently dozing in the armchair in front of the TV, she despaired of ever being able to do anything to change their minds. She began to wonder if she should have stayed put in Paris where women appreciated the value of comfort and sex appeal supplied by the same item. Against her better nature, Sandra also started to feel a little resentful – the business was doing increasingly well, she had provided much-needed work for these people, and how did they repay her? Why, they wouldn't even try her bras on, never mind actually wear them!

And so life went on. Heggarty's rarely sold anything over the counter and any sales that were made were either to people passing through the village or the odd travelling salesman buying something for his wife, or, Sandra often mused, more likely mistress. Once, to her delight, the woman who ran the mobile bookshop came in while somebody minded her van and bought a particularly fetching bra-and-pants set. Although the woman wasn't local she had the same dowdy look as most of the women in the area and yet she'd dared to venture into alluring underwear. How Sandra yearned for her neighbours to make the same break for freedom.

One day when Mrs Weston (no one had ever been invited to use her first name, in fact Sandra wasn't sure she had one), Shirley Rogers and Mary Tennant were doing a shift together, a last-minute, urgent order came through. Le Balcon Blanc had been let down by a supplier and were desperate for Sandra's help. It was a Friday and they needed the stuff by the next morning. It would mean working into the night. With families waiting for them Mrs Weston and Shirley were unable to help out but Mary offered to stay behind. As the other two left Sandra saw Mrs Weston fix Mary with her steely eye as if giving her a warning.

Finally the order was finished. Sandra was to drive it over to the station in order to ensure arrival in Paris by the next morning. As she stacked the boxes into the back of her van she had an idea. She caught Mary preparing to leave and seized her opportunity.

'Mary, you're young, you've got a whole life ahead

of you. Please take this, from me, with my blessing. Just see what a difference it makes.'

The girl looked down and involuntarily her eyes widened as if she was looking at a pot of gold. Sandra was holding the Dove – a fine cotton bra trimmed with satin ribbon. It was the perfect choice for a first-timer – impossibly comfortable yet with a hint of decadent luxury. Mary looked around furtively then grabbed the thing before she changed her mind.

'Thank you,' she mumbled as she ran out of the shop.

Sandra heaved a sigh of relief and prayed to God that the timid girl would find the nerve actually to wear it.

Sandra spent an agonising weekend. She couldn't stop wondering what would happen on Monday morning. Would Mary wear the bra? Would she come to work wearing it? Would it have changed her life?

As Sandra opened up the shop on the first day of the following week she couldn't help feeling a surge of hope. Was this going to be the dawning of a bright new age? Were the recalcitrant bunch that worked for her finally going to see the error of their ways? Despite their persistent capacity to withstand the obvious allure of the goods they daily handled, the women were a conscientious lot and had organised to come in all together to avoid the build-up of a backlog which might easily occur as a result of the rush order.

Once Sandra was sure all her employees would be settled at work she found an excuse to enter the workshop, anxious to see if there was a different atmosphere brought on, she hoped, by Mary's rebellion. Mary wasn't there. It was forty minutes after work was supposed to have started and there was no sign of Mary. Sandra realised with sadness that she'd over-estimated the girl. She should have known that she didn't have the gumption to fly in the face of tradition, to cast off the chains that had bound her throughout her teenage years. The very same chains that she was now going to wear miserably for the remainder of her life.

Just as Sandra was leaving the workshop she heard a commotion in the street outside. She peered out of the window and made out a figure striding towards the shop. It was Mary, she was wearing the bra and people had noticed. Some were pointing, some were shaking their heads disapprovingly, some had their mouths wide open in shock. Sandra watched the girl as she approached. She'd never seen her like this, she was walking tall and proud.

She walked into the shop and spoke with a dignified air.

'Miss Heggarty . . .'

'Please, Mary, call me Sandra.'

'Right, Sandra it is then. Sandra, I want to thank you for opening my eyes. As you can probably tell, I have the Dove on and I've never felt more wonderful in my life. I can't believe it's taken me so long. I'm sorry I'm late but my mother tried to stop me leaving the house when she saw that I wasn't wearing my usual . . . erm . . . underwear.'

'Oh, I hope I haven't caused you any difficulty.'

'No, it had to happen. Someone had to change things round here.'

Mary then made her way towards the workshop with her head held high. Suspecting that there might be a kerfuffle, despite feeling electrified with excitement, Sandra decided it would be best if she held back. A few moments later Mrs Weston emerged from the work-shop and marched out of the shop without giving Sandra a backward glance. She watched her go with some regrets but comforted herself with the thought that you can't teach an old dog new tricks – not every time, anyway.

Bracing herself for a confrontation she turned and gingerly walked into the workshop. As she walked into the room there was a burst of applause. Sandra couldn't believe her eyes. Every one of her remaining workers was standing up, grinning from ear to ear. Shirley Rogers was wearing the Emancipation, a pale-pink satin plunge bra that reeked of demure deca-dence. It was the perfect choice for her: Sandra had always guessed that Shirley had been hiding a sexy light under her bushel. Everything about her now looked emboldened, her face, her smile, her eyes.

Mrs Simms, until now Mrs Weston's henchman, had made a sensible choice, she was wearing a purple version of the more conservative Twilight bra. All the same she too looked like a different woman. Miss Cameron, the village spinster, had become Boadicea in the Challenger, a cream-front cross-over lace struc-ture. She looked ready to do battle with anyone, even Mrs Weston.

Finally Sandra's amazed gaze came to rest on Josie Wigglesworth. She had made the most valiant choice of all – the Midnight Love, a black-lace balcony bra trimmed with red silk. It was one of Sandra's own designs and she'd had nights of interminable passion in mind when she'd created it. Until now, she would have thought that the last person in the whole world who could carry it off and all the courage required to wear it would have been Josie. But she was wrong. In it Josie looked fit for any amount of turbulence of whatever shape or form – she'd be able to handle it, come what may.

There was going to be no stopping them now.

JACKIE KAY

My Daughter, the Fox

W<small>E HAD</small> a night of it, my daughter and I, with the foxes screaming outside. I had to stroke her fur and hold her close all night. She snuggled up, her wet nose against my neck. Every time they howled, she'd startle and raise her ears. I could feel the pulse of her heartbeat on my chest, strong and fast. Strange how eerie the foxes sounded to me; I didn't compare my daughter's noises to theirs. Moonlight came in through our bedroom window; the night outside seemed still and slow, except for the cries of the foxes. It must have been at least three in the morning before we both fell into a deep sleep, her paw resting gently on my shoulder. In my dream I dreamt of being a fox myself, of the two of us running through the forest, our red bushy tails flickering through the dark trees, our noses sniffing rain in the autumn air.

In the morning I sat her in her wooden high chair and she watched me busy myself around the kitchen. I gave her a fresh bowl of water and a raw egg. She cracked the shell herself and slurped the yellow yoke in one gulp. I could tell she was still a little drowsy. She was breathing peacefully and slowly, her little red chest rising and falling. Her eyes literally followed me from counter to counter to cupboard, out into the hall to pick up the post from the raffia mat and back again. I poured her a bowl of muesli and put some fresh blueberries in it. She enjoys that.

Nobody tells you how flattering it is, how loved you feel, your child following your every move like that. Her beady eyes watched me open my post as if it was the most interesting thing anybody could do. The post was dull as usual, a gas bill and junk. I sighed, went to the kitchen bin and threw everything in but the bill. When I turned back around, there she still was, smiling at me, her fur curling around her mouth. Her eyes lit up, fierce with love. When she looked at me from those deep dark eyes of hers, straight at me and through me, I felt more understood than I have ever felt from any look by anybody.

Nobody says much and nothing prepares you. I've often wondered why women don't warn each other properly about the horrors of childbirth. There is something medieval about the pain, the howling, the push-push-pushing. In the birthing room next door, the November night my daughter was born, I heard a woman scream, 'Kill me! Just kill me!' That was just after my waters had broken. An hour later I heard her growl in a deep animal voice, 'Fucking shoot me!' I tried to imagine the midwife's black face. We were sharing her and she was running back and forth between stations. She held my head and said, 'You're in control of this!' But I felt as if my body was exploding. I felt as if I should descend down into the bowels of the earth and scrape and claw. Nothing prepares you for the power of the contractions, how they rip through your body like a tornado or an earthquake. Then the beautiful, spacey peace between contractions where you float and dream away out at sea.

Many of my friends were mothers. I'd asked some, 'Will it hurt?' and they'd all smiled and said, 'A bit.' A bit! Holy Mary Mother of God. I was as surprised as the Jamaican midwife when my daughter the fox came out. I should have known really. Her father was a foxy man, sly and devious and, I found out later, was already seeing two other women when he got me pregnant, that night under the full moon. On our way up north for that weekend, I saw a dead fox on the hard shoulder. It was lying, curled, and the red of the blood was much darker than the red of the fur. When we made love in the small double bed in Room 2 at the Bed and Breakfast place by Coniston Water, I could still see it, the dead fox at the side of the road. It haunted me all the way through my pregnancy. I knew the minute I was pregnant almost the second the seed had found its way up. I could smell everything differently. I smelt an orange so strongly I almost vomited.

When the little blue mark came, of course it couldn't tell me I was carrying a fox, just that I was pregnant. And even the scans didn't seem to pick anything up, except they couldn't agree whether or not I was carrying a girl or a boy. One hospital person seemed sure I was carrying a son. It all falls into place now of course, because that would have been her tail. Once they told me the heart was beating fine and the baby seemed to be progressing, but that there was something they couldn't pick up.

She was born on the stroke of midnight, a midnight baby. When she came out, the stern Jamaican midwife, who had been calm and in control all during the contractions, saying, 'Push now, that's it, good, and again,' let out a blood-curdling scream. I thought my baby was dead. But no, midwives don't scream when babies are still-born. They are serious, they whisper. They scream when foxes come out of a woman's cunt though, that's for sure. My poor daughter was terrified. I could tell straightaway. She gave a sharp bark and I pulled her to my breast and let her suckle.

It's something I've learnt about mothers: when we are loved we are not choosy. I knew she was devoted to me from the start. It was strange; so much of her love was loyalty. I knew that the only thing she shared with her father was red hair. Apart from that, she was mine. I swear I could see my own likeness, in her pointed chin, in her high cheeks, in her black eyes. I'd hold her up in front of me, her front paws framing her red face, and say, 'Who is Mummy's girl then?'

I was crying when she was first born. I'd heard that many mothers do that – cry straight from the beginning. Not because she wasn't what I was expecting, I was crying because I felt at peace at last, because I felt loved and even because I felt understood. I didn't get any understanding from the staff at the hospital. They told me I had to leave straightaway; the fox was a hazard. It was awful to hear about my daughter being spoken of in this way, as if she hadn't just been born, as if she didn't deserve the same consideration as the others. They were all quaking and shaking like it was the most disgusting thing they had ever seen. She wasn't even given one of those little ankle-bracelet name-tags I'd been so looking forward to keeping all her life.

I whispered her name into her alert ear. 'Anya,' I said. 'I'll call you Anya.' It was the name I'd chosen if I had a girl and seemed to suit her perfectly. She was blind when she was born. I knew she couldn't yet see me, but she recognised my voice; she was comforted by my smell. It was a week before her sight came.

They called an ambulance to take me home at three in the morning. It was a clear, crisp winter's night. The driver put on the sirens and raced through the dark streets screaming. I had to cover my daughter's ears. She has trembled whenever she's heard a siren ever since. When we arrived at my house in the dark, one of the men carried my overnight bag along the path and left it at my wooden front door.

'You'll be all right from here?' he said, peering at my daughter, who was wrapped in her very first baby blanket.

'Fine,' I said, breathing in the fresh night air.

I saw him give the driver an odd look, and then they left, driving the ambulance slowly up my street and off. The moon shone still, and the stars sparkled and fizzed in the sky. It wasn't what I'd imagined, arriving home from hospital in the dark, yet still I couldn't contain my excitement, carrying her small soft body over my doorstep and into my home.

When I first placed her gently in the little crib that had been sitting empty for months, I got so much pleasure. Day after endless day, as my big tight round belly got bigger and tighter, I'd stared into that crib hardly able to believe I'd ever have a baby to put in it. And now at last I did, I laid her down and covered her with the baby blanket, then I got into bed myself. I rocked the crib with my foot. I was exhausted, so bone tired, I hardly knew if I really existed or not.

Not more than half an hour passed before she started to whine and cry. I brought her into bed with me and she's never been in the crib at night since. She needs me. Why fight about these things? Life is too short. I know her life will be shorter than mine will. That's the hardest thing about being the mother of a fox. The second hardest thing is not having anyone around who has had the same experience. I would so love to swap notes on the colour of her shit. Sometimes it seems a worrying greenish colour.

I'll never forget the look on my mother's face when she first arrived, with flowers and baby-grows and teddy bears. I'd told her on the phone that the birth had been fine, and that my daughter weighed three pounds, which was true.

'Won't she be needing the incubator, being that small?' she'd asked, worried.

'No,' I'd said. 'They think she's fine.' I hadn't said any more, my mother wasn't good on the phone.

I opened the front door and she said, 'Where is she, where is she?' her eyes wild with excitement. My daughter is my mother's first grandchild.

I said, 'Ssssh, she's sleeping. Just have a wee peek.' I felt convinced that, as soon as she saw her, it wouldn't matter and she would love her like I did.

How could anybody not see Anya's beauty? She had lovely dark-red fur, thick and vivid, alive. She was white under her throat. At the end of her long bushy tail, she had a perfect white tail-tip. Her tail was practically a third of the length of her body. On her legs were white stockings. She was shy, slightly nervous of strangers, secretive, and highly intelligent. She moved with such haughty grace and elegance that at times she appeared feline. From the minute I gave birth to my daughter the fox, I could see that no other baby could be more beautiful. I hoped my mother would see her the same way.

We tiptoed into my bedroom where Anya was sleeping in her crib for her daytime nap. My mother was already saying, 'Awwww,' as she approached the crib. She looked in, went white as a sheet, and then gripped my arm. 'What's going on?' she whispered, her voice just about giving out. 'Is this some kind of a joke? What have you done with your baby?'

It was the same look on people's faces when I took Anya out in her pram. I'd bought a great big Silver-cross pram with a navy hood. I always kept the hood up to keep the sun or the rain out. People could never resist sneaking a look at a baby in a pram. I doubt that many had ever seen daughters like mine before.

One old friend, shocked and fumbling for something to say, said, 'She looks so like you.'

I glowed with pride. 'Do you think so?' I said, squeaking with pleasure.

She did look beautiful, my daughter in her Silver-cross pram, the white of her blanket against the red of her cheeks. I always made her wear a nappy when I took her out in the pram though she loathed nappies.

It hurt me that her father never came to see her, never took the slightest bit of interest in her. When I told him that, on the stroke of midnight, I'd given birth to a baby fox, he actually denied being her father. He thought I was lying, that I'd done something with our real daughter and got Anya in her place.

'I always thought you were off your fucking rocker. This proves it! You're barking! Barking!' he screamed down the phone.

He wouldn't pay a penny towards her keep. I should have had him DNA tested, but I didn't want to put myself through it. Nobody was as sympathetic to me as I thought they might be. It never occurred to me to dump Anya or disown her or pretend she hadn't come from me.

But when the baby-stage passed, everything changed. My daughter didn't like being carried around in the pouch, pushed in the pram or sat in her high chair. She didn't like staying in my one-bedroom ground-floor flat in Tottenham either. She was constantly sitting by the front door waiting for me to open it to take her out to Clissold Park, or Finsbury Park or Downhills Park. But I had to be careful during the day. Once a little child came running up to us with an ice-cream in her hand, and I stroked the little girl's hair. Anya was so jealous she growled at her and actually bared her teeth.

Soon she didn't want me to be close to anyone else. I had to call friends up before they came around to tell them for God's sake not to hug me in front of Anya or she would go for them. She'd gone for my old friend, Adam, the night he raised his arms to embrace me as he came in our front door. Anya rushed straight along the hall and knocked him right over. She had him on his back with her mouth snarling over his face. Adam was so shaken up I had to pour him a malt. He drank it neat and left, I haven't seen or heard of him since.

Friends would use these incidents to argue with me.

'You can't keep her here for ever,' they'd say. 'You shouldn't be in a city for a start.'

'You'll have to release her.'

They couldn't imagine how absurd they sounded to me. London was full of foxes roaming the streets at night. I was always losing sleep listening to the howls and the screams of my daughter's kind. What mother gives her daughter to the wilds? My best friend, Aileen, offered to drive us both to the north of Scotland and release her into Glen Strathfarrar where she was convinced Anya would be safe and happy – the red deer and the red fox and the red hills.

But I couldn't bring myself even to think of parting with my daughter. At night, it seemed we slept even closer, her fur keeping me warm. She slept now with her head on the pillow, her paw on my shoulder. She liked to get right under the covers with me. It was strange. Part of her wanted to do everything the same way I did: sleep under covers, eat what I ate, go where I went, run when I ran, walk when I walked; and part of her wanted to do everything her way. Eat from whatever she could snatch in the street or in the woods.

She was lazy; she never really put herself out to hunt for food. She scavenged what came her way out of a love of scavenging, I think. It certainly wasn't genuine hunger, she was well fed. I had to stop her going through my neighbour's bin for the remains of their Sunday dinner. Things like that would embarrass me more than anything. I didn't mind her eating a worm from our garden, or a beetle.

Once she spotted the tiny movement of a wild rabbit's ear twitching in our garden. That was enough for Anya. She chased the rabbit, killed it, brought it back and buried it, saving it for a hungry day. It thrilled me when she was a fox like other foxes, when I could see her origins so clearly. Anya had more in common with a coyote or a grey wolf or a wild dog than she had with me. The day she buried the rabbit was one of the proudest moments in my life.

But I had never had company like her my whole life long. With Anya, I felt like there were two lives now: the one before I had her and the one after, and they seemed barely to connect. I didn't feel like the same person even. I was forty when I had Anya, so I'd already lived a lot of my life. All sorts of things that had mattered before I had her didn't matter any more. I wasn't so interested in my hair, my weight, clothes. Going out to parties, plays, restaurants, pubs didn't bother me. I didn't feel like I was missing anything. Nor did I feel ambitious any more. It all seemed stupid wanting to be better than the others in the same ring, shallow, pointless. I called in at work and extended my maternity leave for an extra three months. The thought of the office bored me rigid. It was Anya who held all of my interest.

At home, I'd play my favourite pieces of music to her and dance round the room. I'd play her Mozart's piano concertos, I'd play her Chopin, I'd play Ella Fitzgerald and Louis Armstrong. Joni Mitchell was Anya's favourite. I'd hold her close and dance. 'Do you want to dance with me baby, well, come on.' Anya's eyes would light up and she'd lick my face. 'All I really, really want our love to do is to bring out the best in me and in you too.' I sang along. I had a high voice and Anya loved it when I sang, especially folk songs. Sometimes I'd sing her to sleep. Other times I'd read her stories. I'd been collecting stories about foxes. Aileen had bought Anya *Brer Rabbit*. No fox ever came off too well in the tales or stories.

'Oh your kind are a deceptive and devious lot,' I'd say, stroking her puffed-out chest and reading her another *Brer Rabbit* tale. She loved her chest being stroked. She'd roll on her back and put both sets of paws in the air.

But then I finally did have to go back to work. I left Anya alone in the house while I sat at my computer answering e-mails, sipping coffee. When I came home the first time, the wooden legs of the kitchen chairs were chewed right through; the paint on the kitchen door was striped with claw marks. I had to empty the room of everything that could be damaged, carrying the chairs through to the living room, moving the wooden table, putting my chewed cookery books in the hall. I put newspapers on the floor. I left Anya an old shoe to chew.

I knew that no nursery would take her, no child-minder. I couldn't bring myself to find a dog-walker: Anya was not a dog! It seemed so unfair. I was left to cope with all the problems completely on my own. I had to use my own resources, my own imagination. I left her an old jumper of mine for the comfort of my smell while I was out working, knowing that it would be chewed and shredded by the time I came home. When I tried to tell my colleagues about Anya's antics, they would clam up and look uncomfortable, exchanging awkward looks with each other when they thought I wasn't looking. It made me angry, lonely.

Sometimes it felt as if there was only Anya and me in

the world, nobody else mattered really. On Sundays, I'd take her out to Epping Forest and she'd make me run wild with her, in and out of pine trees, jumping over fallen trees, chasing rabbits. The wind flew through my hair and I felt ecstatically happy. I had to curb the impulse to rip off my clothes and run with Anya naked through the woods. My sense of smell grew stronger over those Sundays. I'd stand and sniff where Anya was sniffing, pointing my head in the same direction. I grew to know when a rabbit was near. I never felt closer to her than out in the forest running. But of course, fit as I was, fast I was, I could never be as fast as Anya. She'd stop and look round for me and come running back.

I don't think anybody has ever taught me more about myself than Anya. Once when she growled at the postman, I smacked her wet nose. I felt awful. But five minutes later she jumped right on to my lap and licked my face all over, desperate to be friends again. There's nothing like forgiveness, it makes you want to weep. I stroked her long, lustrous fur and nuzzled my head against hers and we looked straight into each other's eyes, knowingly, for the longest time. I knew I wasn't able to forgive like Anya could. I just couldn't. I couldn't move on to the next moment like that. I had to go raking over the past. I couldn't forgive Anya's father for denying her, for making promises and breaking them like bones.

One morning I woke up and looked out of the window. It was snowing; soft dreamy flakes of snow whirled and spiralled down to the ground. Already the earth was covered white, and the winter rose bushes had snow clinging to the stems. Everything was covered. I got up and went to get the milk. Paw footprints led up to our door. The foxes had been here again in the night. They were driving me mad. I sensed they wanted to claim Anya as one of their own.

I fetched my daughter her breakfast, some fruit and some chicken. I could tell she wasn't herself. Her eyes looked dull and her ears weren't alert. She gave me a sad look that seemed to last an age. I wasn't sure what she was trying to tell me. She walked with her elegant beauty to the door and hit it twice with her paw. Then she looked at me again, the saddest look you ever saw. Perhaps she'd had enough. Perhaps she wanted to run off with the dog-fox that so often hung and howled around our house.

I couldn't actually imagine my life without her now, that was the problem. They never tell you about that either. How the hardest thing a mother has to do is give her child up, let them go, watch them run. I found myself in the middle of the night looking through Anya's baby photograph album. There she was at only a few months with a bottle of milk in her mouth. There she was out in the garden with me holding her in front of the laburnum tree. There was Anya's sweet red head popping out of the big pram. There was Anya at the back of the garden burying her first rabbit. There was Anya and I looking into each other's eyes, smiling.

Much later that night when we were both in bed, we heard them again; one of the most common sounds in London now, the conversations of the urban fox. Anya got up and stood at my bedroom window. She howled back. Soon four of them were out in the back garden, their bright-red fur even more dramatic against the snow. I held my breath in when I looked at them. They looked strange and mysterious, different from Anya. They were stock still, lit up by the moonlight. I stared at them for a long time and they stared back. I walked slowly through to the kitchen in my bare feet. I stood looking at the back door for some minutes. I pulled the top bolt and then the bottom one. I opened the door and I let her out into the night.

LEWIS DAVIES

To the Centre of the Volcano

I

I'M WRITING this play. It's set here in Almeria. Two or three characters. I'm not sure yet. We were happy here once. We drove down with the boy when he was eight months old. We were always good on escaping. She was sick for two days on the ferry. It doesn't affect me. I lie down and I'm OK. Then there was Spain. A whole country stretching out before us into the February rain. The last weeks of winter.

We cut south, avoiding the toll roads, and got caught in a snowstorm on the road beyond Teruel. Two days in a trucker's stop with an eight-month-old baby. I can remember a boar's head above the fireplace with a can of Heineken stuffed between its jaws. Bull-fighters lined the central beam. The pictures over-exposed. The colours fading. Each with his own moment. A TV sat in the far corner. The storm had cut the signal. The barman had tried a few times to get a reception, then gave up, shutting off the power in disgust.

We drank *cerveza* with fish from under the tapas glass. *Atún, boquerónes, bacalao*: eyes cooked dead or cut into chunks. A basket of bread accompanied each

139

order. By nine we were drunk and Malena's eyes sparkled in the lights. The last year had been hard for her. Her work had not gone well. Two months after the birth she had burned all her materials. I could smell the paint, lingering around the cottage on the hill. The people of the valley distrusted us. We wouldn't be there long. They were right.

The snow rushed against the window, drifted against the shattered lorries in the truck park. The men looked at us keenly. The baby, blond and bright, watched everything. I could see it in their eyes. We were once like that, young men lost in a snowstorm with a wife and child. And look at us now. Old men with responsibilities, a job, a truck to drive. Life catches up with you.

The next day the snow stopped. I sat around the bar trying to recover from a hangover. Malena spent most of the day in the room. Joshua was hungry. I could hear his cries along the corridor. Most of the truckers had left by mid-afternoon but we booked in for another night.

Spain was still new again. I hadn't been back since a package tour with my mum and dad twenty years ago. The language was a challenge. I pointed at the food under the glass and waited for evening. A man begged a cigarette from me. He walked with a limp. One leg was twisted shorter than the other. He was an old man who had spent a life in the fields and the sun had been burned into his skin. He smoked desperately as if trying to ward a spirit away from his lungs. He hobbled back to the bar with his prize.

Malena had needed to get away. She claimed the world was closing in on her. No one would let her show her work any more. She didn't want to play the game. Art was for wankers. I hoped Spain would see us together again. Anything to escape another Aberdare winter.

The country was new. I thought we had a good chance. We just needed somewhere to let us live for a while. We just had to keep going. Find somewhere.

We caught the end of Santa Semana in Mazarron. It was the first week of April and the air was warm. The sea a for-ever blue. We walked along the promenade mixing with the crowds. The boy in a pushchair that we had bought in a charity shop in Granada.

The restaurant advertised a local *climatizado*. One waiter served the tables on the promenade. A plastic sheet protected the customers from the wind and spring thunderstorms.

The waiter could speak German, good English and some Dutch. French he would not do. His grandfather had died in France during the Second World War. To the French he spoke in heavy Spanish.

The restaurant served *patatas bravas*, squid, mussels and sardines, beer and wine. It would not serve chips and coffee. The waiter offered us the menu of the day. We said we wanted the tapas and beer. He said that was OK but the menu of the day would have been better.

He struggled with the rush of customers driven off the promenade by the rain. His voice sharp in three languages and the shouting in Spanish. The cook pushed the heaped plates out to him through a window in the wall. He carried a paper table covering over to us and managed a flourish of English as he set the table.

'Would you like to move inside?'

Malena shook her head.

'The rain is going to be heavy.'

'We like it here.'

'It is OK, here is good. Inside would be better but here is good.'

Malena smiled thinly at him.

'Are you ready to order?'

Malena looked at me. It was my turn to order. I always made a mess of ordering. We never got what I asked for.

'*Patatas bravas?*'

He nodded. I struggled on.

'*Uno patatas bravas, una tortilla*, one menu *del día.*'

The waiter smiled. 'No problem.' He scurried back into the restaurant.

Malena grinned at me. I made my excuses.

'It was easier.'

'You don't know what you are getting.'

'There's wine with it and bread.' I pointed at the board.

'There might be meat. What's *conejo*?'

'It doesn't matter. I'll eat it anyway.'

'You always do.'

'What's wrong with that?'

'You always compromise.'

I looked out across the promenade to where the water had turned from blue to grey as the clouds covered the sky. The first drop of rain began to hit the plastic awning. The boy shuffled in his pushchair, still asleep, dreaming.

*   *   *

142

We watched the procession as it merged at the church of San Juan. Serious young men in purple satin robes struggling with a statue of the virgin. She looked white as if sick with the unsteady motion of the parade.

A marching band followed, echoing into a night sky scythed with swifts. The devil birds laughing at the humans and their follies. We bought a balloon for Joshua; his eyes opened wide with delight, looking up into the yellow night.

The parade seemed to follow us around town as we moved from bar to bar drinking. She could always match my drinking. I miss the competition of it, the free carousement. By twelve we were drunk and the boy was asleep again. We walked back down the promenade. People lingered with the night. Holding on to the holiday. A crowd was looking at the beach. The flickering lights of candles played on the sand. As we walked closer we could see the sculptures. Beautifully crafted out of the sand and then coloured with food dyes. A virgin in sand, a cathedral with spires, Jesus with a halo, and taking centre stage, Homer Simpson and his family. They were sitting on a sand settee watching a sand television. A real rug in front of them collected donations from the holiday crowd, *gracias* printed out on the sand. It was the work of a real sculptor, even here in the sand. I could see the hours that had been spent on acquiring the skill. I turned to Malena, looking for her smile at the work, but there was only the crowd. Then panic thudded into me as I saw her jump the wall on to the beach. The sculptor had seen her but he was too slow. Bart got it first. His yellow head shattered into a thousand grains as Malena's fist connected with it. Then

Homer and Marge. I was there by then with the sculptor. I thought he was going to hit her but he only shouted. The crowd bayed at us and Malena was kicking and biting me trying to get at the rest of the Simpsons. I dragged her back as the abuse roared around us. Someone threw a bottle which bounced off my shoulder. Then we reached the pram and the abuse stopped. The baby was crying. Then there was just pity. I held Malena tightly, she cried into my shoulder.

I was driving back to the campsite before she spoke again.

'It's all fucked up. All of it. White virgins and sandcastle Christs. All fucked up.'

The *autovia del sud* is a bleak road but it has the feel of escape.

Two weeks later, we were still driving. We were running out of money and things to say to each other. We had stopped at a square in San José. The Englishman had found us. He had been a shepherd in the Pyrenees but now he ran an antiques shop. He couldn't walk very far now. He had an abscess on his spine. He swam along the front of the village beach in the mornings. He had spoken to Malena in the shop. She was dark and he had tried Spanish, then Portuguese. The Englishman knew the country. We should walk up into the centre of the volcano. He became our first friend in Spain.

The Englishman had a house in the village. We were welcome to the spare room. We could share his bills. Malena stopped trying to imagine herself somewhere else. We were here. Now.

We promised him we would walk to the volcano. It had had taken us three weeks to get around to it.

The path cut down through Presillas Baja. The village was strewn across a spur above the dry valley pouring out from the volcano. We walked on the loose coarse sand which marked the floor of the *rambla*. The Englishman had said it was an hour's walk at most. We found the going hard. The boy was heavy. Ten pounds at birth and three times that now. We had squashed him into my rucksack and tied him in. His eyes followed the valley at first but he soon fell asleep and lolled forward, pulling on my back.

We stopped after an hour. A rusted frame of a car lay abandoned in the centre of the path. Sand and rock had washed around it.

Malena sat on the boot of the car. I remember wondering what a Fiat was doing so far from the road. A lost cause, dreams given up.

She looked away from me, up across the scrub of the mountain. The core of a volcano thrown out thirty million years ago. And now we were here. Two tourists and their child climbing to its centre. Our feet light on the dry flaking earth.

'Why do you think they gave up on it?'

I lowered the boy from my back, not wanting to answer her. She could see the car as clearly as I could. It was a used thing.

'It was an insurance claim. They drove it up here and hoped no one would find it.'

'All this way?'

She brushed some dust from the bonnet of the car. It would have been red once but now it had faded to brown in the sun and rivers of rust ran down from the cracks in its body panels. All the windows had gone and the seats were piled high with rocks.

Her shorts rose high on her legs. The boy snored lightly. She smiled at me. She wanted to play the game.

'All right, there were three French tourists, Hugo, Muriel, and I forget the other one.'

'Haj.'

'OK, Haj. He was a Moroccan. They took the wrong turning in the village and were trying to get to Rodalquilar.'

She smiled at me, flicking her hair back. A sand grouse called from the scrub. The heat surrounded us. I gently put the boy on the ground in the shade of the Fiat. His arms flexed once into the air, grasping for me, before he fell back into sleep. She waited for me.

'Hugo was married to Muriel but in love with Haj.'

'He couldn't find a way to tell her . . .?'

'They drove up into the hills and?'

She waited for me. It was a game to finish first. But it had to be good.

'Threw her into the well at the ruined farmhouse.'

'That's rubbish.'

'Best I could do.'

'It doesn't explain the car.'

She looked away up into the dry hills. Nothing moved. I could see the disappointment on her face. I was close to her now, facing her. She put her arms around me. I kissed her once. Then once again, longer. I could feel the heat on my back run through me. The heat of the car in the sun on my thighs. The softness of her legs, bare and brown. I traced a line with my fingers along the inside of her leg. My fingers touching

146

soft light skin. She curled her hands around my back. I moved my hand up on to her breasts. They were round, still full with milk. I could feel her nipples harden beneath her T-shirt, beneath my fingers. My dick pushed out against the hard cotton of my shorts. The heat of the day filled the valley. She pulled my hand down and looked away.

'Do you think she's in the well?'

'Yeah, of course.'

I followed her gaze. The vapour trail of a jet cut across the blue sky before fading out high to the south.

'I'm sorry. It's just that –'

'It doesn't matter.'

The boy stirred beneath us. His feet scuffing the sand.

II

Spain is very big. It took ages to get where Dad wanted to go. We kept stopping in places he didn't want to stay in. We did see some castles and huge bulls made out of wood. Dad said they were advertising a drink. But he didn't know which drink and we never bought it.

The play isn't making much progress. The Englishman isn't here any more. The man who runs the restaurant claims he could be living with a woman in Bilbao. I wanted to put him in the play. I needed to speak to him again. I drink alone now.

The bar is called Calle Piscina. Nothing special. Six plastic trestle tables and a blue awning to shield the sun. Inside, wooden tables, a straight counter with a glass display case keeping the flies from the potatoes and sardines.

The girl who serves doesn't try very hard. The first day she raised a smile, laughed with Joshua, but after three weeks I've become a fixture. She doesn't smile and shouts at the boy in Spanish when he scurries under the table for his ball. It is out of season and she imagines she shouldn't be serving tables in Presillas, a dried-out village in the desert. I think she's a girlfriend of the cook but whenever they are together a fever curses the tables and the customers evaporate into the dusty village.

The boy's given up on the ice-creams. For the first week he wanted ice-cream three times a day but now the taste has tired him and he just asks for water. I wish I could give up on the wine.

Joshua looks up at me, trustingly. I know it is time to finish this. We have been here too long now.

Dad drinks red wine. He can order red wine. Dad drinks a lot of red wine. Then he starts telling jokes and sometimes he cries. Dads shouldn't cry. People stare at us. Dad just sitting there and crying. But he says he doesn't care. He's crying for Mam. He shouldn't cry for Mam. Mam's dead. I don't cry for Mam any more. Grandma Porthcawl said Mam was in a better place. Dad doesn't believe in God. Grandma Porthcawl said that's why he cries. She said Dad wasn't going to get me back. But he did. It wasn't his fault whatever Grandma Porthcawl says.

The police called yesterday to check my papers. There had been a request to confirm that I was OK. If the boy was OK. I could see the disdain in the officer's eyes. The squalor we were living in. I've never been good at housework. It was one of her complaints, just one of them. I came home once and we didn't have a plate left in the house. She said she was sick of washing them and if I wasn't going to do it we could eat off chip paper every night and throw it away. She had given it all away. Every dish, fork, spoon, pan in the house to the charity shop on Clifton Street. I tried to buy some of it back. There was a set of my grandmother's best Spode. I got four pieces. Two cups, a cracked plate and a saucer. The rest had been sold. Serves me right, she said. I kept those washed until she broke them.

'You stay here long?'

His eyes lingered on the mess in the apartment. Unwashed plates, strewn clothes, pieces of food on the floor.

'No, *un mes*, maybe *dos*.'

He looked around again. He didn't like trouble. He wasn't used to it. Some drunks and some people hitting each other, usually family. He could handle that. I was trouble, tourist trouble. His orders had come from Málaga and from there Madrid. The Consulate had become involved. He didn't like being told what to do.

He checked my passport, then Joshua's. In the photo he was being held by his mother; he was aged eight months. The first time we came away. The officer folded them together and passed them back.

'Mr Hones, your passports are fine. We are a European country. Civilised. The boy will be old enough for school. Here it is free.' He searched for the right word. 'And . . . mandatory.'

He waited for a reaction. Joshua came in from the bedroom. The police had called early. Joshua edged back into the shadows. Afraid of strangers.

'*Hablo . . . en el pueblo.*'

'Yes, you will speak to someone, but in Almeria. Not here. He can go to the school in El Pozo.'

'In September?'

'But you will not be here in September – *un mes, no?*'

'*Si.*'

'Then maybe we don't have a problem.'

'No, I don't think so.'

He looked around the place once more and then spoke to himself.

'*Viven como cerdos . . . pero qué importa?*'

Dad said the volcano was in the mountains. We could climb to the centre when we had a day of good weather. The weather has been good for ages. It's hot and sunny. Sunny and hot. It's always hot and sunny. Last week we had lightning in the night but no rain. The rain doesn't like the coast.

It's a promise. I have to stick to it. We get up early, the sun is still struggling to fill the slopes of *agave* and prickly-pear with enough light for us to see by. The *rambla* has a different light. The shadows play with your imagination. Joshua has brought Scorch along for protection. Scorch is a dragon. A cloth dragon filled with beans. Scorch is going to protect Joshua from the wolves and wild boar. I've tried to tell him there are no wolves in this part of Spain. They've all been shot.

Joshua is a good walker now. He doesn't complain. I can feel the heat on my body, straining. The wine gets to you quickly. I can feel my weight filling me up again. I haven't eaten much since the summer. There didn't seem much point, need. Now it's the wine.

It takes us an hour to reach the farmhouse. We sit down and eat bread and cheese with some apricots. The well is covered up. A lattice of pine posts laid across its mouth to protect the foolish. We call down, listening for the words to expand and re-form in the depths. I wonder if the French tourist is still down there listening.

The *rambla* curves on, always at the bottom of the valley caressing its way to the centre of the volcano. We reach the Fiat. This was as far as the three of us got the first time. The sun was too hot for us. We had not brought enough water. January is cooler, the skies deeper. There are just two of us.

Joshua clambers up on to the bonnet and then on to the roof.

'It's a car.' He looks down at me. 'Why hasn't it got any windows?'

'It's been abandoned.'

'No tyres, no seats, no anything.' He heaves a rock from the top of the car into a thicket of prickly-pear. He looks hard at the car, considering it. 'Can we mend this car? We could go home then.'

'I don't think so.'

'Can we mend our car?'

'No.'

'Why hasn't our car got an engine? This car has got an engine.'

I have to agree with him. The car does indeed have an engine.

Our car is sitting in the village square with its engine missing. Dad asked someone to fix it for him. The man said he had to take the engine away. That was a long time ago. Dad lets me sit in the car sometimes while he drinks in the bar. The radio doesn't work any more. Dad reckons it's because the battery is flat but I think it's because the engine is missing. The car is full of things from home. I found my lion in it on Monday. The lion had been missing since the ferry. Dad said I must have left it in the cabin but I didn't take it to the cabin. I left the lion in the car to guard it. I found it between the seats with a chocolate wrapper and some raisins. I ate the raisins. They were a bit dusty.

We push on up the *rambla* as the heat begins to seep down from the volcano. A hare skips across the broken rocks. Then, where the valley deepens, a line of almond trees. They are just flowering, a pink washed white pouring out from the dry *rambla*.

This would be the place I had imagined. It would be OK for us. Below the trees there is an old squared field. Green shoots rise up from softer earth.

Dad said she was very sick when we visited her in hospital. She looked very sick. She couldn't speak to us. Then I woke in Grandma's house. She said Mam was in a better place. She didn't say where Dad was.

I unpack the rucksack I've been carrying. The camping spade unfolds easily. It was designed for burying your shit in the woods. The soil is soft. I begin to dig. Joshua watches.

'What are you doing, Dad?'

I don't answer, just keep digging. There is no point in asking questions now. I can't talk my way out of this. The hole is about three feet deep when I stop. I think that is enough. Just enough.

Joshua has wandered off. He's trying to dig up some shoots with a stick. I call him over. He looks up, sensing something. I see the fear in his eyes. I wasn't expecting this. I thought I had worked everything out.

Then it hits me. A hard searing pain shoots through my leg and I fall heavily into the dirt. The hole looms up to greet me. The earth is thrust up into my eyes and nose. A clatter of legs and a rich smell of dried sweat and bristle.

I'm three foot down and scrabbling at the sides. I come up for air quickly. The pig has stopped for breath. Joshua is screaming. Caught in the moment, unable to move. The pig is sizing us up. Which one? Joshua is smaller, easier.

I stumble forward slipping on the earth, scrambling to get to him first. I smother-tackle him as the pig hits us again. I can hear the breath in her lungs, fearful for something. Then squeals.

I pick Joshua up and run for the almond tree. The pig, stalled by the sudden movement, hesitates but then kicks into the ground again and rushes for us.

With six feet to go I hurl Joshua into the lower branches. They crack and splinter but he hangs on in fear. The adrenalin fires through me as I jump for the trunk and heave myself up into the tree. The tree sways with my weight. A shower of almond blossoms fall to the ground. The pig grunts around twice at the base of the tree. The tree sways unsurely. I watch her as she looks around sniffing, her glands extended with milk. A squeal from the bushes calls her back into the thicket of prickly-pears.

I can feel my heart crashing through my ribs, the red wine surfaces in sweat. Joshua clambers across the branches to me. He's not crying. He loves trees. I hug him to me.

His head breaks free. He wants to speak.

'I told you Scorch would protect us.'

He is still holding the cloth dragon.

'Yeah, lucky we had Scorch.'

'What's the hole for, Dad?'

I look at him. His blue eyes, my eyes, his nose, my nose. His mind all his own.

'Your mother.'

I pour her ashes into the hole under the almond. Joshua helps me fill in the loose earth. Then we run in case the pig comes back.

We didn't stay long in Spain after that. I sold the carcass of the car. Twenty thousand pesetas. We just had enough to catch the train back from Almeria.

The ferry was huge. The sea surrounded us but we couldn't touch it. Dad said people just went on the ferry for a cruise and wouldn't even get off in Spain unless they were forced to. I loved the playroom. I was the oldest there except Dad. Dad spent all his

154

time in the playroom. He was seasick. He couldn't get off the floor for very long without lying down again.

There was a woman supposed to be organising games for us. There was a list on the wall of all the things we were supposed to do. She only came to see us the first day. She had blond hair and a blue uniform.

She didn't come again. Dad said she was seasick too. I liked the playroom. It reminded me of home.

GIL McNEIL

The Fortune-Teller

'WHAT DOES Rosie want for her birthday?'
'Make-up.'
'Blimey. She's only eight.'
'I know, but it's what she wants. And she wants a Buffy party.'
'Don't tell me: they all run round screaming, wearing loads of make-up, and stab each other in the necks with wooden stakes?'
'Make-up definitely, but no stabbing, I hope. Although with eight-year-old girls you never really know.'
'Sounds delightful.'
'Yes, well anyway. You know that time I dressed up as a tiger for Charlie's Winnie the Pooh party when he was four?'
'Yes, you were brilliant. I'm really sorry he tried to pull your tail off.'
'Well, Rosie was wondering, what with you being her godmother and all, if you'd like to come and do a spot of fortune-telling.'
'What?'
'You know, wrap yourself up in a velvet cloak and pretend to tell fortunes.'
'Bloody hell.'

'I thought you might say that.'

But in the end of course I agree, partly because it seems like a good godmotherly thing to do and partly because the alternative is Laura shelling out a fortune for a 'proper' entertainer, and I know she doesn't have the money. She's bringing up Rosie on her own since Ben left: he went off to India to find himself, and came back heavily into yoga. He's training to be a black belt now, or whatever colour belts you get in yoga. Rainbow-coloured ones probably. Anyway, when he's finished he'll be able to teach other people how to find themselves, and get their legs round the back of their necks at the same time. He says money isn't important, so it's all down to Laura.

I think we should Superglue him to his yoga mat, preferably while he's doing a headstand, but Laura thinks it might upset Rosie. She's probably right, but I still think she's being a bit too grown-up about it all, and a nice bit of revenge always cheers you up. My friend Leila once biked a pig's head she'd bought at her local butcher's round to a man who'd recently dumped her – and it cheered her up for weeks.

'All set for tomorrow then?'

'I think so. I'm dropping Charlie off at my mum's, but he's still in a hyper sulk about not being invited. He went on hunger strike yesterday, but it only lasted ten minutes. I got the crisps out.'

'Oh, very cunning.'

'I know, it never fails. God knows what I'm going to do when a packet of crisps doesn't do the trick any more: I can just see me standing outside the sixth-form disco waving a packet of crisps at midnight.'

'Oh don't. I really don't want to think about it – it's hard enough persuading Rosie to get dressed now. What's it going to be like when she's a teenager?'

'It's going to be hell.'

'Oh, you're such a help. You've really cheered me up now.'

'Good. I spent half the morning trying to track down a pack of tarot cards, you know, so I'm not feeling too chirpy myself. I ended up in one of those New Age places, with some nutter behind the till telling me about when she discovered she had second sight. She was totally barking. Anyway I've got one, and I've taken out all the really scary ones.'

'Good thinking. I've got a sort of glass ball thing – it's a paperweight really but it'll do for a crystall ball. And I'll fix up the spare bedroom as your grotto.'

'I'm not sure I like the sound of that. Will I have to sit on a toadstool or something?'

'Stop it. I thought I'd drape loads of scarves about, and bring up some chairs from downstairs. Will that do you?'

'Sure, as long as you stash some gin under my chair. I've got a feeling I'm going to need it.'

'Sort of help the spirits flow, kind of thing?'

'Very funny. Oh, and I've bought a load of aromatherapy candles too. I thought that if it turns out I'm crap at the fortune-telling thing at least they'll all be nice and relaxed. And I've sorted out my outfit – my long black skirt, with a black velvet top, and a scarf I got from the hippie stall in the market, covered in bits of mirror. And I got loads of beads and crystal bracelets, and dangly sparkly ear-rings. I was aiming for Gypsy Rose Lee, but it's gone a bit more Danny La Rue.'

'Sounds brilliant. I can't wait to see you. Oh that reminds me, I must get a new film for the camera.'

'If you think you're taking pictures of me looking like a complete nutter you can bloody well think again.'

'Oh don't be such a spoilsport.'

'I'll see you tomorrow, and I'm warning you, if I see a camera there'll be trouble.'

'Charlie, come on. Get in the car. We're going to be late.'

'Mummy, can I take my Lego dragon to Nana's?'

'Yes, now hurry up.'

'I can't find it.'

'What?'

'My Lego dragon.'

'Well, why did you ask to take it then?'

'I hoped you'd find it for me. Honestly, Mummy, you're horrible, you know, really horrible.'

'Charlie. Get. In. The. Car. Now.'

He walks slowly towards the car.

'I'm not sitting in the front with you. You look very stupid, you know.'

I am in full Madam Zorba kit: Laura made me promise to arrive in my costume just in case any of the girls arrive early.

'Thanks, Charlie. Sit in the back then. But hurry up, or we'll be late for Nana.'

'I hate you. I want to come to the party. When I have my party I'm going to have an Angel party. He's got black hair, and a leather jacket, and black trousers, and he's a vampire. And he bites girls. And you can't come to my party, you can only do the cake.'

* * *

159

Mum gives me a long look when I drop him off, and says she hopes none of the girls at the party are easily frightened. And then Charlie launches into his Life Is So Unfair speech again, but is diverted when Mum says she's bought a little present for him. My enormous sparkly ear-rings are making my earlobes ache already, and I'm getting some seriously funny looks from other drivers.

I'm trying to remember all the snippets Laura has given me on each of the guests as I'm driving along. Gabriella, long blond hair, ballet, horrible snooty mother, nasty to other girls. Emily, lovely, mad about animals, and she's Rosie's best friend. Georgina, likes to be called George, mad about football. Flora, sweet but highly strung. Clever, as in boffin clever, can go on for hours about philosophy and genetics, but not terribly good with buttons or zips. And she has a ferret. Christ, I've just thought, I hope she doesn't bring it to the party. All I need is a ferret disappearing up my skirt.

At the traffic lights I realise that I'm muttering to myself, and this combined with my unusual ear-rings is unsettling other drivers. The woman in the passenger seat in the car next to mine stares at me with a kind of appalled look on her face and closes her window.

Laura becomes almost hysterical with laughter when she sees me, and I have to pretend to sulk to get her to stop.

'Sorry, you look great. Honestly. It's just, well, you really look the part.'

'Thanks. You owe me big time, you know that, don't you?'

'Yes, Danny.'

'Really big time.'

'Yup. Will it involve dressing up, do you think?'

'Oh, I'm certain it will.'

'Great. Can't wait. Now if you'd like to follow me I'll show you your grotto.'

'Laura,' I say, as I follow her up the stairs.

'Yes, Dan.'

'I hate you.'

The spare bedroom looks amazing. There are scarves draped everywhere, and a little table with the glass ball on it, and two small lights draped in red chiffon. Rosie comes up for a quick inspection, and says it's all brilliant. And she wants her fortune told too, which is daft really as she knows it's me, but I guess anything's possible when you're eight. She adores my earrings and is on the point of launching into a serious bid to be allowed to borrow them for the party when the doorbell rings. She hurls herself downstairs to greet her first guest, and soon the entire house is full of the sound of small girls screaming with delight, and running about in a generally over-excited manner. Christ. This is going to be a long day. I light the candles and wait for the first guest to appear.

A very small girl, Amelia, is ushered in. She looks terrified. I try my best not to speak in a scary voice, and ask her to sit down and pick three cards. She does, and I notice her hands are shaking. I'm about to march downstairs and say that frightening small girls out of their wits is not my idea of party fun, when I realise that she's staring at me expectantly, waiting for my verdict on the cards. I desperately try to remember

Laura's tips on Amelia but can only dredge up something about dogs. So I say I can see she is deeply loved, and she sits up a bit higher in her chair and looks pleased. Then I say I can see something about animals but it's not clear what, and she's off.

She's got a rabbit, called Snowy, but wants a Great Dane, only her mother isn't keen. I bet she's not. I tell her that her future is linked to animals and that she has a special gift, which goes down extremely well. She says she's going to be a vet when she grows up, or maybe a deep-sea diver, so she can help save sharks because people are very cruel to them, you know. I pretend to consult my crystal ball and then tell her I think a vet is more likely and she says that's what her mum says too: a coincidence she seems to find highly remarkable.

George is next, and is very pleased when I appear to know all about her prowess with a football from staring at three tarot cards. I gaze into the crystal ball for a bit and tell her she's a very special girl, who's not afraid to do things even if other girls don't do them. She nods, and then says in a very small voice that actually she thinks she would be better if she was a boy, because she's not very pretty or anything. I tell her she's going to be extremely beautiful when she grows up, and what's more she'll know all about football, which will be a lethal combination as far as most grown-up boys are concerned.

She's clearly thrilled with this, and says can she ask me a question, only it's something really important. I brace myself for something really challenging and she says, 'Will I have long fingernails when I grow up, really long pointy ones?'

I tell her she will, and she will also have high-heeled sparkly shoes for when she's not playing football, and she skips off delighted.

Next three girls come in together, Zoe, Nicky and Sophie, because they're all a bit too scared to come on their own. It turns out they all love animals, and it's a bit hard to work out which one likes what, but I foresee a rabbit, a small pony and three Labrador puppies, which seems to go down well. Sophie says when she grows up she's going to have a pink coat and a pink car and a pink house, and curly hair. And she'll eat chocolate every day, and drink Coke. We all pause for the full marvellousness of this vision to sink in, and then I say that I can see she will also be doing something important with her life because she has hidden talents, and mustn't hide her light under a bushel. Thankfully nobody asks me what a bushel is, and they go off chattering about Labrador puppies and what they're going to call them.

Emily is ushered in, and is delightful, just as Laura said she'd be. I tell her that she has a special gift with animals since this always seems to be popular. She blushes and says when she grows up she's going to live on a farm and have ducks and chickens and owls. And she won't eat lamb, or any other meat, come to that. It will be a vegetarian farm. And everyone can come to stay, her mum and her dad, and her sister, but not her big brother Sam, because he's a pig. I say he'd probably like it on the farm if he's a pig, and I can see she thinks this is extremely witty.

Then I peer into the crystal ball and tell her that she's going to be happy and have a long life, and I close my eyes as if to concentrate harder. For some reason I get a very clear picture of a goat, so I tell her she will have lovely goats on her farm. But she says oh no she won't, she doesn't like them, they're smelly and poke you with their horns. My one crack at truly 'seeing' something has been a dismal failure, which is a bit of a relief really, so I mumble something about how her farm will be lovely, and goat-free, and she trots off downstairs to rejoin the party.

Clever Flora is next. She gives me a very quizzical look and then launches into a passionate monologue, the gist of which is that fortune-telling is illogical, because it implies the future is already fixed, which is obviously rubbish. I'm very tempted to tell her to bugger off, or foresee something horrible, but this wouldn't exactly be in the Party Spirit – and anyway she's the one with the ferret. For all I know she's tucked it into her party frock and will order it to bite me if I give her a hard time. So I mutter something about fortune-telling meaning different things to different people, and thankfully this seems to satisfy her.

She sits down and says shall she choose some cards then? She chooses five, all of which have horrible-looking symbols on them, and she goes a bit pale. I reassure her that they are in fact excellent cards and clearly she's a very special girl who will grow up to achieve great things. She's pleased and gives me a short run-down on her latest theories about time travel, and how it might be possible to invent a new species of hamster by mixing up DNA from different species.

I look at my crystal ball and feel a strong desire to put the ferret issue to rest once and for all. I say I can see a small animal who's very important to her, but it's not here at the party, is it? Please God she says no.

She's very impressed with this, and tells me all about her ferret which stupid Daddy made her leave at home even though he loves parties. She begins a long speech about the magical world of ferrets while I nod, and privately think that Daddy has been very clever indeed, and then Laura comes in and says the other girls are getting fed up waiting. Flora gets up to leave, but then rushes back over to me and throws her arms around my neck and says thank you, it was lovely, and really really interesting. What a sweetheart.

Gabriella is next, with Natasha. They both have long blond hair, big blue eyes, and simpering grins. I feel very tempted to predict warts. I say they're both obviously very special girls, at which they both nod, but then I add that there's a faint cloud around them which suggests that they are not always as kind as they could be. Then I get a bit carried away and say all the horrible things you do to other people always come back round to you in the end. I sincerely hope this is not actually true, because if it is I'm in for a very bumpy old age. But at least its wipes the smirk off their faces.

They both frown slightly, but then Gabriella rallies and says, 'What about my ballet? Miss Jenkins says I have real talent.'

'Oh yes,' I say, 'I can see you dancing.'

And she nods with a tiny smile of satisfaction that I'm finally starting to deliver the goods. She tells me that she knows she'll be beautiful, because her mummy has told her, and her daddy says she'll be a princess, and Natasha says she's going to be a princess too. I tell them I'm sure they will, but they'll still have to be kind, or they'll be very unpopular princesses. They don't seem too sure about this last bit, but skip off quite happily with confirmation that they're going to be princesses.

Then Rosie comes in and says it's all brilliant, they all love it, and will I tell her fortune now because I'm obviously really good at it. She chooses her cards, and I say they're the best cards I've ever seen, and she's destined for a truly spectacular golden life full of happiness and joy. She's delighted, and wants to know if she'll get a dog, and have long curly hair like Gabriella, and a house with a swimming pool. I say yes, a huge swimming pool, and loads of dogs and fantastic hair, but she'll also have a brilliant career which will make her truly happy and earn her a fortune.

Oh good, she says, because then Mum can give up work and come and live in my house and do the cooking. Then she says, 'And Dad can come round too sometimes, can't he?' And she looks very carefully at me.

I say yes, of course, and he'll be very happy and proud, and everything will be lovely. And she smiles and says thank you, and gives me a big hug. Wish I was a proper godmother and had a proper magic wand to wave.

'You were great, they're all thrilled.'

'You're welcome. It was quite sweet really, all those eager little faces. The only dodgy bit was when I saw the goat.'

'I beg your pardon?'

'Emily was going on about a farm, and I saw a goat.'

'What do you mean you saw a goat?'

'Well, I had my eyes closed, and I suddenly got this vision of a goat, but it turns out she hates them. Good thing too really – it'd be pretty tricky to discover you're a psychic in the middle of a children's birthday party, wouldn't it? I mean you'd probably have to tell the police or something. And you'd never be surprised on your birthday again, would you?'

'I haven't been surprised on my birthday for years.'

'No, neither have I, unless you count the kind of surprise where you realise that no bastard's going to whisk you off to Paris for the weekend, and you've still got to do the washing up. I get loads of those kind of surprises.'

'So do I.'

'Great, isn't it? But you know what I mean, I bet being psychic can be a real drag. Although I suppose it could come in handy sometimes. It'd be brilliant in supermarkets. You'd know exactly what was in your fridge.'

'Yes, and you'd never spend three hours driving the wrong way round the M25 looking for Gatwick.'

'Look, Laura, I've told you before, if it's a circle it can't matter which way you go round it, can it?'

'Not if you've got all day, no. But if you're late for a flight it bloody well does.'

'Yes, well, it was delayed so it was fine, wasn't it? Although if I was a psychic I suppose I would have known that, wouldn't I? Or maybe I did, which is why I didn't panic.'

'You looked like you were panicking to me. Running after that bus in the long-term car-park screaming Stop You Bastard Stop looked pretty panicky from where I was standing. I think you've spent too long stuck up here with these bloody candles. Do you want a cup of tea or something, or some food? I've got to get back downstairs and stop them demolishing the living room.'

'OK. What food have you got? No, don't tell me. I can see sausage rolls, fairy cakes and jelly. See, I do have powers.'

'Wrong again. Not a sausage roll in sight. Now stop going on about being psychic, or I'll send them all back up again for a second sitting. Stay put and I'll get you some food. They'll be off soon.'

She brings up an assortment of food with a Buffy theme – vampire biscuits with red icing, and sausages on cocktail sticks in a pool of ketchup, so they look like they've been recently slaughtered. She's really got into it. Actually it looks pretty revolting but it tastes fine, and I nosh away quite happily, relieved that I've not turned out to be a psychic, and won't be called up by police forces nationwide to solve horrible crimes. Then Laura comes back to say there are only a couple of girls left, so I can creep out if I want to. Which I do. My ear-rings are killing me. She gives me my Buffy party bag for Charlie.

'Thanks again for today, you were great.'

'You're welcome.'

'I'll ring you later.'

'All right, and I'll tell you about your costume for Charlie's party next month. I'm thinking polar bears, *Gorillas in the Mist*, or maybe *Star Wars*. You could be R2 D2. Or that gold one, a bit of gold body paint and you'll be fine.'

'Goodbye, Danny.'

*   *   *

Charlie is delighted with his Buffy bag, and adores the vampire teeth which he insists on wearing all evening. His supper goes everywhere: really wish I hadn't decided to make spaghetti bolognese. I finally persuade him to go to bed with the usual combination of bribery, threats and bedtime stories. I'm back downstairs doing the washing up when Laura rings.

'You'll never guess where I've been this evening.'

'Acapulco?'

'No. Casualty.'

'God, why?'

'We had to go and get Clare, Emily's mum. She rang just after you left to say she was going to be late, because she was stuck waiting for an X-ray, so we went and picked her up. You'll never guess what happened.'

'What?'

'A goat made her crash her car.'

'Stop it.'

'No, really. Spooky, isn't it? She was driving round to pick up Emily, and she turned a corner and there was a goat slap in the middle of the road, so she swerved to avoid it and drove straight into a hedge. She just missed hitting a great big tree. Her airbag went off and everything, and her neck hurts but she's fine.'

'Thank God for that. Where on earth did the goat come from?'

'Oh it got out from one of the back gardens. The owner came charging out apparently, almost hysterical with apologies. The police came and everything and insisted she went to hospital. They said it could have been really serious and had a real go at the goat woman, who burst into tears, so Clare said she ended up calming her down while they waited for the ambulance.'

'Bloody hell.'

'Yes, I know. So, maybe you're psychic after all. What can you see in store for me tomorrow then, any wayward farmyard animals? Any tall, dark and handsome strangers? I could really use one of those.'

'Couldn't we all. Honestly though, it is a bit weird when you think about it, isn't it?'

'Now look, I know what you're like, don't start going all twilight zone on me, it's just a coincidence, you know.'

'I bloody well hope so.'

'Don't you think if you did have some sort of weirdy gift, it would have revealed itself before now?'

'I suppose so.'

'Like that time you lost the car keys when we went to Alton Towers. Or that time you thought you'd lost Charlie in Woolworth's, but he was in the pick-and-mix eating all the sweets. Or that time –'

'All right, all right, I get the point. God, you make me sound like a disaster zone.'

'No, but I don't want you going all loopy on me. Look, I'll ring you later in the week and we can fix up a night out. Unless you already know where we'll be meeting, and what time, in which case I'll just see you there.'

'Actually I've just had another vision. I can see myself in my car, with Charlie in the back, fast asleep. I'm driving somewhere. Oh I can see it now, I'm driving round to your house, to slap you hard. I think it's going to come true. I really do.'

'Sorry. I'll stop now. But thanks again, you were

great. And trust me, you're not psychic. Give Charlie a kiss from me.'

I'm smiling as I walk up the stairs, thinking about goats, and Buffy party bags, and sure enough Charlie has crept into my bed. He must have waited until I'd gone downstairs, just like I knew he would.

EMMA DONOGHUE

Enchantment

P ITRE AND Bunch knew each other from the old
time. They were Louisiana crawfishermen, at
least as long as the crawfish were biting. These days,
what with global warming and so forth, the cages were
mostly empty, and it was hardly worth the trouble of
heading out to Mudd Swamp every morning.

The two men were having a smoke at the Bourdrilleaux Landing one May evening, and discussing
whether there was any such thing as a coloured Cajun.
Pitre mentioned, not for the first time, that what
flowed in his own veins was one hundred per cent
French wine.

'Every ancestor I ever have was a full-blood
Acadian. Cast out of Nova Scotia back in 1755 at
the point of a British gun.'

'Maybe so,' said Bunch, grinning, 'but you were
born in the state of Texas.'

'About one inch over the border,' growled Pitre. He
was twenty years older than Bunch, and grizzled like a
mouldy loaf.

'Well, whatever, you know, I'm a live and let live
sort of Cajun, my friend,' said Bunch, sucking the last
from his Marlboro. 'I was born and reared in these
swamps, but I'm willing to call you brother.'

'Brother!' snorted Pitre. 'You're a black Creole with a few Sonniers for cousins, that's not the same thing at all.'

Just then a candy-apple red jeep came down the dirt road. Four old ladies spilled out and started taking photographs of the boats. Pitre asked them in French if they wanted to buy some crawfish, then mumbled it again in English; he hauled a cage out of his boat and held it up, with the few red creatures waving inside. The ladies just lengthened their zoom lenses for close-ups.

'Are you fishermen?' one of them asked excitedly, and Bunch said, 'No, ma'am. We're Federal agents.' They peered at his dark, serious face and twittered even more, and one of them asked if she could have her picture taken with him, and afterwards she tipped him ten dollars.

'I don't think the Bureau's gonna approve, *cher*,' commented Pitre as the tourists drove off waving through the windows of their shiny jeep.

'I'll put it in the Poor Box on Sunday,' said Bunch.

Pitre let out a sort of honk through his nose, and got back in his boat, and said something about checking that alligator bait he'd left hanging off a tree.

'You marinade the chicken good?'

'It stinks worse than your wife,' Pitre assured him, and drove off, the snarl of his engine ripping the blue lake like paper.

When he got to the other side of the cypress swamp, the shadows were lengthening. His gator bait dangled, untouched except by the hovering flies. Pitre cut the rope down and hung it from another tree at the south edge of the basin, where he'd seen a big fellow the year before, thirteen feet if he was an inch. He wondered how much gators were going for an inch, these days. You could sell the dried jaws to tourists, too. Tourists would buy turds if you labelled them *A Little Bit of Bon Temps from Cajun Country*.

It was cool, there under the trees, with the duckweed thick as guacamole, making the water look like ground you could stretch out on. All the other guys had gone home; Mudd Swamp was his own. Pitre leaned back against an empty crawfish cage and rested his eyes. The air was live with small sounds; a bullfrog, the tock-tock of a woodpecker, the whir of wings.

He thought it had only been a minute or two, but when he opened his eyes they were crusted at the corners, and the evening was as dark as a snakeskin around him. He couldn't read his watch by the faint light of the clouded moon. He supposed he was hungry, though he couldn't feel it. Yes, maybe he could fancy some fried oysters. The outboard motor started up with a cough, and Pitre manoeuvred his way through the flooded forest. He veered right by the big cypress with the wood-duck box nailed on to it, then picked up some speed.

The stump reared up beneath his boat like a monster. Pitre flew free. The engine died, and then there was only the wash of ripples, almost silky. Pitre reared up and shook the duckweed off his face, retched for breath. The water was no higher than his waist. You could drown in a couple of inches. He tried to stand, but one of his legs wasn't working. He told himself to stop splashing around. Gators were drawn to dogs, or to anything that moved like a dog. Pitre was shuddering with cold now; it sounded like he was sobbing. He turned his face up to the mottled sky. *Que Dieu me sauve*. A tag from a prayer his grandmother used to say. *Que Dieu me sauve*.

The moon came out like the striking of a match. Vast and pearly, it pushed through the branches of a willow tree and lit up the whole swamp. Pitre looked round and saw exactly where he was. His boat was only the length of a man behind him, not even overturned. He crawled over, got himself in after a couple of tries. There was a water hyacinth caught in the bootlaces of his smashed leg. He heard himself muttering, *Merci merci merci*. The motor started on the first try.

Before Pitre was off his crutches he'd started putting up signs. The ones nailed to electricity poles along the Interstate said simply *Swamp Tours Exit NOW*. Along the levee road they went into more detail: *Explore the Wonders of Mudd Swamp 2 + ½ Miles Further*, said one, and another, *Pitre's Wildlife Tours Twice Daily Next Left*.

Bunch rode the older man pretty hard for it. 'What makes you think anybody going to want to get in your beat-up skiff and go round a little swamp no one's ever heard of? When they could be cruising in comfort in Atchafalaya Basin or Lake Martin?'

'If you build the signs, they will come.' Pitre pursed his chapped lips and banged in another nail.

Bunch snorted. 'And what's with that marker you've hung up on the big willow that says *Site of Miracle*?'

'You may mock,' said Pitre, fixing Bunch with his small eyes, 'but I know what I know.'

'What do you know, *mon vieux*?'

'I know I was saved.'

'Here we go again.'

'And now,' said Pitre, wiping his forehead, 'I've been called by the Spirit of the Lord to turn away from killing.'

'Killing? Who've you been killing?' asked Bunch, pretending to be impressed.

'Crawfish, I mean.'

The younger man let out a whoop of delight.

'I've been called to lead tours of the wonders of creation,' said Pitre, thrusting a blurred photocopied leaflet into Bunch's hands.

He read it over smothered chicken at his uncle's Cracklin' Café in Eunice. It made him laugh out loud. Old Pitre couldn't spell, for one thing. *I will tell you and show you also, a great variety of mammals, fish, and foul.*

As Bunch drove back to the Bourdrilleaux Landing that afternoon to check his cages, he noticed that *French Spoken* had been added in fresh paint to all the signs.

Sure enough, by the beginning of June there was a little queue of tourists at the landing, most mornings. They shaded their eyes and gawked at the glittering blue sky, the lushly bearded trees. They were from Belgium and Mississippi and Quebec, all over the map. They giggled and flicked dragonflies out of each other's hair.

'Hey, Pitre,' Bunch called as he drove up in his truck one day.

The other man walked over, counting twenties.

'I've got to hand it to you, my friend, you've

176

drummed up more trade than I ever thought you could. You or the Spirit of the Lord!'

Pitre nodded guardedly.

'How many tours a day you doing now?'

'Four,' said Pitre, 'maybe five.'

Bunch whistled sweetly. 'Five tours at two hours long? At your time of life? What say I give you a hand, before these tourists wear you out?'

'I'll manage,' said Pitre, and turned back to his boat.

In the middle of the night Bunch had a bright idea. He picked up a box of cheap pecan pralines in Grand Coteau, transferred them to his wife's old sewing basket, and sold them to the Mudd Swamp Tour queue at two dollars a pop. When he turned up the following day with a basket of alligator jerky, a party was staggering off Pitre's boat, their eyes bright with wonder.

'It's so green out there!' said one of them, and her friend said, 'I've never been anywhere so green!'

Pitre came over to Bunch with his arms tightly crossed. 'Get away from my clientele.'

'Your what?' laughed Bunch.

'You heard me. Parasite!' Pitre cleared his throat wetly. 'I'm trying to do the Spirit's work here, like I've been called to –'

'You've been called, all right, Pitre. Called to make a quick buck!'

Pitre turned his back and jumped in the boat. It bobbed in the water, and the tourists squealed a little.

By the time he got them out under the cypresses he had recovered his temper. The sun was a dazzling strobe, and the sky was ice blue. Iridescent dragonflies skimmed the water, clustered in a mating frenzy.

'Lookit there, folks,' Pitre said under his breath, pointing through the trees at a great white egret on a log, its body one slim brush-stroke.

'It that a swan?' shrieked one little girl. At the sound, the bird lifted off, its huge snowy wings pulling it into the sky.

Pitre's visitors knew nothing about the wonders of creation. He considered it the least he could do to teach them the names of things. He showed them anahinga cormorants and glossy ibis; 'Go to the State Prison, you'll find a bunch of guys serving time for shooting ibis, that's the tastiest meat,' he said sorrowfully. He pointed out water hyacinths in purple bloom, a turtle craning its neck on a stump, and a baby nutria wiping its face with its paws.

'So where's the alligators?' asked a New Yorker with a huge camera round his sunburned neck.

'Well, as I told you at the start of the tour, I can't guarantee you'll see one,' said Pitre. 'They mostly look like logs. Yesterday's tour we saw three, but it's colder today; they don't come up much till it's sixty degrees or thereabouts.'

'There's one!' yelped a small boy, pointing at a log.

Just then Bunch roared by in his boat, which was ten years newer than Pitre's, with a fancy air-cooled outboard on the back. Cutting the motor, he floated within ten feet of the tour. 'Morning, all.'

'Crawfish biting?' asked Pitre, cold.

'Some,' said Bunch with his gleaming smile. 'You folks seen that big-fella gator over by the houseboat?'

It sounded like bullshit to Pitre, but of course his party clamoured to be taken over there right away, where the nice young man had said. Pitre spent fifteen minutes edging the boat round the shoreline, peering at dead wood and doing slow hand claps to attract any gators in the vicinity. 'I'm sorry folks, I try my best for you, but there's no guarantees in this life,' he said at last. 'We must learn to be grateful, you know?'

But the tourists were not grateful, especially when he admitted that no Louisiana alligators had ever been known to kill a human being. His party were not content with blue herons and watersnakes, or a fifteen-hundred-year-old cypress, and even when he rounded up the tour by taking them to the *Site of Miracle* sign and narrating his rescue from drowning by the God-sent appearance of the full moon, they seemed unimpressed. When they had driven off in their various SUVs, Pitre saw that there was only seventy cents in his tip jar.

Monday was wet and chill, but on Tuesday the sun came up strongly again. Pitre sat by his boat all morning, squinting into the distance. His throat was dry. At noon a group drove up in a Dodge Caravan.

'Over here,' he called to them hoarsely. 'Pitre's Tours, that's me.'

'No, I think we're booked on the other one,' a lady told him brightly.

He was about to tell her that there was no other one, when a motor started up behind him with a flamboyant roar and he turned and saw Bunch, wearing a fresh white T-shirt that said *Bunch's Enchanted Swamp Tours, Chief Guide Virgil Bunch*.

'This way, ladies, gentlemen!' cried Bunch.

Pitre just stared.

'What's enchanted about this swamp?' asked a fat man, looking up from his guidebook.

'Wait and see!'

Once his party was on board, Bunch roared out into the middle of the lake as fast as the motor could go, then headed into the flooded woods and ducked in between the stumps. He bumped into a floating log to make the boat jump and the tourists yelp. Then he cut the engine and said, 'My friends, welcome to paradise! This just happens to be the only Enchanted Swamp in all of Louisiana!'

He had paid the older man's techniques the compliment of extensive study, and had decided that the whole experience needed a little bit of personality and pizzazz. Bunch began the tour by claiming ancestry from every culture that made up the tasty gumbo of present-day Acadiana: the Cajuns, the Creoles, the *gens de couleur libre*, even the Chitimacha Indians, 'Who took what they needed and left the balance at peace with itself, you know?' He assured his party that the twenty-foot, flat-bottomed aluminium skiff they were sitting in had been personally designed by him to reach the parts of the swamp where other boats just couldn't go.

'Has this boat a name?' asked one Frenchwoman.

'Sure does,' Bunch improvised. 'It's called *The Zydeco*.'

Another of his techniques was to present everything in the best light. Instead of telling his tour party that blue herons were very common in this part of the river system, he instructed them to keep an eye out for any flash of blue in the trees, because they just might be lucky enough to spot the rare blue heron, who brought ten years' good luck to anyone who glimpsed him. Finally, catching sight of the head and shoulders of a little gator basking on some driftwood, Bunch made his eyes bulge with amazement, and told the tourists that this fellow must be fifteen feet long.

'No!'

'No way!'

'Mr Bunch? Virgil? Did you say fifteen?'

'They're just like icebergs, that way,' he whispered, paddling the boat near enough for them to take photographs. 'For every inch you see, there's a foot underneath the water. Not too close!' he told one little boy. Rolling up his jeans, he showed them an old scar on his shin from one time he'd had too much rum and fallen over someone's guitar case: 'Gator bite.'

One lady took a picture of his scar.

'The only sure way to keep them from attacking,' said Bunch, taking out a squashy paper bag, 'is to give them some snacks.' And he started lobbing lumps of rancid chicken at the alligator, who snapped at one or two before sinking beneath the surface.

On the way back, he gave his happy party a high-speed summary of *good ole Cajun humour* and *joie de vivre*, not to mention *laissez les bon temps rouler on the bayou*, winding up with a dirty joke about a priest. Finally he produced his tip jar, which had an alligator jaw glued on top, and they crowed with delight and stuffed their notes through its wicked teeth.

That night Bunch was eating steak and listening to the Breaux Bridge Playboys at Mulate's when Pitre walked in. The older man took one look at him across a crowd of Canadian college kids, then turned and walked back out the door. So that's how it was now, Bunch thought.

The summer turned hot, and there was more than enough business to keep both men busy. Pitre didn't alter his methods. He simply turned up at nine every morning and sat there in the sun waiting for custom, pretending his competitor didn't exist. The sun cooked him to red leather. That was the downside of being a hundred per cent pure white Acadian, Bunch thought with amusement, but he didn't make a remark like he would have in the days when they were still speaking.

Bunch himself had bought a cheap cellphone so tourists could book their tours with him direct. He got his sixteen-year-old daughter to make him a website with ten pages of photographs of alligators, and linked it to every listing on Louisiana tourism. *See local indigenous wildlife in its natural ecohabitat which makes it a photographer's dream. Fishing also available.* Bunch's real stroke of brilliance was finding a medium-sized gator with a stubby tail and feeding it meat scraps daily, until it would come when he called. *Your guide will explain from personal experience what it is to live off the swamp by spring fishing and winter trapping as the tour progresses for a full one and a half hours.* After a few weeks he scrawled *Performance of Live Cajun Music Included* on his leaflets, threw a small accordion into his bag and upped the fare from $20 to $25.

Whenever he felt his spiel was getting a little flat, he'd spice it up with a tall tale about a six-foot catfish or a ghost. He took great pleasure in transforming Pitre's near-death experience into a tale he called the Swamp Man. 'My *grandpère* used to say the Swamp

Man was a crawfisherman, stayed out too late one night, crashed his boat into a tree in the dark and drowned in no more than two feet of water. What's he look like? Well, kind of decayed, you know – holes for his eyes, and dripping weeds all over him . . .'

Pitre overheard that story, one day, as he was drifting along with his own tour, a tangled clump of grey Spanish moss in his hands, explaining in his hoarse monotone that this was an airborne plant that did no harm to the trees it hung from. He didn't look in Bunch's direction. Bunch watched Pitre's stiff shoulderblades as the boats floated past each other and the tourists waved in solidarity. You had to hand it to the old man, he had self-control.

Pitre told it how it was. He didn't think the Spirit wanted him soft-soaping things. He told his tours that the trees in Mudd Swamp were slowly dying and not being replaced because the government's levee kept the water at an artificially high level all year round. Yes, the birds were pretty, but their waste was poisoning the trees from the top down. And a nutria was no relation to a beaver, it was more of a rat.

What bugged him the most, as the first summer of his new life wore on, was that his customers were always asking him where the restroom was – as if an open skiff or a knot of trees could be hiding such a thing. He wrote at the top of his leaflets, *NO RESTROOM FACILITIES*, but the tourists didn't seem to take it literally. One of them, when Pitre had explained the situation, said to her husband, 'Let's go, hon. I've never been *anywhere* that didn't have a restroom' – and they marched back to their car.

One July afternoon, after the dust of the departing tourists had settled, Bunch walked over to Pitre. 'I was thinking of renting a Portolet,' he remarked, as if resuming an interrupted conversation.

Pitre slowly shifted his gaze from the cypress forest to the man in front of him.

'You know, for the clientele?' said Bunch. 'But they cost, you know, because the company has to drive all the way out here to empty it and stuff. What say we go halves, split the difference?'

'What say nothing,' said Pitre through his teeth. 'What say nothing.'

'Oh well, *cher*, if you're going to be like that,' said the younger man with a shrug. 'Though I don't think the Spirit of the Lord would like your attitude . . .'

Pitre's face never flickered, but the remark had got under his skin. He headed out to the swamp that evening, on his own, to see if it was any cooler than the land. When he got to the Miracle tree, he let his boat float. Pitre squinted up at the willow tree, but it looked much the same as all the others: a swollen base, tapering to a skinny top. He tried to sense what it was that had touched him, that moonlit night when he'd been within an inch of drowning. A feeling of being marked out, prodded awake, as distinct as a fingertip in the small of the back. He'd been so sure about his new calling, at first, but now it seemed as if he'd mistaken some small but crucial marker a while back and gone astray.

A few days later there was a Portolet standing in the shade of a live oak by Bourdrilleaux Landing. It looked like a small grey plastic alien craft. Pitre pretended not to notice. At noon, he was emptying the boat of one group and filling it up with another when a girl ran over. 'Uh, I wanted to use the restroom,' she began, with that way kids had of talking so that everything sounded like a question.

'No restroom,' said Pitre automatically.

'I tried the one over there, but it's like, locked! It says, *For use of Bunch's Enchanted Swamp Tours only.*'

Pitre could feel his teeth clamping together. 'That's a mistake,' he muttered. 'Very sorry, ladies and gentlemen. You'll just have to wait.'

'I can't wait two hours,' wailed the girl.

'That's the trouble with you young people nowadays,' Pitre told her. 'Nobody's got any self-control of themselves.'

That family drove back to the hotel, and he didn't get any tips that day either.

In August it was hitting a hundred by ten in the morning.

Bunch bought a cap with a visor to keep the glare out of his eyes. He took to claiming that his name was authentically Acadian. 'Sure is, ma'am. Used to be Bonche, you know, back in Canada, but when the English kicked us out at gunpoint back in 1755, my ancestors had to change it to Bunch to avoid persecution.'

He varied his tall tales to keep himself from getting stale. He always took his tours past a duck blind in the middle of the lake, but sometimes he said it was a man-made nesting sanctuary for orphaned cormorants, and other times he called it a shelter for canoeists caught out on the lake in a lightning storm. Once – just to see

185

if he could get away with it – he claimed it was a Dream Hut for young Chitimacha boys undergoing spiritual initiation.

'The Swamp Man? That's a terrible story,' he said on all his tours, lowering his voice as if he was almost afraid to tell it. 'This crawfisherman, back in old-time days, it was a long hard season, and he was desperate to know where the fish were biting, so he did voodoo, you know voodoo?'

Fervent nods all round.

'I bought a how-to book on it in New Orleans,' confided one old lady.

Bunch darkened his tone. 'So this man, he conjured up this spirit, and it was the devil. He didn't know it but it was. This man struck a bargain that his crawfish cages would always be full, you know? So now the devil had a hold of his soul. And the very first time the man went out fishing, it was in the evening, getting dark, and he bent down to pull up his first cage, and it was so full, it was so heavy that it pulled him right down!'

The tourists looked into the oily sheen of the water, shuddering.

'He drowned in there, but he never really died, you know? The flesh rotted off his bones, that's all. And if you ever come out here in the evening, just when it's getting dark, well, all I'll say is, don't put your hand into the water, because the Swamp Man will grab hold of it and pull you in!'

Two girls moaned theatrically. They weren't really afraid, Bunch knew; in this day and age it was hard to really scare anybody.

As trade fell off a little in the worst of the heat, he couldn't have done without his cellphone. It meant he

186

could sit around in the shade at the Lobster Shack, drinking homemade root beer, till he got a call to say there was a group wanting a tour. Whereas Pitre squatted in the dust at Bourdrilleaux Landing every day like some kind of scarlet lunatic, under a limp banner that said *Pitre's Holy Spirit Tours Anytime.*

One morning Pitre turned up at Mudd Swamp at eight; he'd had a pain in his jaw all night that had kept him from sleeping. His stomach wasn't right either. He sat down in his usual spot and tried to pray. The problem was that he'd never got the knack of it in his childhood. And now he was a man of the Spirit, he still didn't know quite what to say, once he'd got beyond *Oh Lord, here I am, like you told me.*

By noon not a soul had turned up. Pitre's tongue was stuck to the roof of his mouth. He'd forgotten to bring any water. His boat floated motionless beside the landing, not ten feet from the other man's boat, which had a duck decoy glued on the prow and a freshly painted name: *The Zydeco.* Pitre narrowed his eyes at the dirt track that led down from the road. There was no shade; the sun bored into his head through his eyelids, his ear holes, his cracked lips. In the long grass he saw a sledgehammer and recognised it as his own; he must have left it there after banging in a sign. He lurched to his feet at last. There was something he could do, anyway. He picked up the sledgehammer and staggered under the weight of it. He cradled it against his shoulder. At the landing, he climbed down into the *Zydeco*; it skittered under his feet. His heart was sounding strangely. He hoisted the hammer over his head and brought it down.

Pitre was in the bottom of the boat. He couldn't tell

if he'd managed to hole it. The light was behaving like water. He had stopped breathing for a while. He couldn't tell whether something had gone wrong with the whole world or whether it was just him; he seemed to be under some kind of dreadful enchantment.

The hospital let him out the next morning, mostly to shut him up. When he got back to the Landing, Bunch was waiting for him. The *Zydeco* seemed unmarked, and the sledgehammer was nowhere to be seen.

'Understand you called me an ambulance on that cellphone of yours,' Pitre said flatly.

'That's right,' said Bunch, as if they were chatting about the weather.

Pitre stared past him, at the cypresses, their heavy greenery. 'I received a message,' he said, jerking his chin upwards.

'Again?'

He ignored that. 'We don't want another Cain and Abel situation.'

'I guess not.'

'In a spirit of brotherhood,' Pitre said, then paused to clear his throat, 'I propose that we unite our tour companies.'

Barely a smirk from Bunch.

'No use both doing six trips a day when we could each do three.'

'I take your point,' said the younger man. Then, after a minute, 'Did the doctor say you had to take it easier?'

Pitre stared him down. 'No,' he said, 'it was the Spirit.'

'Whatever, my friend,' said Bunch, letting his teeth show when he grinned.

MICHÈLE ROBERTS

Please Excuse My Husband – He's a Vegetarian

I T WAS not easy, being a vegetarian in France.

Harry could just about manage in Paris, and other large cities, but in rural society he was done for. On their holidays, he and Nicolette mainly stuck to picnics. Simple enough at lunchtime, when you could turn off down a B road and park near a bridge over a river or at the entrance to a forest, get out the folding table and chairs, and enjoy your Camembert, baguette and tomatoes with no one looking at you and criticising. Harder in the evening, though, when he wanted both to avoid the mosquitoes and to eat something hot. Often enough Nicolette was forced to smuggle their little camping stove and aluminium cooking pots into their hotel room and rustle him up some clandestine spaghetti, rather than face the incomprehension of the *patronne* in the restaurant downstairs.

'It's not that I want to argue about it,' Harry complained, 'I just want something to eat. They're so intolerant, the French, of anything different.'

'Oh darling,' Nicolette said, 'it's just not in their culture, that's all.'

When they were driving south in the summer, Nicolette was sometimes able to persuade Harry to stop for lunch at a *routier* café. She liked the masculine ambience, the atmosphere of cigarette smoke and the sports news blaring on the TV and the long tables lined with hungry lorry drivers. She liked all the men looking at her as she walked in. French men really noticed women. However much they were concentrating on their *bifteck* and *frites* they lifted an eye and appraised her face and frock and legs while she bobbed her head and murmured, '*Bonjour, messieurs*.' Then as the meal progressed she would peep at them sideways and eavesdrop on their conversations and smile shyly if they caught her eye.

The hors-d'oeuvres presented no obstacle. You helped yourself from the array of cold dishes on the buffet. While Nicolette inspected the homemade rabbit pâté, the *rillettes* and *saucisson* and soused fillets of mackerel, before settling on a selection of crudités so that she didn't look too meat-loving and greedy, Harry would pick out some olives, gherkins and hard-boiled eggs (he ate eggs, as he ate butter and cream and cheese – to hell with rennet being made from animals) and some sliced tomatoes, or perhaps some grated celeriac in mayonnaise.

With the main course came the real problem. While the *routiers*, and indeed Nicolette too, could choose between three or four meat dishes, the most that Harry would ever be offered, once his eating requirements were explained, was an omelette. Even in quite posh restaurants, or perhaps especially in quite posh restaurants, harassed waiters had no time for Nicolette's super-polite requests that her husband be given something off the *menu du jour* and way off the *carte*. A blank look and a shrug and much sighing would, if

Harry was lucky, eventually be followed by the offer of an omelette.

Harry graded his omelettes on a scale of one to ten. Some came in at eight, plump and creamy and rolling in melted butter, with slices of mushroom inside and a sprinkling of parsley on top. Some came in at nought: those incorporating cubes of bacon – someone in the kitchen trying to jazz things up or just be kind to the poor benighted Englishman – and which had then to be sent back.

Sometimes, if Harry was very fortunate indeed, the waiter would become inspired and suggest a plate of steamed vegetables before or after the omelette. Harry knew he should look grateful and not fed up. Nicolette would smile sympathetically. Out of solidarity with him she would forswear liver and onions, or sausages and lentils, or sweetbreads, or pork simmered with cream and apples and calvados; she would compromise and order fish, usually poached salmon or trout. Nothing with legs, nothing still with its face on, with eyes that looked at you. The waiters would shake their heads over the pair of them and slap down the basket of bread and the carafe of wine with contempt.

Nicolette was sure it was contempt. She was very sensitive to what other people thought of her and hated upsetting or offending anyone. She yearned to fit in and not attract criticism. She was ashamed of English tourists who loafed around foreign cities in beachwear, skimpy shorts and vests in shrieking colours, with too much sunburned red flesh on view. She wished that Harry would wear shoes rather than trainers. She herself favoured sandals, and neat linen skirts and blouses that went well with her pink cheeks and blonde hair. Similarly, despising those same tourists who expected everyone else to speak English, she had gone to evening classes for some years and taken language lessons and was now quite proficient.

Harry liked French wine and the French climate and the French way of life (mainly) but claimed he had no ear for languages. What he had instead was a built-in resistance to learning anything he didn't see the point of. Important things came naturally and spontaneously. Sex, for example. You didn't have to learn that, did you? Nicolette had the gift of the gab and good luck to her. So it was Nicolette who, sitting down and shaking out her napkin, would smile sweetly and address the waiters in her best French, very formal and correct, with much deployment of please and thank you, but it was no use, once the moment of ordering the food arrived and she had once more to go through the rigmarole of pleading that Harry be given something he could actually eat, she would become flustered and anxious and begin trying to use the imperfect subjunctive and then flounder completely and start blushing, and the waiter would look first baffled, then impatient, and finally irritated and contemptuous. The *patronne*, that busy goddess circulating the dining room, making sure that everything was going smoothly, would be summoned, and would courteously enquire what was the matter.

Nicolette eventually learned never to utter the word vegetarian. Instead she would say timidly, 'I am afraid my husband cannot eat meat or fish. He is unable to.'

Madame would assume that some digestive or gastric disorder, probably located in that venerable organ the liver, was at issue, and would briskly announce,

'So why not an omelette? Or a plate of steamed vegetables?' And continue on her tour of the tables. People's eyes would swivel; they would stare at the mad English. Nicolette would feel their eyes boring scornfully into her back. She would bend her head humbly over her sliver of unadorned trout and eat it as unobtrusively as possible.

Matters improved once Harry retired at sixty-five and he and Nicolette made the big decision and moved to France full-time, because now Nicolette could cook Harry's favourite dishes at home. Many of these were in fact French classics. Onion tart for instance, or potatoes baked in cream, or leek soup, or stuffed pancakes, or asparagus soufflé. They were obviously, also, vegetarian dishes. It was just that in French people's presence you hadn't to call them that.

They settled in the north-west, within easy reach of the Channel ports at St Malo and Caen Oustreham. Really, the landscape was quite like that of Somerset. The climate was a few degrees warmer though, and less wet. They bought a cottage with just enough land to create a manageable garden. Nicolette planted vegetables and soft fruit, apple trees and a vine, all kinds of herbs. Harry sent group e-mails to all their friends back home: we're living our dream. He took photographs of the local churches, went for long walks in the forest, did some bird watching, played bridge over the Internet with chums in Australia and Canada, and enjoyed nothing more than sitting on his bench outside the front door watching the sunset with a glass of beer at his side. Nicolette felt restless but tried not to show it. She missed her teaching job. I'm only fifty-five, she said to her reflection in the mirror; that's not old, is it? She couldn't cook and clean all day long but what else could she do? She settled for weekly ballroom-dancing classes in the village hall, and also gardened ferociously. She pruned and lopped and chopped. She supervised all the workmen who came to do repairs. Such sweeties they were, the electrician and the carpenter and the plumber. So appreciative of the aperitifs she offered them.

Their neighbours in the farm up the road, Monsieur and Madame Bonnefoi, invited them in for a drink one evening, then pressed them to stay for dinner. Nicolette felt obliged to refuse and to explain why.

'But what would happen to all the animals if we didn't kill and eat them?' exclaimed Monsieur Bonnefoi. 'There would be far too many of them, don't you see?'

Nicolette geared herself up once more to rehearse Harry's pacifism towards dumb beasts, his love of nature and his respect for the ecological movement. In the light of the havoc caused by intensive farming methods, dubious supermarket practices, BSE, and the outbreak of foot and mouth, surely that made sense?

She swigged her sweet vermouth. She didn't like it much, but it was what her hostess was drinking. Women here, she had learned, were not expected to ask for pastis or whisky.

'Harry just prefers vegetables,' she offered.

The neighbours smiled.

'Ah, he is a herbivore?' they said.

They were pleased with themselves. They smiled and shrugged their shoulders and exchanged significant looks. Nicolette had seen that shrug many times before. It said: what kind of man is this? Can he really be called a man at all if he doesn't eat meat?

Harry sprawled in his chair, oblivious. Madame Bonnefoi had set out an array of little savoury treats to accompany their drinks. Harry had refused the plate of bits of crackling, the cocktail sausages, also the pizza-flavoured crisps and bacon-flavoured mini-biscuits, but had accepted the second whisky with alacrity. Now he was full of edgy *bonhomie*, bored, wanting to be off home, not listening to anything anybody said because he couldn't understand it, but instructing Nicolette to translate for him as soon as he had something he wanted to say. She began to give him a whispered version of the conversation so far. Harry interrupted her.

'Hang on, old girl. Let me say something for once. Just tell them that being a vegetarian is brilliant for your sex life, all right?'

He punched the air with his empty glass. Nicolette laughed shrilly. She translated what he'd said. The Bonnefois roared with delight and toasted their new English neighbours afresh. Monsieur Bonnefoi slapped Harry on the back and told Nicolette how lucky she was.

Harry discouraged Nicolette from accepting any other dinner invitations, because it was so boring for him having to sit there all evening in silence while everybody talked in French, having to prod Nicolette to say for him whatever he wanted to say. Having to eat omelettes and steamed vegetables. So Nicolette visited her new neighbours in the daytime.

To cement their friendship, she and Madame Bonnefoi regularly exchanged small gifts. Nicolette gave

Madame Bonnefoi bunches of flowers and herbs from her garden, and Madame Bonnefoi gave Nicolette a couple of trout from the stream, still twitching and thrashing in their plastic bag, a pot of goose fat, and some duck's blood for making *boudin*. She let Nicolette watch the pig being slung up by the hind legs from the fork-lift truck to be butchered, and showed her how you scoured off the bristles with a blow-torch. She showed her how to kill poultry – hang them by their trussed legs on the barn door then cut their throats – and demonstrated various methods of skinning rabbits once you'd killed them. One way was to gouge out the eyes, take a knife to the sockets, and peel the skin off from there. In a few minutes the fluffy white fur was tugged off and the naked head and body were filmed with rapidly seeping red.

Sometimes, on frosty December mornings, Nicolette heard the hunt go by, the yapping of the excited dogs as they poured across the rigid silver of the bare-furrowed fields, the exultant repeated call of the hunters' horns. Wrapping herself in her quilted jacket, she would hurry to the open door and strain her eyes against the sparkling light for a view of the escaping prey. The hunters wore olive-green coats and sturdy boots. They waved to her from where they stood in the lane, gossiping, guns crooked over their arms. Monsieur Bonnefoi would bring home his share of the dead beast, and Nicolette would watch his wife cut it up and parcel it for the freezer. Boars had to be culled, Madame Bonnefoi instructed her, because they savaged the crops. They had to be put down.

Harry was found murdered one afternoon in

January, his throat expertly slit from ear to ear. The gendarmes asked Nicolette whether her husband had had any enemies, and she replied that, as a vegetarian, he had certainly found it difficult to fit in.

MAEVE HARAN

Mysterious Ways

'WHY THE devil should I want a babby when I've got a lovely young wife like you?'

Anne closed her eyes to block out the covetous look in the eyes of her ancient husband. Sixty if he was a day, white-haired and whiskered, with the crowning glory of a mole on his chin sporting three hairs, which he stroked as if they were finest fox fur.

'Babbies be mewling, puking creatures that take a wife's thoughts away from her husband.'

Anne herself was young and lustrous as a hothouse peach, her pale-gold hair, released from its ties, rippled down almost to her knees, and her eyes brought to mind the lake with the sun shining into its summer depths.

When her brother had told her she must marry an old man, Anne had wept. If her father were alive he would have saved her from marriage to a man who wanted her young body to warm his old, cold flesh. Her brother had brutally reminded her that their father and their mother were under the earth and that bargains like this had been made since time began. Her youth and beauty for her ancient husband's wealth and manor house. 'And a fine manor it is too,' her brother had told her. 'Twenty rooms, lead-paned windows, fine hangings and a gaggle of servants. He'll give you bairns and a comfortable life. You should be grateful.'

But Anne's husband hadn't given her bairns, nor did he want to, and she cared not at all for comfort.

Her husband was speaking again in his high querulous voice. 'Isn't it enough that I worship the ground you walk on, would strew it with rose petals and never dull thy youthful bloom wi' child rearin'? There's plenty would want to be in your position.'

Anne's husband was right, of course. Many's the lady who'd give her silk dresses not to have to produce child after child every year till her womb was worn out like a dried-up gourd. But Anne was twenty and she wanted a child with all the yearning of a chained-up she-wolf. Whether it was God's lore or blind longing, she knew not. Only that she longed for a child, to hold and love with all the pent-up desire she had never felt for a man.

Sometimes she thought he did it to spite her. He seemed lecherous enough for three men, but always he interrupted the act before the seed could enter her. She saw that his own desire for her was like a greedy child's and she knew her longings were doomed to failure.

She tried to forget about her need to be a mother and made sure she was a good wife, that she kept a good table, provided the finest Rhenish wines (in fact giving her husband her own portion too that he might fall asleep instead of getting that look of lechery in his rheumy eyes).

There were many things to keep the young Lady of the Manor busy. Her father had been a gentleman farmer and she took pleasure in the management of the fowls and the milking. She had learned the skills of the dairy at her mother's knee and loved the cool shade of the place, its sense of purposeful endeavour. And the fact that it was female.

Her husband rarely strayed into the dairy.

She had been married three years, and her management of the dairy had gone as smooth as . . . indeed as smooth as milk. Until this week. Now, overnight, the milk had started to curdle.

'What say you, Sarah?' Anne asked one of the servant girls, who had also grown up a farmer's daughter. 'What ails the milk?'

Sarah was plain, her face as flat as a cow-cake, her mouth above her white starched collar pursed like a cat's arse. 'They do say' – she lowered her voice to a whisper – 'that tis the fault of Hepzibah Jones, of the bold face and manner to match.'

Anne glanced around her. She knew that Hepzibah was the newest of the manor's dairymaids. She had been the object of much jealousy when the smallpox had ravaged the village two years ago. So many pleasing complexions had been ruined. But not Hepzibah's. She glowed with so much brazen beauty that even Anne, with all her pale comeliness, couldn't help but envy and wonder.

'Some said 'twas witchcraft,' whispered Sarah.

Witches, as was well known, could turn the milk sour as well as avoid the pox.

Next time it happened, Anne called together farmhands and milkmaids alike and asked who knew why the milk might turn.

'If tis not a witch,' stated John the cowman, 'then it

can only be one other. Some female who is with child, whether she knows it or not.'

'Is any of you with child?' Anne asked the milk-maids. 'If so, I shall not take from you your livelihood but find another task more suited to your state.'

Three of them blushed and hid their faces in their smocks. Only one stared at them unflinchingly. It was no surprise that this was Hepzibah.

'And what if I be?' the girl demanded rudely. ''Tis a lie that being with child can turn milk sour.'

'But what will you do?' Anne asked the bold Hepzibah after she'd sent the others about their business. 'When your time comes? How will you live without a husband to give you his name and his protection?'

'My mother will help with the babe.' Hepzibah stood tall and proud.

'But what of the father?'

Hepzibah laughed a strange, defiant half-snarl. 'I baint sure how much use *he'd* be.' She cast a sudden look at Anne. 'Don't pity me, mistress, 'twas something I chose and don't regret. My father left us to fend for ourselves, and his father before him. We have no use for husbands in our household. 'Tis a bairn that I desire, not some horny, clumsy oaf of a man.'

It was a message that echoed in Anne's own heart. She watched the young woman's proud, strong face. Hepzibah was not like the other dairymaids. She had been shaped on a different anvil.

Anne, lonely in her cold marriage, felt the spark of friendship flicker in her breast. 'It is not pity I feel,' she said in a low voice, watching the other's face, ''tis envy.'

Hepzibah laughed. 'Why would you envy me, mistress, with your fine big house, and your silk clothes, and shoes so soft they feel like velvet?'

'You will have a child, Hepzibah, a babe of your own to hold and love. Is that not cause for envy enough?'

'And what of the hate of the village women who will look at their menfolk and wonder which it was that toiled between my legs, and spit at me for it.'

'I would give not a shrivelled fig for their hate if I had a child to hold.'

Hepzibah heard the pain in Anne's voice. 'But what of thy own husband, mistress? Will he not give 'ee the child you long for?'

'He would rather spill his seed on the ground, in contravention of the Holy Bible, than share me with an infant child.'

'Then you should pray, mistress, and tell God of your troubles. For the Lord will surely listen to so just a complaint.'

Anne glanced at the girl in surprise. She didn't seem the God-fearing kind.

In June, Hepzibah's confinement came.

Anne visited her and held the baby in her arms. It was a fine lusty boy with dark hair that stood from its tiny head in a peak and unfathomable blue eyes.

As she held it to her chest, Anne wept and knew that, deep inside her soul, a bird was fluttering that would have to be set free or she would die of longing.

'There is a legend,' Hepzibah said, watching her, 'that says if a husband's seed takes not root in your womb, go up and visit the giant carved on the hillside on Midsummer night and the moon goddess will tip her white milk into your lap, and make you fecund.'

'What nonsense, Hepzibah!' Anne scolded. 'An old wives' tale.'

Anne pushed such profane flummery aside. She would try once more to get her husband to do his duty without being prey to pagan wickedness.

But her husband pleaded he had an ague and would sleep alone till it left him.

She had near forgotten the heathen nonsense when Hepzibah returned to the dairy, leaving her infant in her mother's care.

'Do you know what night it is tonight?' whispered Hepzibah.

'Hepzibah,' scolded Anne, 'banish thy blasphemy else the milk truly will turn sour with such talk.'

'But, mistress,' Hepzibah wheedled, 'tis not just Midsummer night but a full sphere to boot.' She pointed to the faint round moon which had just appeared, pale as a ghost, beyond the hillside where the carved giant had slumbered for centuries.

That night Anne spiced her husband's mead with honey to make him drink deep. Mead was the drink of folk on their wedding nights, so her old nurse had told her. And now she helped him to his bedchamber, and off with his clothes, and into his nightshirt.

He stood before her with his spindly legs. She could see from the lie of the cambric that he was waiting eagerly for her.

Together they lay down in the great bed, chill despite the warmth of the June evening, and moved together. But at the last, just as Anne's hopes were soaring (she knew 'twas that time of the month when she might fall the easiest) he took himself from her and spilled himself upon the linen.

Something rose inside Anne, cold and angry and yearning, and she felt like baying at the moon for the unfairness of it.

Downstairs the hired women, Sarah and Ruth, were whispering as they did the last of their chores. Anne, still clad in her night attire, crept downstairs and leaned on the door to listen.

Sarah's voice, louder than Ruth's and with a bitterer edge, spoke first. 'Remember Becky Robbins, you know that had five girls and yearned for a male child,' offered Sarah, drying her hands on her apron, 'she went there, to the giant, and laid upon his member.'

'Tis not the truth!' exclaimed Ruth.

'Aye, tis so,' Sarah nodded, 'and nine months to the day she had her boy!'

'With help of Swanley's shepherd, more like,' Ruth laughed. 'He be always roaming up there tending his flock. 'Twould be him who did the deed, and no giant, or I'm an unbed maiden.'

Anne slid back into the shadows, her breath shallow and panting. It was nonsense and she knew it to be so.

'Why not venture up there?' she asked herself, not realising her words were spoken out aloud. 'A carved giant's member will be as much use as my old husband's.'

'Hush!' Sarah had heard someone speak and laid a hand on Ruth's lips. 'Someone is out there.'

'Tis only the old dog scratching at the moon,' Ruth replied. And together they took themselves up the back stairs to the small room where the servants slept.

Anne found her cloak and pulled on her shoes. They were fine lady's slippers, not for scrambling up hillsides, but her stout pair were upstairs in their bed-chamber. Better not to risk going back for them.

Outside the moon was bright as a church candle. Anne hid herself in the shadow of the house. How could she venture out in that light? She would be seen by every villager in the county.

And then, like a gift, a dark cloud crossed the moon and, waiting no longer, she ran across the lawn, through the knot garden, and away towards the hill behind.

The night was the strangest she had known. One moment the bright of the moonlight, next the deepest darkness of hell. Should she go on? Was it not pagan folly, this story of the giant, and probably sacrilege too?

But now the giant was in view, a huge figure the height of a church steeple, his outline white like the drawing of a child, grass growing within. He held a club, but 'twas not that that caught the eye, but his manhood. It stood erect and powerful, carved in chalk, ten paces wide and who knew how many long?

From a distance his shape was clear, but the closer the eye, the less distinct it was, just so many lines of chalk in the ground. Except that member.

Anne stood, fighting the desire to laugh or cry at her own wildness, to believe an old wives' tale like simple serving girls. She was about to turn, to go back to her home and husband when, without warning, a vaster cloud covered the moon and the sky was black as tar.

Anne shivered, even though it was near to the summer solstice, and all at once, the cloud shifted, bathing the landscape in a white blinding light. Anne felt herself move forwards, upwards, up that hill towards the light and the giant, and yet, looking back, she knew she had made no willing choice to do so.

At the crest of the ridge she stopped, closing her eyes, shutting out the glow of the moonlight reflected on the chalk. There was awe in this place. Not the awe she sometimes felt in church. Something older and primitive, from the times when man's life had only just begun.

She knelt down at the place where Sarah said Becky Robbins had lain down before her and afterwards had got a son.

She willed herself to concentrate, to gather all her energies into that one spot in her womb, to open herself up, like a ripe fruit split in two, for the power to come down upon her.

Yet no power came. There was the light and silence, silence so deep it thundered in her ears, and somewhere in the distance the bleat of a sheep. Nought else. No ancient powers of fertility. No fecund God. No pagan Angel Gabriel.

Anne flushed at this thought and stood up. What had she truly expected?

There were tears in her eyes, of stupidity and sadness, at the emptiness of her life, barren, alone in her great house with her jealous husband who did not want to share her body with an infant, to let a babe suckle her breasts in place of him.

She stopped at the base of the hill and glanced up at the giant one last time. Before she could turn she felt a hand grasp her chin and turn her face around. And she found herself looking into the laughing eyes of a fine gentleman. Anne gasped. He wore no loin-cloth made of the skin of an animal like the giant, but a silk frock coat with a waterfall of lace at his neck. His face was clean-shaven and his dark hair, unpowdered, hung softly round his face.

This was a living breathing man of her own times.

His eyes were dark with a wildness about them to match her own, yet they filled Anne with no fear. Standing here, the stranger's eyes burning into hers, she knew that something pre-ordained and outside her control was about to happen.

In her deepest sex, excitement crackled.

He said nothing, but raised a finger to his lips on which glittered a diamond ring, then took her by the hand.

He led her, in the bright white moonlight, towards a stile and into the field beyond. She was half across the stile when he lifted her, laughing, and carried her through the burgeoning corn. She could feel the ripening ears caress her skin like the soft touch of a feather.

Almost mid-way through the meadow he stopped and slid her down. Anne looked about her, awe-struck. Although they were deep in the waist-high corn, here it was scythed flat, as though a chamber had been fashioned, secret, and protected from prying eyes. Here, with a new gentleness, he laid her down upon his cloak which was lined with scarlet silk. Should she shout and scream and demand he respect her vow of holy matrimony? She opened her mouth to protest but not a word escaped.

As his hands roamed, above, below, between, setting her skin afire, and her blood singing, she knew this could not be Swanley's shepherd. Was it then some young blood, or a highwayman out for payment in kind?

Beyond, high on the hill, the giant was still on his

hillside and Anne forgot all logic and gave herself to the rapture of the moment. She had known the hands of but one man on her pale flesh, her husband's, and they were cold, like the sliding of a slug.

This night was no silent submission, but a glorying of the flesh, a flowering, an awakening so intense it left her shaking and spent. And the stranger still was smiling.

Sleep overtook her then. Not the fickle, shallow sleep from which she woke constantly in that big, cold bed, but a deep, warm blanket of sleep that tucked itself around her, holding her as if she were in her mother's arms.

She woke with a start. The moon had gone, chased away by the sun which had already climbed beyond the giant's hill. Panic filled her. The house would have risen and be in consternation, searching for its mistress like an anxious dog.

The stranger had gone. There was no sign that a real breathing man had ever pleasured her. She tried to remember a word he had spoken, but with a shiver she knew there had been none.

Anne did up the buttons of her nightdress. All around her the hay glistened with dew – and yet her nightdress was as dry as if her nurse had warmed it by the fire. Shaking her head, too overwhelmed by the mystery of the night, she ran home.

As she reached the gate to the knot garden a bell began to toll, and she stopped, relief bringing a peal of laughter to her lips. It was the bell summoning the village to church. Today was the sabbath, God's own day. If she ran up the back stairs she might yet avoid discovery.

Their bedchamber was still in darkness as she slipped into their bed. Was it only last night that they had made the beast with two backs, and he withdrawn his seed, miserly even with God's ordained gift?

She listened to the household beginning to waken. Sleep overtook her then, languorous and enveloping, and hours passed before her eyelids flickered and she took in the silence of the house. Next to her the bed was empty. The clock on the wall told her that it was midday and her head pounded from the mead. A knock on the door made her start. It was Hepzibah, holding a jug on a platter, smilingly lazily.

'Where is Sarah?' Anne asked.

'Gone to church.'

'And my husband?'

'He too. Tis the saint's day. Even thy husband must go then. I told them you had a fever.'

A fever.

That was it, of course. She had had a fever, no more. She had been delirious, her imagination playing tricks.

'I have made you a tisane of feverfew. For the headache.'

Anne drank deeply. Deep inside her she felt a strange tightening and gasped. It was against all possibility but she knew as certain as she had known her own birth-date. The quickening of the seed. The beginning of life. She climbed out of her tall bed and knelt by its side, the tears falling down her face and dampening the fine cambric of the sheet. 'Thank you, Lord,' she whispered.

Hepzibah simply smiled.

The birth took place in March, just as the first spring flowers were announcing the end of winter.

Anne's husband had watched her belly grow with anger and suspicion. How had this happened when he was so careful to withdraw at the moment of danger?

Anne had smiled with her strange new glow of contentment and told him that it took but one seed to take root and his must have the valour of Hercules.

Her husband scowled and asked the servant girls if Anne had been alone with a man in their recollection.

Sarah and Ruth said no, their mistress was dutiful and devoted. And Anne gave him no other cause for complaint. His house was a model of good order. His servants busy and quiet-voiced. He could hardly protest to her brother or the priest since Anne was not flouting but fulfilling the wifely ordinances. So, with ill grace and some distrust, he accepted what others congratulated him for.

The birth was not a difficult one. Anne's husband, though squeamish, stayed at her bedside throughout, much to the sighing of the midwife, who judged that men, having done their part, should stay away and let the women wail in private.

It was suspicion, not love, that drove him to be there.

The babe was a bonny one. A fine boy with fair hair and eyes that seemed to see all creation. The most beautiful child the midwife could remember in all her years tending women's travail. His skin was smooth and gold, with none of the look of a bruised plum like so many new-birthed babes she'd helped into this naughty world.

As Anne wrapped him in the shawl that Sarah had knitted for him, she smiled at his dark eyes, and the jut of his brow, and knew her life was at last complete. This was indeed the force that glowed and sparkled like jewels and gave life meaning, even her own empty loveless one.

'He has no look of me,' complained her husband.

The midwife looked from babe to Anne's husband and back again.

'Aye,' she said, 'he does.' And she pointed to a tiny mole on the child's chin. There were no hairs protruding, but it was in the selfsame spot as her husband's own. 'Thus the father, so with the son,' she said as she put him to Anne's swelling breast.

It was enough. Grudgingly, her husband accepted the child as his own.

As for Anne, she could have been no happier if she had given birth to the Christ-child. He was the apple of her eye, the sun in her hemisphere, the reason for every beat of her heart.

By the time his first birthday came, Anne had forgotten that night of midsummer madness. It had been nothing but a wild dream, the product of too much mead and too great a longing. The child did indeed belong to her husband, and the mole on his chin proved it.

She was with Ruth and Sarah, supervising the laundry, with the child, already able to sit up, playing at her feet. His beauty and good temper delighted her. He was a golden child indeed.

Later they toasted him with cakes and ale.

She had bidden Hepzibah to come and bring her son as a playmate.

Hepzibah arrived, her apron rolled down in the spring sunshine, revealing the crack between her breasts, on to which Anne saw her husband's eye settle with the ease of a bird on a perch.

'He's a handsome boy, by my troth, just like his father.' She caught Hepzibah's eye as her husband bent down to pat the child grudgingly. 'But what's that pretty bauble round his neck?'

Anne dropped to her knees, the colour draining from her rosy lovelorn cheeks like spilt milk.

Around her baby's neck was a golden chain with a tiny figure on it. Yet she had placed nothing there. She knelt to consider it, her heart pounding.

It was a golden giant wielding a club. 'Some trinket sent by a well-wisher,' Anne insisted, her terrified gaze locked on to Hepzibah's bold one.

Anne picked up the child and held him to her, drinking in his beloved smell. Gently, she removed the chain and put it in her bodice, next to her breast.

'Next time,' whispered Hepzibah, as Anne's husband took himself off to some urgent task on the farm, 'go thither at the winter solstice.'

Hepzibah patted her stomach. Anne saw that it was swelling again, tight and round as a fruit. 'Then 'twill be a girl child.'

'You were right.' Anne smiled slowly, and held the baby even tighter. 'God works in mysterious ways.'

And she began to toll the days until the winter solstice was upon them.

CELIA BRAYFIELD

Spam

A T 2 A.M., Maeve composed an e-mail. The process was simple, satisfying and not offensive to her son. At that point in her life not many of the things she could have done had these advantages.

'Dinner with Clive and Sally tonight,' she informed her friend Annie, a universe away in Somerset. 'Another mercy meal, fixing up the poor little widow. And before I went I asked myself, will he – this *he* they are putting forward as suitable to fill my void – will he be another one that's just separated and hates his wife? Or totally boracic and after the insurance money? Or one of those who wants to have Jon's wife because they'll never have his talent? Or gay and they haven't realised? And guess what – this one was *all of the above*.'

She paused and took a swig of her late-night tequila slammer. Tequila, she was discovering, was good for life-rage, and there was no real need to slam it, it tasted just the same without. And a slam might disturb The Boy, who was probably on his own computer upstairs, and, when annoyed, would appear to growl insults and grunt for money. So she drank her tequila unslammed. But on nights like this she felt like slamming something.

'To complete my happiness, Clive said he'd walk me home because he had to take the dog out. Remember that huge farting Labrador they used to have? And on the way the dog crapped and he dived in with the plastic bag to be a good citizen and scoop the poop. And then, when we got to my house he grabbed me, said he'd always fancied me and how about a shag? I mean, in those words. With the bag of poop dangling off his wrist, for God's sake. Aaarrrrgh! It was still warm, I felt it touch me. Gross, gross, gross. Men!'

Maeve finished the drink and poured herself another one. Bottle on the desk, bit of a give-away, better wipe off the ring-marks before The Boy saw them and demanded his share.

'I don't know how these things work out in Somerset,' the keys rattled in the silent room, 'but here in London there are no men. There are only boys and arseholes. Men have gone extinct. What's really sad is realising that Jon was probably an arsehole too, and if he was still alive I could have sussed that and made peace with it. At least he would have been my arsehole.'

Maeve hit the Send button and a motherlode of misery went up into space, pinged off a satellite and came down in a small stone cottage in Somerset, when Annie logged on before breakfast, as those in the media are nervously habituated to do even after they have downsized and gone regional.

'Here there are neither men nor arseholes, but only sheep,' Annie wrote back. 'And the boys are all after my daughter. So I've given up. But come and see our cottage anyway. When did you last get parole from that think tank?'

'Can't remember. Going round tank so long I feel like a goldfish,' Maeve answered her. 'If I have to work one more weekend with one more focus group on work–life balance I shall go mental. How's Saturday 4 U?'

'Fine,' wrote Annie. 'We can't walk on the Downs because of foot and mouth but we can send the kids to the pub and have the place to ourselves for a natter.'

God has a terrible sense of humour. If you doubt this, look at the children born to ardent feminists. When they met, Maeve and Annie had been as ardent as they came.

Each had triumphed over the male-oriented admissions system of the same ancient university and accepted places at the heartiest of once-male colleges. There they joined the Women's Group and snuggled into sisterhood as enthusiastically as other students burrowed into their duvets.

When Naomi Woolf came to talk on the politics of lipstick, they sat shiny-eyed together in the audience. They marched on International Women's Day. They saw *Thelma and Louise* three times. They went for tattoos, oriental characters meaning 'peace' on the left shoulder for Maeve, a lizard in the small of her back for Annie.

With a laundry-marking pen, they wrote poems on the obscenity of men on the doors of the Union toilets. These poems Maeve and Annie wrote from experience, for they agreed that there was no need for a modern feminist to reject men, but that women should empower themselves, reclaim their sexuality and have as much fun as possible.

In this manner some years passed in thrilling ideological purity. The true nature of God was still unknown to them. Maeve and Annie embraced the challenges of the workplace, becoming, when they chose to define themselves through their work, a researcher in a highly regarded left-leaning think tank and a producer of nature documentaries destined for cable TV.

Partners were accepted in due course, and pair-bonds formed. Jon was a photographer, and Maeve sincerely admired him on many levels. Annie, a little bewildered, found herself chosen by a wildlife reporter from among the millions of females who admired his bum as he scrambled up gum trees after goannas.

So they had grown sharper, slicker, thinner and almost world-weary, maturing in the confidence that they had got life right. With every credit card in the name of Ms they felt stronger and braver and more certain that they were not, and never would be, victims of anything. The worst that befell them then was that Maeve visited a Chinese masseur who told her that her tattoo said 'muesli', not 'peace' at all.

Before long they had babies. Maeve with the stroppiest 5-kilo baby boy ever born, brought the concern of the hospital psychiatrist upon them when she named him Rose. Annie had Sam, the most flirtatious, most clingy, most pink-crazed little girl ever to dream of growing up and getting a job in Claire's Accessories.

They tried, Maeve and Annie. They embraced these challenges too, first with spirit and then with determination. Sam was given Lego and she ignored it and whimpered for Barbie. Rose immediately rejected his name and told people he was Ron. When Maeve gave him a doll, he threw it in Camden canal. When it floated, he fished it out, tied it to a brick and threw it back. Another boy saw him, so he said he was playing Mafia and the doll was sleeping with the fishes.

Having now reached the age of hormone madness, the children of Maeve and Annie remained passionately fixated by outmoded gender stereotyping. Sam spent hours painting her nails and The Boy had become just another add-on to his own computer, a pallid alien who only spoke to swear or demand money.

Sam was irritating, but The Boy was a problem. He seemed bent on a life path leading directly to jail. His school work was frighteningly bad, he seemed unable to extract meaning from a book. Out of school, it was worse. Already, he was a Chelsea supporter. Maeve naturally did not believe that biology was destiny, but she could not deny that her son seemed doomed by testosterone to graduate from transgression to exclusion before moving on to criminality.

In the cottage garden the ex-children snarled briefly at each other before Sam returned to *EastEnders* and The Boy went upstairs and plugged himself in.

'This is lovely,' Maeve complimented her friend, although she was getting too urbanised to appreciate inglenooks.

'Well, we can afford it,' Annie admitted. 'I can grow vegetables and do B and B if it comes to that. The market for fortysomething TV producers ain't getting any easier.'

The kitchen had an ancient stone-flagged floor, on which a round shape about six feet in diameter was roughly drawn in black. 'Are you having a rug here?' asked Maeve, wondering if rural poverty could cause a woman's style sense to atrophy.

'You will not believe why that's there,' Annie predicted.

'Try me.'

'The woman who owned this house before was into witchcraft.'

'Witchcraft?' Was this not to be expected in a rural environment? Poverty, inbreeding, witchcraft, surely they all flourished together out here, under the spindly new hedges planted to qualify for the EU subsidies?

'She did her spells right here. It's a circle, look, drawn on the floor. You draw a circle to cast spells in.'

'What spells? What was she like, this woman?'

'Oh, perfectly normal. And a lecturer at the university. Bio-medical science, not at all flaky. That was why they were moving. She told me she'd done a spell for a husband, and it had worked, so they were both selling up and buying a place together.'

Envy, stout as a kitchen knife, stabbed Maeve in the heart but she covered up the wound. 'Perhaps we should try it.' She gave a sharp laugh.

'Oh, don't worry, I have.' Annie was so bubbly, so unashamed, that Maeve scented the truth before she was officially notified. 'The first full moon I got, I was down here with my white robe and my cauldron.'

'It was only her old nightie,' sneered Sam from the fridge, where she had materialised in search of Diet Coke. 'She looked pathetic.'

'Really, it's just about connecting with the goddess.' Annie was concerned to get the frozen expression off her old friend's face. 'Re-establishing femaleness as being as holy as maleness. Going back to pre-Christian spirituality, before goddess worship became unacceptable in a patriarchal culture.'

'You've gone back to reading Fay Weldon,' Maeve accused.

'You used to like Fay Weldon,' said Annie.

'Fuck!' said The Boy, who had hit his head on the low lintel of the doorway. He brought with him the foul miasma of an unwashed teenager, ripe trainers, hormonal secretions, seborrhoeic encrustation. 'Look, if I've got to go to some pub with this girl, I'll need some money. They don't exactly do happy hours round here, do they?'

'What happened to the money I gave you this morning?' Maeve demanded.

He shrugged, angrily dragging his hair over the bruised part of his forehead.

'You can't have spent it already,' she protested.

He snarled, 'I have to live, Mum. You've got loads, you've got Dad's insurance. Ten pounds is nothing.' She gave him another note and he mumbled away without thanks.

'It's just a phase.' Annie tried to comfort her, opening a bottle of wine. 'They must grow up eventually.'

'Who says? Where is that written, that a man has to grow up? If Jon had ever grown up he'd have got past being a war-zone junkie, packed in hitchhiking on helicopters and he'd be here now.'

'One day he'll just turn into a lovely chap. It can't go on for ever, can it?'

'Can't it?' countered Maeve, for whom life and pain and loneliness were one long indistinguishable tunnel of grey, and everything bad seemed to go on for ever.

219

They sighed. They filled their glasses. The night drew in, a wistful early autumn night that raised a white mist out of the shaggy lawn.

'The thing about the spell,' Annie confided eventually, 'is that it worked.'

'How did it work?' Maeve teased her. 'You turned a sheep into a prince or something?'

'It's not like I'm going to be a full-time crone. But after I did it, I met someone. At work. Two months ago. Sam's a bit anti, or I'd have asked him over tonight.'

'Well, good for you.' Maeve raised her glass to her friend's new suitor. 'But I'm sure it would have happened anyway.'

'And it's still early days,' Annie added, hating to publicise her happiness when her friend was grieving. Outside the moon, lopsided as if it were pregnant, hoisted itself through the withering leaves of an old apple tree.

A few days later, Maeve poured her nightly slammer, sat down in front of her screen at 1 a.m. and learned that she had mail. As a wife, she had always had mail. Life in those golden times had been three times as full, so she had done much on-line, shopping, booking, ordering and whatever. Then there had been personal stuff, people inviting them. Since Jon had travelled constantly, she used to write ten refusals a week.

Now that she was a widow, she most often got nothing. It felt pitiful to check the mailbox the whole time in the hope that some server error had maliciously dammed up a warm flood of human communication addressed to her.

'Greetings', said the subject line. Her heart shrivelled, expecting to be disappointed. Spam, it was going to be spam. Anything that looked friendly always was.

The message was wreathed in ivy and written in a Gothic font. 'The Cyberwitch salutes you,' was the first line. 'Click here to join her in celebrating the rites of the Triple Goddess. Visit her site and sample the natural wisdom of ancient times.'

There was no Unsubscribe URL so Maeve hit Reply and wrote 'Unsubscribe' in the subject bar. That usually fixed things. Funny that some hocus-pocus site had targeted her just a little while after Annie had revealed her own dabbling. That was the verb; one *dabbled* in witchcraft. One did not splash around in it, wallow in it, get obsessive, rip off the clothes and dance skyclad in the moonlight on Midsummer Eve. No spells please, we're British. She laughed at herself and capped off the tequila bottle.

'Greetings,' wrote the Cyberwitch the next night. 'Visit my site and learn of the eight festivals of the Goddess! Mabon is upon us, it is time to prepare!'

So frustrating to be spammed with nothing to be done about it. Maeve mailed the message to her ISP, suggesting that they tighten their security against such timewasting rubbish.

On the third night, the Cyberwitch returned with animations. In the ivy border on the message, the leaves twinkled with stardust. At random intervals a shower of silver sparks shot across the top of the screen. Around the edge of the Start menu, a lithe black cat appeared and prowled towards the far side of the screen, where it sat down, wrapped its tail around its feet and blinked its yellow eyes. 'Free yourself from old conflicts!' promised the message. 'Find your own self-determined spiritual path! Click here and discover your own inner wisdom!'

What the hell, thought Maeve. Where's the harm? Why am I buying into those old patriarchal attitudes that persecuted witches just for being free-spirited women? And she clicked.

Maybe it was the promise of liberty. Maybe it was the word 'self-determined'. Maybe it was the memory of Annie's happy face. Maybe it was the cat. A cat, after all, is an evocation of curiosity. And it was just curiosity. She was not about to go dancing round her kitchen in an old nightie.

Maybe it was the animation. Great images. High-quality movement. Until then, Maeve had assumed that the Cyberwitch was some needy housewife in some godforsaken small town in the New World, some person with a name like Charlize out in a place called something like Moose Balls, Alaska. The animation said not. It said professional work. It said that a woman who passes her days circulating in a highly regarded think tank might respectably visit a site adorned with such artistry.

'MABON IS UPON US!' the site announced. 'This is the autumn equinox, the festival of the harvest, the time of abundance. It is the time to celebrate and give thanks to the Goddess for the fruitfulness of life, to throw out and clear away what is unwanted.'

You could click on an ear of corn to learn the correct spells to say on Mabon eve. You could click on a pumpkin to learn the appropriate rituals. You could click on a crescent moon for a full list of the eight festivals of the Goddess. Click on a snail, and a really quite erudite essay on the use of the double-spiral motif in prehistoric art filled the screen. And if you wanted a personal spell, you could click on a cauldron.

What personal spells could this Cyberwitch offer? Nothing relevant to the life of a high-achieving urban post-feminist. Hah! That would be something to see. Maeve clicked once more. The cauldron did a little dance, rocking its fat sides while the page loaded.

'The Cyberwitch is all-knowing!' it promised. 'The Cyberwitch is totally aware. With her connection to the eternal forces of birth and rebirth, she will devise her spells individually to bring about the changes you want in your life. Register with the Cyberwitch and a spell will be e-mailed to you personally each day. Just enter the question and the Cyberwitch will access the wisdom of the Triple Goddess on your behalf.'

There followed a registration form. Maeve had downloaded an automatic form-filling cookie. Some things in life were so simple. Just a password and another click and the form was completed, even the credit-card numbers. The registration fee was $20. Individual spells, upon request, were a further $20 each.

A box appeared to command: 'Enter your deepest wishes.'

'I wish Jon was still alive,' she wrote. That'll test you, Cyberbitch.

'Error 101. The Cyberwitch regrets that the cycle of birth and rebirth cannot be disrupted. The seeds of the new cycle are contained in the old. Ask the Goddess to reveal these mysteries to you.'

Hah! Just as she thought. There was an OK, so she clicked on it, and found herself back on the wishes screen. This time she entered. 'I wish my son would bloody well grow up.'

The screen cleared immediately, and the words 'WISH ACCEPTED' flashed through a flurry of shooting stars. Then a new screen appeared announcing, 'Your spell will appear in your mailbox shortly. Blessed will you be by the Cyberwitch.'

While she waited for the mailbox to load, she tried to visualise The Boy as a socialised young adult. It wasn't easy.

'Blessings from the Cyberwitch. Your individual spell is ready to use,' advised the subject line, when the message popped up. Maeve read it with a cynical smile. It seemed to involve entering a trance, visualising a blue light around The Boy, and saying some oogy-woogy prayers. 'May the Great Mother watch over (insert name). May she/he be guided from the inner realms, where endlessness of time and space reach out to embrace the furthest stars.'

'Your personally designed spell is time-sensitive and will operate for three days only. Should you wish to renew the spell after this time, at a cost of a further $20 for each three-day period, click here.'

Personally designed. Humph. Not with the she/he and the 'insert name'. Still, the trance instructions were pretty much the standard meditation technique. Maeve had always found that calming, though since Jon died she'd been too damn angry with destiny to get anything out of the standard bag of stress-busting tricks.

Where would be the harm in trying it? What would be the worst that could happen? She'd feel silly, that would be as bad as things could get. Not very silly, so special postures were required, just a bit of walking around in a circle. It wouldn't work, of course. Not any more than any other visualisation exercise. It might help her sleep. Better for her than tequila, anyway. Maeve printed out the spell and rummaged in a drawer for a candle. The whole thing only took a few minutes. Yes, she felt silly. Silly in a girlish sort of way that was really rather pleasant. She went to bed and slept well.

At 6.30 a.m. a terrible crash woke her up. A crash on the ceiling. A crash from The Boy's room. He had fallen out of bed. This happened sometimes, when he was drunk. He was too big for her to pick up now. Maeve drifted back to sleep.

At 7.30 a.m., some music woke her, a sizzling riff from a saxophone, percolating up from the kitchen. She must have left the radio on. Time to get up anyway.

In the kitchen sat The Boy. He smelled like his father used to smell, the cool-cheeked aroma of a freshly washed male. The radio crooned quietly. The whole kitchen smelled good. She detected coffee, and a whiff of toast, and detergent. The tumble dryer was whirring. On the table was a newspaper and The Boy seemed to have been reading it. When she came in, he got up.

'Morning, Maeve,' he greeted her. 'Sorry, I've got to run. Lecture at ten. Can I pick up anything for you on my way home?'

'I can't think, I'll text you,' she promised him, dazed by the unfamiliarity of it all.

'Have a nice day,' he said. The front door closed quietly behind him.

Maeve had to sit down. 'I don't believe this,' she muttered. 'This is just a fluke. He wants money for something, that's what this is. He'll ask me tonight, you bet.'

The Boy did not ask for money. He ate, put his plate in the dishwasher and disappeared to his room. The next day was pretty much the same, though he stayed out in the evening. On the day after that, he washed some more of his clothes and when her on-line supermarket delivery arrived, he put the groceries away in the cupboards. On the fourth day, Saturday, he got up at five in the afternoon, asked for money for the pub, swore at her when she refused, stayed out until dawn and threw up in the front garden.

Maeve scrolled back to her spell message and clicked on the button to Renew. A little trance, a little muttering, a little walking around – could it really have created such a spectacular change? Apparently so. The Boy reverted to the new, clean, co-operative mode. She was halfway to giving Annie the good news, but remembered her own scepticism and faltered. Annie, however, soon asked Maeve to put a date in her diary for next May. 'A traditional country wedding,' she promised. 'Luckily the Vicar cannot oblige us because I am divorced, so be prepared to jump over the bonfire.'

After a few weeks, in which life seemed less grey and she slept a little better, Maeve went back to the wish screen and entered, 'No more arseholes.' This was not successful. 'Error 1023. The Cyberwitch cannot process negative desires. Reframe your intention positively and retry.' But the blank box was difficult to fill with anything that really expressed what she wanted, so she let it go.

True to her word, the Cyberwitch also sent daily spells, most of which were ridiculous, although it was nice to have mail every day, and strangely soothing to read all the mumbo-jumbo about the wine of life and the bread of connection, under the pretty little animation showing the phases of the moon. Once a week a free sermon on pagan practice was delivered, and some of them were quite interesting. She particularly liked the treatise on the Inner Realm and the Creation of Entities. 'A thought form ensouled with archetypal strength and nature, having an independent existence beyond the human imagination.'

The festival of Samhain saw the site redesigned with apples and hazelnuts, which gave way to holly and mistletoe at Yule, snowdrops at Imbolg and daffodils at Eostar. There seemed no reason not to decorate the house in keeping. And paint the bedroom a different colour, a light lavender she'd always hankered after despite Jon being sure it would make him look jaundiced. In fact, it was quite flattering.

When she came to put things back on bookshelves, Maeve decided to find somewhere else for the photographs. Her and Jon on their wedding day, her and Jon on honeymoon, Jon getting his award from the Foreign Press Club. She kept them in a box, ready to go up somewhere downstairs when she had a chance to get organised. Doing a spell every three days – and the lapses had such distressing results that she became committed to the routine – took up quite a portion of her time now. It was definitely worth the effort. The Boy, struggling with A levels in everything related to IT, actually achieved an A for a piece of coursework.

Was it right to bewitch your own child? Did she really, truly, seriously, believe that that was what she was doing? The Cyberwitch – maybe she really was all-knowing – offered an incantation for guilt. 'Write the name of your shame on a candle and let it burn out, consuming your guilt as it burns.' Well, that was easy enough.

By the time Beltane was looming, and soon after it the date of Annie's wedding, and the Cyberwitch was twittering about the spirituality of pleasure, Maeve felt ambition rising in her veins. What the hell, it was only $20. She asked for a spell to create a new partner. 'WISH ACCEPTED' flashed up immediately.

It was elaborate. The circle was required, and a ritual bath, plus a cauldron, and a knife, a piece of silk thread, a dish of earth, some flowers, and a peeled wand to represent a wooden phallus, which needed to be anointed with oil, preferably sandalwood or rosemary. The trance itself was recommended to last half an hour, with a lengthy visualisation invoking the Lord of the Day, a tall man dressed in animal skins.

'In our culture, images of the male are so tied up with violence and authoritarianism that you may encounter psychic resistance,' warned the Cyberwitch. 'Extensive trance-work will allow this playful and creative deity figure to emerge in due time manifesting his archetypal attributes, wild joyousness and life-upholding actions.'

'This spell is not time-sensitive. For best results, it should be performed with a waxing moon in the first half of the year.' Maeve selected the night after the last new moon before Annie's wedding. A wedding, she remembered, was always a good place to make a connection.

In view of the effects of global climate change, the wedding reception was held in a barn, transformed by a local catering company into a pavilion of elegance fluttering with cream satin ribbons. Annie's new husband was the image of the old, only a little plumper, with deeper laugh lines, and without the slightly embalmed look that a man gets when his face is his fortune.

'And you, young man,' he said to The Boy. 'What are your plans for your life?'

'In my gap year, I thought I'd go to Peru,' announced The Boy.

'Uh!' gasped Maeve, with whom this thought had not been shared.

'Lucky Daddy and Mummy, being able to afford it,' rumbled the bridegroom.

Maeve, almost vibrating with surprise, demanded, 'Who says I can afford it?'

'Oh no,' said The Boy graciously. 'My father isn't with us any more, I'm afraid. He died a couple of years ago. And I'm not relying on my mother to pay for me. I've done some extra work this year, I've saved some money. And we have some airmiles. She won't have to pay for anything. I've looked into what it costs. It'll be OK.'

'Have we got really enough airmiles for a return ticket?' asked Maeve, not wishing to look like a heisted parent in public.

'More or less. I can pay extra in cash. Don't worry. And I'll have enough left to start me off at uni.'

Maeve meant to say something about his exam results but all that came out of her mouth was a noise like that of a small dog asking for food.

'Kids today, eh?' The bridegroom gazed fondly at Sam, a sulking vision in rosebuds and pink net. 'They've got so much get-up-and-go. So independent.'

When he had gone, The Boy turned to Maeve and said, 'I meant to tell you, Mum. You don't mind, do you? I mean, you'll be OK without me?'

'Of course I'll be OK,' she said, reminding herself that only a few months ago it had seemed unlikely that he would ever be good at anything except under-achievement. 'Just – no helicopters, OK?'

Perhaps it was because The Boy had unsettled her, but the event was not living up to its promise. She scanned the room half-heartedly, looking at the weather-bronzed, drink-glazed faces of Annie's male friends, and saw no one resembling the Lord of the Day among them.

In the weeks that followed a light cloud of disappointment settled over her. The spell was not working. The Boy was leaving, and the house would soon be empty. A woman who has lost her husband tragically cannot let go of her only son with ease.

As if attuned to her mood, a message arrived in her mailbox to announce, 'The Cyberwitch will cease operating on 30 June. Remember you are a child of the Great Mother and may the Guardian Spirits protect and keep you. Thank you for your support.'

When The Boy was gone, in the manner of mothers, she set about his room with the Hoover and dusters. The last spell had expired just before his departure, so she expected the worst. Old trainers under the bed, three or four pairs of them. Seven unrelated socks. A can with mould in it. Five CDs without covers, three covers without CDs. Several important-looking documents from UCAS at the back of the wardrobe, three with ketchup on them. At least £3.65 in small coins.

On his desk, folders containing college work. She was curious to see this project marked A, this breakthrough piece of coursework on which were predicated his creditable grade predictions and his university offer, indeed all his future success. She began to search.

It was a purple folder. Its content was familiar. Its title, in Gothic print on the front, was *CYBER-WITCH: a site for the modern witchcraft practitioner*. The section on market environment suggested that 'witchcraft is the fastest-growing religion in the UK, with over 30,000 known adherents. The profile is primarily ABC1 women in the 35–45 age-range.' When he wanted, he could be really nifty with his pie-charts, The Boy.

Maeve wanted to cry. She wanted to throw the folder out of the window. She wanted to ring up Annie and tell her the whole pathetic story, and get some sympathy for a woman exploited by her own son to the tune of – she pulled over his calculator and worked it out. Why, the little sod had taken her for over a thousand pounds.

'A very friendly site,' said his tutor's comment. 'Excellent use of graphics and animation.' Annie was still on honeymoon. Maeve still wanted to cry, but she had to agree with the tutor. Why, the Cyber-witch had been the best friend she had had for months on end. So – well – comforting. And so convincing. And really informative.

The section headed 'Resources' cited some books. *The Wiccan Handbook. Hedge-Witchcraft for Beginners. Casting the Circle, A Book of Rituals*. Well, he had read some books at least.

Perhaps it was the trainers, or maybe the dust, but she needed air. She left the mess and went down to the café on the corner to mull over her discovery. Was it so bad that she had been deceived? Wasn't it her own gullibility that was as much to blame? And at $20 every three days, wasn't he right that she had the money to spare for whatever he had wanted? Quite clever, really, to find a way of extracting money that she would consider acceptable.

But hadn't she found a way of getting him to behave that he had considered acceptable? The washing. The exam results. The happy home. There had been benefits to them both. The terrible model of the parent-teenage stand-off had been broken and they'd achieved a very workable peace. The end might possibly justify the means. So why this feeling of rawness? Why the sensation that was not quite pain, more like piercing disappointment?

The day was hot and she felt breathless, so she took off her cardigan, feeling the sun warm on her shoulders. She was crying, just a little. She dabbed her eyes with a napkin, leaning forward to allow another customer who was coming to sit behind her to squeeze through to his table.

I really wanted that spell to work, she acknowledged to herself. Bloody hell, all that drawing a circle and anointing a token phallus and sitting in a trance for ages. You bet I wanted it to work. And since it was all rubbish, all my son's oh-so-clever life-enhancement scheme, all just a plan to plug him into my credit card, it was all a waste of time and I've got nothing to hope for, nothing at all, ever.

'Excuse me,' said the man who was sitting behind her. 'I hope you don't mind me asking, but what does your tattoo mean?'

Half her mind experienced a flash of red rage and said immediately that this was the cheapest, stupidest, most cheesy pick-up line she had ever heard, and she must have heard it at least a thousand times. The other half suggested that she should maybe turn round and check out the situation before reacting.

She turned. The man was leaning comfortably back in his chair. He wore a leather jacket and he seemed tall.

'It means "muesli",' she said. It was impossible to say this without smiling. 'I didn't know that when I had it done, of course.'

'What did you think it meant?' He asked this in way that was amused but still kind and definitely interested.

'"Peace",' she answered. 'The person who did it said it meant "peace".'

'You were conned, then,' he said, almost sadly. He was young, at least, younger than she was. But *definitely* interested.

She paused on this. What the hell. 'That's me,' she agreed. 'Just gullible, I guess.'

MEERA SYAL

Now You See Her . . .

L OOKING BACK, it was sort of inevitable really that
Mum went into Sukhbir's star-spangled MDF
painted wardrobe and didn't come out again. Not
my fault she went in, you understand, because that
was her job, as the podgy assistant to the even podgier
Sukhbir the Surprising (Magic N Mimicry for the Over
Sixties), but who was to know she would vanish into
thin air leaving behind a handful of sequins and a
Vick's inhaler?

I can't say I was delighted when Mum announced
she would be taking on a second job as a magician's
assistant. For a start, magician's assistants are supposed to look like Debbie McGee, pert, blonde and
vacant, with big hair and straight teeth and high-cut
Lycra leotards and toned thighs. They aren't supposed
to look like a middle-aged Indian woman with a bad
perm and a slight overbite with legs that, in tights,
resemble a condom stuffed with walnuts.

'I won't be wearing anything revealing, Seema beti,'
Mum wittered. 'Sukhbir only does old people's homes.
They don't like loud noises or anything with strobe
lighting so I will look friendly rather than . . .'

'Sexy?' I snorted.

Mum pursed her lips. I noticed the fine lines that

234

were beginning around her mouth and eyes, her eyebrows that resembled startled caterpillars now that she'd given up tweezing and dyeing her hair.

'What for?' she would shrug when I pointed out that forty-two was not old, look at Madonna, and that she had to make some kind of effort if she was going to find herself another bloke.

'I've been married once. Once is enough for anyone,' she sighed.

I hated that sigh, like a deflated balloon, full of loss and hopelessness. I was scared that if I stood in the way, if any of that whiny wind touched me, ruffled my hair, shivered my sleeve, I would catch something. The something I saw in some my aunties' faces, even the married ones, which reminded me of broken strings on an instrument, and smelled like the suitcases on top of Mum's wardrobe, stuffed with silk saris she never wore any more and tattered black-and-white photographs from India, a faraway musty sad smell of missed opportunities and half-forgotten songs.

'Besides,' Mum continued, 'my job at your uncle's warehouse doesn't pay enough, and when you go to university this September . . .'

'If,' I reminded her.

'*When* you go to university, all those expenses . . . I don't think your father is going to help much with that, so . . .'

'So you are working for your brother, ask him for a raise!' I spat back, knowing that Mum was trying to imply everything was Dad's fault, as usual. I mean, I still can't work out what made them get married in the first place as it's obvious to me that they're chalk and cheese, pickle and paneer. It's not as if they even had an arranged marriage (or assisted marriage as they're known nowadays, like helping an old lady across the road, as opposed to kidnapping her and forcing her to hitch up with a distant cousin who keeps goats).

Mum was very proud of the fact that she and Dad fell in love at college and had loads of fights with her parents before they would agree to them getting hitched.

'I should have listened to them,' she would sigh again. 'Parents can sometimes see more clearly than their kids who are just dizzy and blind with excitement.'

But I could see what Mum must have seen in Dad. He's still a looker; even though the long curly hair is going a bit thin on top, he's still got the dimples and the charm and that voice . . . The Punjabi Bob Dylan, that's what he called himself, that's when Mum fell for him, seeing him playing and singing in the college courtyard. Suppose it must be quite an experience, hearing 'All Along the Watchtower' on a harmonium. She fell for an artist, and who expects artists to have any money anyway? So I've never expected wads of dosh from him. In fact, I respected the fact he followed his dreams. That's maybe why he doesn't have crow's feet and grey hair like Mum. He had the guts to plough on with his music, and even though he's just a part-time DJ on a local radio station, he's still got, well, joy.

I told Mum that I'd rather have that than a regular cheque every month and she laughed right in my face.

'Ha!' she spat, and she really did look very unattractive when she did that, with all the fine lines bunching into full-blown call-the-Botox-surgeon-right-now-wrinkles, and her boobs and belly jiggling in the ridiculous glittery cocktail dress that she'd chosen for her assistant's uniform.

'Ha! You think it's romantic, starving for your art, huh? Not so romantic when you have kids to feed as well. Why do you think so many of the great artists are men, huh?'

'Because women are too busy shouting at their kids?' I muttered.

'No! Because only men can afford to be that selfish . . . my painting, my book, my music . . . me me me. For women, once you have had a child, it's us us us. You won't understand until . . .'

I didn't wait to hear the end of her usual bum-numbingly boring mantra. As if the world would suddenly make sense once I'd sprung a sprog. I had a size 16 mother squeezing herself into a size 10 dress so she could go and wave wands in front of a bunch of drooling crumblies and she was lecturing me about maturity.

I called Dad from my mobile and told him about Mum's latest crazy scheme and he laughed a lot and made me feel slightly better.

'That's your ma, once she's got an idea in her head.'

'But why can't she work in Tesco's or something? Something less . . . shameful?'

'Because, my darling girl . . .' My dad paused and inhaled sharply and I knew he was lighting up a cigarette even though he'd promised me he had given up. 'Because . . . she is too proud to ask that konjoos brother of hers for more money. I mean, this is the guy that gave us a set of second-hand saucepans for a wedding present . . . and monitors the amount of bog roll used in his guest toilet – and secondly, because

Sukhbir's a family friend and he's probably paying her under the counter, no tax, no questions asked, you see?'

I saw.

'So you don't think,' I ventured, hearing Dad scuttle around for an ashtray probably, 'you don't think she's doing this because she's having some sort of menopause . . . you know, dressing up for some attention or . . . oh God, maybe she's looking for a toy boy or something – I don't know.'

There was a long gap whilst my dad choked and rattled like an old boiler, trying to catch his breath.

'Your . . . your mother? T . . . Toy boy?'

'Yeah, OK Dad,' I smiled. 'Don't try and say anything else or you might cough up some lung. I'll see you on Sunday then.'

'Yeah yeah,' he gasped. 'I'll play you a new tune I did today, s'good, Seema, could be jingle, I think. Flog it to Guinness or someone and baboom.'

'Baboom. Yeah, Dad. Bye.'

I knew from experience it was pointless trying to change my mother's mind. I hadn't managed to stop her turning up at the school gates with mittens when there was a sudden cold snap, or cans of pop when it suddenly turned warm. Sweet when you're six, sick when you're sixteen. She got away with it at first, the sympathy vote, her being a single parent and 'foreign' to boot. But once everyone else's parents began catching up with us, every term bringing forth another crop of affairs, desertions or just the Growing Apart thing, it became harder to explain Mum's behaviour. I tried everything: crying, shouting, Venn diagrams, even once sneaking out through a side entrance and leaving her waiting for me at the school gates, which just ended with her calling the police, who in turn got out their helicopter and team of frogmen. They were all quite annoyed when they found me at home in my slippers watching *Countdown*.

'She needs to feel she is doing her best,' my Auntie Bimla explained. 'You know, she has to be both parents to you, so she tries twice as hard.'

'I have got a dad,' I reminded her.

'But he's not here, is he? He only gets the fun bits, the icing on the cake. Your mother has to make the cake and wash the plate afterwards. Poor Manju.'

Poor Manju. Vicharee Manju. Such bad kismet, hai hai. I know all the catch-phrases her so-called friends sob out in between eating their way through a family-size biscuit barrel on their visits over here. I think they actually enjoy it in some perverted way and I've told Mum so, descending like a huge flock of sari-clad crows for their monthly pecking session.

It always starts with the What Went Wrong questions: 'Such good-looking people, both of you, from such good families . . . Maybe it was the money – if Manju had been allowed to finish college . . . Maybe it was England, back home the families would have kept them together . . . Maybe it was another woman, these blondes go like rabbits.'

And then it was the What Might Go Wrong scenarios: 'How will she find another husband, now she's shop-soiled goods? . . . What if she falls ill suddenly, and all we find is her decomposed body, half eaten by wild cats? . . . What will become of poor Seema? How will we show our faces when she ends up selling her body for crack?'

239

At this point Mum would usually disappear into the kitchen and while she deep-fried mountains of homemade snacks, the crows would huddle together, making plans for their fallen sister.

'There is one agency in Hounslow, they welcome divorced people with children, as long as she's not too fussy . . . Hah! They found my second cousin a match there, the man had a colostomy bag but also his own house and car, she was lucky . . . Please someone take her along to their beautician. Who wants to marry a woman with open pores and chin bristles, huh?'

Then Mum would enter pushing her hostess trolley and everyone would ooh and aah at the tiny hand-pinched samosas and the golden pillows of pakoras and the glistening orange laddoos plumply dripping with butter, and that's when I would usually come in from my hiding place from the hallway, load up my plate and attempt a quick getaway, although who manages that with the Mafia around?

'Hai! Look at how Seema is growing so nicely, such a pretty girl if she would stop scowling . . . How old now? Seventeen? So what are your future plans, beti?'

Mum would sit up then, sniffing the air, catching the whiff of hungry carnivores around a defenceless (unmarried) meaty snack. She would clear her throat, the dumpy woman in beige, the sparrow amongst the birds of paradise, and she would say, 'Seema is going to university. Then after that, we shall see . . .'

So I left her to it, basically. Left her prancing around the sitting room in her lurid Lycra, practising pirouettes and dodging imaginary knives, doing whatever magicians' assistants do for their warm-ups, because I had more than enough to cope with. I mean, you would think she might spare a thought for me, in the middle of revising for my A levels. You would think she might remember to feed me occasionally as I sweated over my textbooks, but no, once she'd done a couple of 'gigs' as she cringingly called them, her evenings were spent jigging around downstairs doing God-knows-what to the strains of 'Fly Me to the Moon' (the Julie London version, at least she picked up some smidgeon of taste from Dad).

You would think she would understand my raging hormonal problems, given the amount of crappy American self-help books by her bed with shiny happy covers like Tampax ads: *Make Friends with Your Flab! Pelvic Floor Exercises for the Hopeful Celibate! Raging Womb – One Woman's Story of Redemption!* In fact, the only book she seemed to have read properly was a stark paperback with a one-eyed bandaged teddy bear on the cover. It was called *Children of Divorce Speak Out.* (No exclamation mark, obviously an intellectual read.)

As I picked it up (not that I was snooping, I was looking for the hairdrier), it fell open to one particular page where someone, Mum I presumed, had boxed in a whole paragraph in bright-red pen. It said, 'Children of divorce, whatever their age, will instinctively, perhaps unconsciously, look for someone to blame. Sadly, it may be themselves; mostly, it will probably be you. How you cope with this will of course be dependent upon the age of the child and on your own parenting skills. But the questions will inevitably come. Do you feel ready to answer them?'

And then further down the page, a couple of lines, underscored so heavily that the red ink had bled right through the page, 'Some children will inevitably idealise the absent parent, often at the expense of the parent with whom they live. Past conflicts, which they may have even witnessed, may be glossed over or simply be magicked away with a wave of a child's angry wand. It's not that children can't handle truth, their truth may be different from yours. And you both have to be ready for it.' And in her fat curly writing, Mum had written in the margin: SEEMA. Followed by three exclamation marks.

Well, I just flipped. I mean, the cheek of it, when all through my childhood it's been me hiding the truth from Mum, protecting her from herself mostly. Not telling her about the nicknames following her behind her back, Mrs Mop (from my schoolmates, because of once turning up in her slippers), Eeyore (from Dad, because of her I've Just Sucked A Lemon expression), Mata-ji (from her friends), who mockingly call her Revered Mother even though she's younger than most of them, because ever since I can remember, my mother has moved, spoken and behaved like an old woman. I'd never told her of Dad's confessions on the telephone, where he would admit that he had fallen out of love with her because she simply Let Herself Go; that he would stare at the pictures from when they first arrived in London, at the laughing woman with the glorious black mane of hair, black almond eyes and psychedelic miniskirts, and wonder who'd spirited her away.

And so I was going to tell her The Truth. I was going to wave this stupid psychobabble book in front of her face and tell her everything. I stomped down the stairs towards the strains of Julie London and was really miffed to find the door to the sitting room locked, as

I'd planned quite a dramatic entrance. I didn't even know that door had a lock. I banged on it yelling for Mum over the music. The song snapped off hurriedly; then I heard these weird noises, strange popping sounds like restrained sneezes or muffled fireworks, and then whispers, naughty-schoolchildren mutterings and guilty giggles from behind bunched fists.

'Mum!' I shouted. 'Open up! Who's in there?'

There was a moment of silence and then this spooky single note that seemed to reverberate around the hallway, even though it was obviously coming from behind that door, a note like a distant siren, or the string of a harp, sweet yet heavy with a powerful undertow that threatened to pull you along with it, high yet the bass from its vibration made my breastbone tingle, unearthly yet so familiar that somewhere a vague memory began forming in my backbrain of a scene on a seashore somewhere, somewhere where I stood with my parents and smelled tangy salt air and felt shells nestling under my toes, and just as I thought I had remembered where we were . . . the door opened and Mum stood there smiling. Her face was flushed and her dress had fallen off one shoulder, revealing a greying bra strap underneath.

'Yes?' she enquired like a distant shop assistant.

I glanced around the room. Furniture had been moved. There was a smattering of what looked like soot in the fireplace, odd as we have a push-button gas fire, and a vague smell of burning hung in the air.

'Who was here?' I demanded.

'No one, beti,' Mum smiled, looking more like herself now, apologetic, eager to please.

My blazing temper had gone; now I felt tired and

nasty. I threw the book on Divorced Children on to the sofa.

'I was thinking . . . I want to go and live with Dad for a while.'

I braced myself for tears, hysterics, threats.

Mum just stared back at me calmly, still smiling politely.

'I see.'

'I've been thinking about it for ages, I've discussed it with Dad, he's fine about it and with my exams and everything and you doing this new . . . job.'

I was babbling now. That wasn't cool.

Mum stepped in.

'You want to think about it overnight, beti?'

I nodded, too surprised to say much else.

'OK,' Mum continued smoothly. 'Why don't you come tomorrow night and see the show? You haven't been yet. Then we can have something to eat and talk about it. Yes?'

I didn't answer right away as I was staring at something that had caught my eye, moving quickly between the television and the sideboard, which had now stopped and was staring at me with inquisitive pink eyes.

'It's at the Happy Pastures Residential Home, you know the one, at seven-thirty tomorrow. Yes?'

The rabbit looked at me, smiled in a toothy kind of way, and winked. I rubbed my eyes, opened them and it was gone, leaving behind what looked like a puff of blue smoke.

'Yes, Mum,' I said croakily, and thought it best I went to bed.

*   *   *

By the time I arrived at the Happy Pastures Residential Home, the audience had already gathered, or should I say, been wheeled in by over-jolly ladies in overalls, beaming despite the pervading smell of boiled vegetables and medication. Wrinkled people in comfy shapeless clothes were seated in rows, unnervingly silent as Sukhbir the Surprising finished setting up his props.

The most surprising thing about Sukhbir was why a fat middle-aged Punjabi man wasn't mortally ashamed to be wearing a sequinned white jumpsuit. Magicians, to my mind, should wear black capes and have curly moustaches. But apparently his brother used to be in a '70s bhangra band and why waste a good costume, Sukhbir laughed in explanation. He laughed a lot. Maybe the result of playing to half-dead audiences for most of his magical career.

My heart sank as I watched Sukhbir set up his 'tricks': the fake bunches of flowers, the hankies that come out in a string, the table for sawing the lady in half, my mother in half, I realised with a slight tingle. And of course the star-pasted cupboard on castors, where my mother in her spangly dress would be magicked away (in other words, concealed by a hidden curtain across a false back), and then remarkably reappear while the old people, if they could manage it, would clap with arthritic hands.

Someone tapped me on the leg. I looked up to see an old lady with a shock of white hair like a halo and blue watery eyes who wheezed into my face with pepperminty breath.

'Have you got children?'

'No,' I muttered.

The old lady smiled sympathetically with baby gums and whispered, 'I always say that as well. Saves face all round eh?'

There was another tap on my shoulder and it took me a moment to recognise my mother. She'd piled her hair into a stiff beehive which sparkled as it caught the overhead lights. Her lips had been painted crimson red and shaped into a cupid's bow and her eyes . . . I don't know how she'd done it because I find liquid eyeliner really tricky, but she'd somehow managed to shape them into Cleopatra-like crescents, black sweeping lines above and below the lid which met in a perfectly shaped bow, and on her lids, a greeny-bluey iridescent shade shimmered as she blinked. The sea, I remember thinking. Or a mermaid's tail.

'Come sit nearer the front, Seema beti, you'll have a better view.'

'No, Mum, I'm fine here,' I replied, not wanting to walk next to her at this moment.

'So,' she smiled, 'have you decided?'

'Um, yes,' I said, 'I think I'll go to Dad's for a bit . . . just a few weeks or something . . . he said I can stay as long as I want.'

Mum hardly reacted. She swallowed slightly and then blinked once, slowly. I glimpsed the swell of waves before she opened her eyes again.

'OK, beti,' she smiled again, less brightly this time. 'It's up to you.'

I nodded, embarrassed now, wishing she'd stop staring at me so intently, unshed tears brimming above the perfect black lines.

'Mum,' I began wearily.

'Showtime!' she laughed suddenly, switching on a

246

smile that was pure Las Vegas, and tripped away on her high gold sandals. 'See you!'

I didn't reply. I don't know why.

By the time the finale came, I was desperate to get away. Sukhbir had manfully produced bouquets, released doves, stuck and unstuck a pair of metal hoops and dismembered and then reassembled my mother to a totally silent audience. He had begun the evening by cheerfully filling in the silences following his tricks with 'Olé!' and occasionally 'Caramba!'. When the Spanish didn't work, he moved on to other languages, or at least the few phrases he'd picked up from holidays abroad which sounded vaguely uplifting. 'Coq au Vin!' he'd yell as a dove flew up into the rafters. 'Due Cappuccini Per Favore!', 'München Gladbach Über Alles!'. Eventually he simply lapsed into Punjabi expletives, telling the rabbit who refused to get into the hat that he'd slept with its sister and hoped that its manhood would shrivel up and drop off very soon.

All through the show, my mother never stopped smiling and posing; she did look quite pretty when she smiled, although it was very flattering light.

And then Sukhbir announced through gritted teeth, 'Ladies and gentlemens, and now our grand finale . . . in which I will make the lovely Manju completely disappear!'

Mum trotted forwards as Sukhbir flung open the door of the painted wardrobe and pulled back a blue velvet curtain revealing an empty space behind it. He knocked the back wall of the wardrobe with a flourish and then swung it on its castors towards my mum. She stepped into the wardrobe, waving and beaming like a royal on walkabout, and then fixed me with a gentle

247

smile and blew me a kiss. Sukhbir drew the curtain in front of her, shut the door and then twirled the wardrobe around faster and faster, muttering to himself and making wavy fingers at the audience.

Underneath his muttering I caught another sound layered below, that single note again, the vibrating harp, or maybe this time it was more like the sound of rushing water. Or possibly feedback from the speakers. Then Sukhbir stopped the wardrobe with one pudgy hand, flung open the door, pulled back the curtain and naturally, as per schedule, my mother was not there. One person clapped somewhere at the back of the room, a careworker, I think. Sukhbir bit his lip and then banged the wardrobe's back wall, nothing in here, nothing up my sleeve, we'd seen it a hundred times. He slammed the door shut.

'And now, let's see if the lovely Manju will come back and wave you all farewell!'

Sukhbir spun the cupboard twice, opened the door, pulled back the curtain. Mum wasn't there. He did this five times. It was only after the sixth time, after Sukhbir had searched the wings, dismantled the front door of the wardrobe, and made a call on his mobile phone, that the audience finally applauded. My mother had really really gone. I stood up on unsteady legs. The audience were now cheering. Sukhbir sat down in his white jumpsuit on the unhinged splintered wardrobe door and burst into loud, heartbreaking tears.

No one took my mother's disappearance seriously at first. Once the police had taken statements and established that Mum hadn't been suffering from any mental disorders or recent tragedies, and that her handbag had gone with her, they concluded that she'd 'done a runner' and would be back when she'd cooled off.

'We have a couple of AWOLs every week nowadays,' one of the officers confided as he tidied up his paperwork. He had the face of a disappointed bloodhound; his jowls shook every time he emphasised a point.

'One day they're perfectly normal, the next, they just snap and they're off. I mean, who hasn't felt like that sometimes? Now are you sure there was nothing recent that might have . . . you know . . . tipped her over the edge? Any arguments or . . . fallings out?'

It was only when Dad arrived that I remembered me and Mum discussing my move to Dad's place, although it had hardly been an argument. I was going to mention it but things suddenly got a bit heated as Dad strode into the foyer of the residential home. Dad was miffed anyway, because he'd had to leave the radio station in the middle of his slot, I found out later, so the first thing he said was, 'What the bloody hell has Manju done now?'

Then there was an animal growling from a corner, a flash of white jumpsuit, and suddenly Sukhbir the Surprising was sitting on top of my dad's chest, pummelling away with his chubby fists, sobbing into Dad's face.

'You are not good enough to touch the *diamanté* on her sandals!' he wailed as Dad lay there, too stunned to react. 'She is an angel among pigs! A ruby in the mud! None of you understood that! And now she has gone! Gone! Gone!'

By the time the jowly policeman had peeled Sukhbir

off Dad, all the fight had gone out of him. He slumped in a corner, like a deflated barrage balloon, muttering in Punjabi and wiping his nose on his sequinned sleeve. Dad brushed himself down, and then pretended to fly at Sukhbir, although I noticed he was hanging on to the policeman's arm, relying on him to hold him back. I also noticed for the first time that Dad had a comb-over; a curly patch of hair had lifted from his forehead, revealing a shiny balding patch underneath. He'd kept that quiet.

'Were you two having a . . . a thing?' Dad shouted, bravely standing behind the policeman. 'Is that it? Or maybe –' He shot the policeman a look. 'Maybe you did away with her, after she turned you down . . . she did turn you down, didn't she?' Dad added, a brief flash of panic flitting across his features.

Sukhbir laughed. Not his usual hearty earthy chuckle but a hollow bitter snort as he raised his eyes to Dad, black marbles glittering in his fleshy face.

'Your mind . . . always in the gutter. Some women you have a "thing" with. Some women,' and here he raised his bushy eyebrows at Dad, 'you treat as a thing. And some women . . . very special women –' And then, annoyingly, Sukhbir burst into tears again.

I wanted to know what happened with these very special women. I almost asked. But Dad was standing, just staring, staring at Sukhbir with such a weird expression on his face, that I thought it best to keep quiet. Then the policeman told us all to go home and get a good night's sleep.

Dad insisted we go back to his place. I pointed out that Mum might already have sloped back to her place . . . I nearly said Our Place until I remembered that I was supposed to be moving out . . . but Dad reckoned she would probably be knackered and slightly embarrassed and would appreciate not being asked too many questions right away. And besides, he added, it was ages since I'd been round there.

Once we'd arrived, I remembered why. Although it is a nice roomy two-bed flat, it looked and smelled like a student bedsit. There were clothes, CDs, papers and take-away cartons strewn everywhere and it had a slightly musty smell, like old damp socks, and indeed there they were, draped over a radiator.

'I thought you had a cleaner, Dad,' I said, trying not to sound like a nag, one of his favourite complaints about Mum.

'I did,' Dad replied, flinging objects at random into a nearby cupboard. 'But she kept moving things and I could never find anything so what was the point?'

I stepped on to an ashtray which was overflowing with cigarette butts. I looked up and caught Dad's eye. He looked like he was daring me to say something.

I bit my tongue and said instead, 'Why don't we go over to Cedar Road?' Good move, saying the address instead of Mum's place/our place.

'Well, you're the one who wanted to move in so what's the problem?' Dad snapped at me.

He actually snapped at me! I felt tears pricking my eyes, hating myself for feeling so pathetic. I began picking the socks off the radiator, and had just discovered that they were all odd single socks when I felt Dad's arm snake around my shoulders.

'Sorry, baby,' he muttered. 'I'm just . . . you

know . . .' 'I'm a bit worried as well,' I began, but Dad butted in.

'Angry . . . really angry at your mum for doing this . . . I mean, it's so . . . irresponsible.'

I had never never heard Mum's name and that particular adjective in the same sentence. Suddenly I felt very tired.

'I think I need to sleep, Dad,' I told him.

Dad rushed off and brought out some crumpled sheets and a blanket which he began laying on the couch. The couch!

'The other bedroom's got all my gear in it,' Dad apologised. 'My sound system, synthesiser . . . don't worry, it'll all be shifted before you move in properly!' he called as he drifted off.

A memory flashed through my mind, of a posse of fat relatives visiting from India who spent their time either eating, bathing or sleeping. Mum had immediately given up her bedroom for them and slept on the couch for two weeks. I had slept in my own bed. Of course Mum had done that for them, for me, because that's what parents do for their kids, I'd assumed.

I glanced through my dad's half-open bedroom door. He had a king-sized double with bright-red sheets. It looked much more comfortable than the bloody couch. And then, on the far bedside table near the window, I spotted a neat pile of belongings. It was the neatness that gave it away. A hairbrush, some cotton wool, and a box of tampons. Dad came out of the bedroom carrying a pillow, closing the door behind him.

'My bed's um . . . messy right now, baby. You'll be OK here, won't you?'

I lay awake for ages, spooked by the unfamiliar night sounds of clanking pipes, traffic and Dad's pneumatic snores which sounded like an asthmatic drilling for oil. I went through all the reasons Mum could have left (me moving out, depression about her cellulite, unrequited love for Sukhbir, although that was scraping the barrel) and then the ways she could have done it (removing the false door at the back of the wardrobe, a secret trapdoor under the wardrobe, a secret compartment at the top of the wardrobe where she could have hidden whilst we all panicked outside. But all the sensible logical reasons didn't add up to Sukhbir's expression when he opened that wardrobe door. He was puzzled, then shocked, then disbelieving. But there was something else hidden in the creases of his chubby face, a something that kept me awake all night. He was frightened, as if he'd been half expecting it, as if his worst nightmare had come true. I left my mobile on all night in case Mum phoned. She didn't.

By the end of the third week, when Mum hadn't returned, I bought a new mobile, one of those digital ones that can supposedly pick up signals in Antarctica. The first week had been absolute chaos. We had newspapers and local TV cameras swanning around, not because Mum was a missing person because, like the policeman said, that wasn't news any more. It was the way in which she'd disappeared. It was quite a tricky job for the reporters and I could see why, because it was how I felt about it too. One the one hand, it was a serious business, a mother abandoning her family. (The reporters were slightly disappointed that I wasn't younger. They turned up expecting to do shots of some cute toddler with a tear-streaked face holding a clumsy crayon drawing saying Cum Hom Mama!) On the other hand, it was ridiculous and darkly amusing, to disappear in the middle of a disappearing act. 'Bizarre' was used quite a lot. Also 'Absurd', 'Mysterious' and, according to a journalist from the *Fortean Times*, 'A Sinister Conspiracy'. His theory, of Mum slipping through a hole in the time-space continuum was 'interesting but unhelpful' according to the local police, who stopped calling once the reporters had gone for good.

We'd moved back to Cedar Road in the first week as well, as I'd refused to clear up the debris, and Dad had refused to pay the huge amounts that every cleaning firm had quoted him for fumigating the premises. There was also the small matter of the Blonde Nutter who'd turned up in the middle of the night in Dad's flat, brandishing her key and complaining loudly that her Poopikins hadn't called her for a whole forty-eight hours.

When Dad tried to explain that he was having an Emotional Crisis because Mum had gone missing, the Nutter yelped, 'But that's what you wanted, isn't it? Now we can get married!'

It was at this point that Dad lost it, screaming and chucking stuff around, which the Nutter joined in with, only at a much higher decibel level.

I just picked up my duvet and went to sleep in the bath, hearing them spit and yowl at each other, her screaming, 'I knew it! She's just an excuse! You never loved me!' Dad screaming, 'Get off my case, man! You're a totally psycho trip, you know that?' Funny how he reverted to being a hippie prat when he was angry.

I lay on the hard cold enamel and remembered lying in my bedroom, listening to Mum go through her usual night-time rituals, bolting the front door, watering the flowering jasmine on the hall table, boiling a last kettle for her Bed Tea as she called it before padding up the stairs, humming 'Fly Me to the Moon' in a distracted happy way. I realised how safe it had made me feel, ten o'clock and all's well with the world. Another world, another lifetime.

At first we were bombarded by visitors, all with that same expression of confused grief and ghoulish excitement. The sari-clad crows turned up in force bearing gifts of tupperware filled with home-made Indian food.

'You have to eat, Seema beti!' as if the chicken tikka and rice would bring her magically back.

They kept pawing me and hugging me, fighting for turns to crush me to their cushiony bosoms and pat my head, promising me that, 'You will never be alone, beti, we are here.'

Normally that would have been enough for me to pack a bag and do a runner as well, but gradually I began to look forward to their daily visits. Maybe it was just the physical thing, of seeing other women with Mum's burnished skin and black eyes, who smelled like her, that faint whiff of cardamom and talcum powder, or hearing the occasional Punjabi phrases tucked in between flawless, slightly accented English.

'Why she couldn't have talked to us, hai mere dil! It's been too much for her, vicharee, thenu puta,' and at this point they would shoot evil glances at Dad who would scarper into another room.

Dad tried his best to charm them at first, accepting their sympathy with a tortured brave smile and a brief flash of his dimples. But they remained extremely unimpressed, which surprised both me and Dad. I mean, Dad's always got out of every situation by making people, mainly women, laugh. But the sari brigade didn't laugh. They tutted and sniffed and huffed and muttered every time Dad attempted a dimpled grin or a cheeky-chappie quip and instead pawed and patted me ever harder until Dad gave up.

'He's really upset,' I told them as I attempted to roll out a chapati which sadly resembled a map of Africa. (They'd decided I needed to learn how to cook for myself so every day I had to learn a new dish, and acquired a new set of burns with it from the hot griddle or the steaming pans.) 'He's upstairs every day on his synthesiser playing all this sad music,' I tried to convince them.

They clucked as one, ruffling their saris like matronly hens. 'Now he's sorry!' they tutted. 'Big help, singing his moony-shoony songs! Women need solid things, Seema beti. Bread. Central heating. Strong arms around them. Any idiot can sing a song . . .'

And then would come the keening, the nightly dirge, sent out as a homage to my mother across the ether, all of them holding each other and singing their grief to the sky.

'Hai Manju! We are sooo lonely without you! Where have you gone? Where?'

It amazed me, actually, the number of people Mum seemed to have acquired without me ever knowing. They all turned up in dribs and drabs, waifs and strays looking for their missing owner. The old Polish lady from two doors down, who told me how Mum would pick up her pension for her every week and mowed the lawn for her every fortnight. The rosy-cheeked woman from the next street, who arrived with a toddler hanging from every limb, for whom Mum would babysit every Wednesday afternoon.

'I'd just go shopping, nothing special. I just needed two hours away from the madness. She understood that, your mum.'

The lollipop lady from my old school whom Mum had got hooked on Indian sweets.

'Ooh I loved them sticky orange ones, them what you call 'em, jalebis . . . she brought me a bag every Friday, she did.'

The librarian with whom Mum discussed the latest paperbacks over a snatched cup of tea and fairy cake, the ice-cream man always parked outside our house on his rounds because 'She'd run out like a little kid for her ninety-nine, used to tickle me,' and various local snot-nosed youths on bicycles who'd rung the doorbell to ask if the 'Smiley lady with the funny pyjamas' was back yet.

I got quite good at whipping up tea and snacks for the various visitors, quite enjoyed it in a weird sort of way, maybe because all of them had really come to talk about Mum and these little bits of her were better than nothing at all. Dad would harumph about the kitchen, unwrapping yet another packet of bourbon creams and moaning, 'See, that's your mum all over. Time for every loony and lame duck that wanders by, always too busy –'

For Me, he wanted to add. I could see it written on his face and at that point, he really did look like a spoilt kid, pouty and pissed off, and I realised then that he didn't get it. But I did, maybe for the first time. How strange it was, strange and amazing that all these people knew their little bit about Mum and together their little pieces made a huge jigsaw that I never knew existed. A glorious multicoloured picture, like one of those Magic Eye things which close up, just looks like squiggles and mess, but once you change your perspective, how the foreground mess dissolves and there, suddenly, you see the mountain, or the unicorn, or the ocean, which has been there all the time, waiting to be discovered.

And the picture became even clearer once I'd rummaged through Mum's bedroom, looking for clues, for some answers. The expensive French perfumes, not in their packaging but opened, used, lined up on one of her wardrobe shelves. The poetry books in her bedside table drawer: Sylvia Plath, Christina Rossetti, Dorothy Parker, strong bloody women hiding amongst her vitamin pills and tweezers. The folded piles of Indian suits and saris, piercing emerald greens, hot fuchsia pinks, silver lotus embroidery, tiny gold sequinned elephants marching across silk hems and organza scarves. All the bright wicked daring things behind closed doors, waiting waiting. But nevertheless, they were there.

Is that where she had gone? Gone somewhere where she could read about scarred hearts and wear burnt-orange saris with skin smelling of rose and jasmine, where the elephants could march in peace? I'd always seen Mum as a desert: dry, barren, boring, somewhere to be driven through quickly with the air-conditioning on full blast. But suddenly, now all I saw was sea, deep, unpredictable, in which everyone swam, expecting that the summer would last for ever.

By the fourth week, we'd all changed. The visitors were less frequent and more silent, hope fading, fears growing. Mum's distant brother, who'd already got a replacement for her in his factory, wrote a cheque, and posters began appearing in the press, around the neighbourhood, of Mum's face with HAVE YOU SEEN THIS WOMAN? in bold black lettering above it. Sukhbir the Surprising announced his retirement and returned his membership of the Magic Circle. It made page three of the local freebie paper, whilst Mum's picture was on page one. I pointed out to Dad that it was an old picture so who would recognise her from that? One of the ones from the last days of their marriage, where her hair was still black and her smile, though slightly less wide, at least reached her eyes.

'Doesn't matter,' Dad said stubbornly. 'It is definitely her. People will know.'

Every night, on his radio show, Dad would make the same announcement before signing off. He would tell his listeners that Mum was missing, describe her, give out contact numbers and then always end with, 'Manju, please get in touch, baby. Whatever it is, we can work it out. Love you, baby.' Then his voice would crack and Julie London singing 'Fly Me to the Moon' would snap on, with its weirdly cheerful string intro and Julie's smoky voice asking us to let her play amongst the stars.

By then I was back at school and was something of a tragic heroine, with loads of people who normally avoided me coming up to squeeze my arm and then move away nervously, as if losing a parent so carelessly and weirdly might be infectious.

My headmistress called me into her office and asked how I felt about my A levels the following week, given my 'difficult personal situation'. I told her that I was fine and would do them like everyone else. I could see she was disturbed by how calm I must have seemed, a hard-hearted bitch who didn't care much one way or the other. Actually I couldn't begin to tell her how much I cared. Because, above everything else, Mum had been obsessed about me getting my exams and because of that obsession, I felt sure that next week, on Monday, on the day of my first exam, she would come back.

The night before my first A level, I cleaned the entire house, hoovered, dusted, put fresh sheets on Mum's bed, cooked her favourite meal of saag alloo and rice, and sat down with my sociology textbooks, trying to concentrate but failing pretty miserably as I jumped at every approaching car and footstep outside. I heard Dad come in, finished off a chapter and then padded downstairs. He was sitting in the freshly hoovered lounge, feet on the coffee table, muddy shoes on the carpet, a half-eaten plate of saag alloo on his lap, flicking from one channel to the other.

'Cup of tea, baby,' he said without turning around.

I started shouting. I don't remember what I shouted but it was enough to make Dad jump up, tip his food on to the sofa, which made me shout even more, but I think the words Lazy, Insensitive and Selfish figured quite strongly. At the end of it I was panting for breath and Dad was standing in front of me, not looking cheeky or boyish any more, but sad, tired and old.

'You know what?' he said. 'You are just like your mother.'

I'd ended up in Mum's classic pose with my hands on my hips, feet splayed in old slippers, dressing gown falling off my shoulder, holding a cup of tea and feeling this lava of rage and uselessness gradually simmer down, leaving ashes and this horrible sensation that there was no one in the world that understood me and that I knew, deep down, I was very very worth knowing. That I deserved that.

'Yes,' I said finally, 'I am just like my mother. Is that a problem?'

Dad caved in. Everything seemed to collapse inwards slowly, his skin sagged, his eyes drooped and brimmed up, his shoulders slumped. He came over and squeezed me, a big daddy-bear hug, and I felt like a kid again, a kid with an old lady's head and shuffly slippers.

And then it came back, clear and sharp, the memory, a snapshot of us all on the beach in Bournemouth. I'm so small that Dad looks like a giant; I have a good view of his hairy knees with his jeans rolled up above them. He's holding out a yellow spade with a tiny green crab on it which skitters from one side to the other in a mad sideways dance. And Mum is just behind him in a white sun-dress dotted with little flowers, the camera up to her laughing face.

'Oh Seema!' she laughs. 'Oh my Seema!'

And I remember that we were happy once, all of us together, and remembering this is so painful that I feel sick and dizzy for a moment, trying to push it away, as always. But I breathe through it. I let Dad hold me and I let myself remember this time. I remind myself of how good it was, of how they tried, instead of hating them for failing. A line popped into my head from infants' school assembly: A Child Made Of Love. Well, me and Jesus then. Not bad company to be in really. I felt wise and impressively mature as I patted Dad on the shoulder.

He sniffed again and mumbled into my neck, 'Any chance of that cup of tea now?'

My A levels lasted a week and a half. The days rolled by in a cycle of nerves and diarrhoea; before the exam I was worried about the exam, after the exam I looked for Mum at the school gates and the stomach cramps would begin when she wasn't there. My mate Jenny took to walking me home, just letting me talk and rage and sniffle until I felt OK enough to go inside.

'Do you feel your mum's abandoned you?' Jenny asked, appropriately enough just after our second sociology paper.

She wants to be a therapist but I told her she has to get rid of the cheesey smile first, otherwise her patients would simply end up attacking her with a heavy object.

I shook my head. 'No, I've never worried about her really wanting to leave me. Maybe that's me being big-headed but . . . she wouldn't. At first I thought she was trying to teach me a lesson, so I was angry. Then I felt sad because I realised . . . well, loads of things.'

'And now?' Jenny asked.

I gulped. I didn't want to say it but I sort of did want to as well, because maybe saying it would stop it being true, stop it happening.

'Well,' I began, trying to speak past the golf ball that had risen in my throat. 'It's been a month and we haven't heard and – something might have really happened to her . . . she might be . . .'

Actually I couldn't say it in the end. But Jenny knew and she held my hand, just like when we were in the playground all those years ago, when we'd laugh because our mums would always be waiting at the school gates with those silly funny grins on their faces, lighting up like lamps when they glimpsed us running towards them, ready to take us home.

Put down your pens!' she said and the whole room erupted into cheers. Everyone was throwing their jumpers, pencil cases, good-luck mascots in the air. The last exam, the last duty to our school, the last day of being kids before moving on to college or university or the year out before university where you could bum around hot countries smoking too much dope and discovering the meaning of true happiness from some smiling limbless beggar. I just wanted to leave. I gathered up my stuff, avoided Jenny who was sobbing and laughing into some lad's shoulder, and began the long walk down the gravelled drive towards the rusting iron school gates.

There were a few anxious parents waiting behind the gates, more parked up, folding up newspapers or on their mobile phones. And somebody in a turquoise outfit that shimmered like sun on sea from even this distance. Somebody standing in her usual place with her hands on her hips, not waving, just waiting. I dropped my bag and started running. Most exercise I've done in years as a matter of fact.

For a moment, just a moment, I hesitated, as I got nearer, puffed out, a stitch beginning, because I wasn't sure. She had Mum's face, Mum's body, but the skin glowed like brown buttermilk and the hair gleamed like polished plumage and the sari clung to a body that was curved and inviting as a velvet sofa and the eyes . . . so that's what they really looked like when they were full of laughter and tenderness and well, joy. And when I finally reached her and the arms enfolded me, I felt little currents running between us, electric sparks, a completed connection.

'Seema,' she said. 'Oh my Seema.'

Well, of course I never got a satisfactory explanation other than It Just Happened and lots of I'm Sorry, betis, and everyone else had the same reaction of relief followed by annoyance and then disbelief when Mum refused to give anything else away. Dad offered to stay with us to help Mum over what he called The Rehabilitation Period but Mum said she'd already done it, thank you, and instead invited him for Sunday lunch and told him he would have to bring a pudding.

Once everyone had been bundled out with promises of dinners and visits following very soon, I ran Mum a bath, putting in loads of lavender and jasmine and leaving out a silk nightie I'd found stuffed in a drawer. As I picked up her shoes from where she'd left them in the hallway, rather snappy sandals with delicate blue embroidery, a load of sand fell out of the toes. Fine golden sand, the kind you see on holiday posters, and a single shell, iridescent under the hallway light, with a pointy whirly top like the dome of the Taj Mahal.

I didn't ask her about it until weeks later, when we were snuggled up under a blanket watching some trashy quiz show. Mum had her application forms strewn around from various local colleges, having finally decided on a sandwich course in homeopathy and car maintenance. The room was still heaving with bunches of flowers, sent by various well-wishers – orchids, sunflowers, baskets of spring blooms.

'Shouldn't they have died yet?' I asked.

Mum shrugged. 'They're not ready to yet, beti.'

Then I took out the shell. 'Remember this?'

Mum looked and smiled, a dreamy faraway smile, and I suddenly smelt salt in the air, a sharp tang, and a breeze ruffled through the room making the flowers nod and smile with her.

'Oh that,' she said, and took it from me, little sparks suddenly fizzing around the ends of her hair and gone so fast, I suppose I could have imagined it.

She wasn't going to tell so I didn't push. Everyone's entitled to their secrets. I don't even ask now when she disappears downstairs behind the locked lounge door and I hear her singing along to 'Fly Me to the Moon', whilst all the lights in the house flicker to the beat, and little fireworks dance outside my window, keeping me company until I sleep.

CHRISTOPHER BROOKMYRE

Mellow Doubt

I HAVE OF late, but wherefore I know not, lost all my mirth. Or to put it more plainly, I haven't quite been my usual carefree, smiley, mass-murdering self for a while now, and it's starting to make me feel . . . a little lost.

There are a number of evident and plausible reasons for this.

When I look in the mirror, I no longer see the face my mind expects. This isn't any pretentious and self-pitying psychobabble, I should stress: I paid a maxillo-facial surgeon a shitload of money to *ensure* that I no longer see the face my mind expects; and that, more importantly, I no longer see the face so very many people in so very many countries would dearly love to get into with a floor-sander and a bucket of hydrogen chlorate. I don't look radically different. With the bruising and swelling gone, the features and proportions are halfway familiar, but the lines and contours seem softened; blurred almost, so that I resemble what could best be described as a Japanese anime version of myself. I look different enough, though, let me tell you. Walk into the bathroom for a pish in the middle of the night, catch a sideways glimpse of *that* in the mirror and you're swapping your cock for a Glock, if you haven't already jumped backwards into the bath. When it comes to undermining your sense of identity, having your own coupon replaced would do it every time.

But that's not it.

I'm sitting, as I do most days, outside a bar overlooking the beach. Resting on my table are a beer and a book, though again, like most days, I'm too distracted by what's going on in front of me to read it. Today, however, *un*like most days, my attention is enticed by something other than the cornucopia of sun-worshipping females parading between the terrace and the sea. These last have captured my eye but not my mind, a pleasant and picturesque backdrop to my necessarily ugly reflections; soothingly incongruous, disposably irrelevant. I didn't come here for the reasons everyone else does. I'm not on holiday and I'm not looking for parties, romance or even just sex. I needed to be somewhere fluidly transitory, where people come and go and the locals don't bother learning your face because you'll be history in a fortnight. I also needed to be in a place where wearing sunglasses from dawn to dusk does not look suspicious or even affected.

This is my life: for now, for as long as needs be. For ever, if necessary. Not so bad, you might think, and yes, I can afford it. Money is not an issue. I was always prepared for this possibility, every day, on every job, though I never considered it an eventuality, and certainly not an aspiration. I didn't do the things I did so that I could afford to loll in the sand for the rest of my days. You lie in the dirt long enough later on; what good's a head start? I did what I did because it electrified me every moment I was awake, and I did what I did because I was the best in the whole wide fucking world.

I have killed more people than I could accurately count: four hundred at a rough guess. I have brought down aeroplanes, sunk cruise liners, even trashed a fully armed military base. I had the police of half the planet trailing in my wake, presidential sphincters tweeting at the mention of my name. So all things considered, it is not my idea of the good life to be just another nobody vegetating here in the sun, my back resting against a pile of cash, like a moron lottery winner or some Cro-Magnon cockney gangster. This is my life now and it represents, to say the least, a bit of a come-down.

But that's not it.

I am watching a man and a young child, little more than a toddler, play on the sand with a lightweight football. They are using a pushchair and an ice-box as goalposts, the child running up unsteadily to take a shot as his father crouches in the centre of the target. The child connects, giving it a clumsy but firm toe-ender. The ball wobbles in the air as it flies, lending plausibility to the man's transparent attempt to appear wrong-footed. He collapses to the ground, flailing an arm as the ball bounces past him. The child jumps, hands raised. The man thumps the sand, feigning the anguish of defeat.

Here in the bar, there is no need to fake it. I have lost all that I have lost because I was – I am – defeated. In my line of work, you don't lick your wounds then return to the fray with renewed determination; not when defeat means that the world knows your true name and your true visage. In defeat you may live, but not to fight another day. You may live to become faceless, to drink beer in a reassuringly crowded holiday resort, and to contemplate the person you will never again be.

The sting of humiliation fades with time, but the loss remains, joined soon by a colder, more sober process of recrimination. The apportioning of blame – so often an opportunity for deflection and plain old denial – was simplified for me in that none of my comrades survived. That only left myself and the man who laid me low. As my adversary he was responsible for my defeat but not for my failure, so, much as I detest him and much as I resent what he has done to me, I know it would be foolish and unhelpful to focus my anger upon him. Sitting in this bar, on this beach, I have come to understand that there are occasions when the pursuit of vengeance is simply undignified. Yes, I could kill him, but what would that prove? That I am the bigger man? That he was wrong to cross me? No. Because the truth is that I crossed him, and no two ways about it, I got my arse felt. Twelve of us, professionals, armed and prepared, against . . . well, best not dwell upon the details. When you lose despite such odds in your favour, you have to accept that you humiliated yourself. Seeking vengeance only compounds it. Let's be honest, there *is* no retribution for a humiliation of that magnitude. Nor is there possible reparation to those who were counting on you.

I failed. Me. *I* was gubbed. *I* was humiliated. My reputation was effectively erased, as surely as I knew my identity would have to be also. Even my memories have been all but stolen: when I look back upon the things I have done, I can no longer view my victories as anything other than a prelude to my ultimate defeat.

But believe me, that's still not it.

My nemesis, my embarrassingly improbable nemesis, did all of this to me. He destroyed my great scheme, wiped out my crew and even cast me down to what he reasonably assumed would be my death. However, my greatest wound, the strike that has had me reeling ever since, he delivered with mere words.

There are four teenage males running along the sand, lanky and awkward, suffering that phase nature has the decency to hide inside a cocoon in other species. They bellow guttural laughs as they bear down obliviously upon the man and his child. The child instinctively moves closer to the man as the group approaches, seeking security, protection. The man smiles down, offering reassurance with a ruffling of the hair, but his eyes remain vigilantly upon the teenagers, positioning himself to deflect any accidental contact.

The man is about my age, I estimate. He looks younger when he smiles, but his true years are revealed as his face sharpens in ready defence. The child resembles him facially; I can see that even from here. Even if he didn't, there'd be no questioning the relationship: the man is alertly attendant upon the child, but the clincher is that the child looks up at him as though the world is his to command.

'How does it feel to know you'll never see your son grow up?' I asked him, Larry, my improbable nemesis, when I thought I still held the power of life and death.

'You tell me.'

Now, I've analysed and deconstructed this little exchange many, many times in order to exhaust every avenue of interpretation, but even as I did so I knew I was merely trying to find an escape-clause in the small print. I had a gun pointed at his head, so he had to say *something* to buy himself some time, surely? Granted, but it was still a hell of a thing just to pull out of your arse at zero notice. And as he said it, there was a cold sincerity about him, a conviction that couldn't be entirely accounted for by mere anger or hatred. Under the circumstances you could hardly have described it as smug, but it was definitely the look of one who knew he had something on me; he wasn't only telling me I had a son I've never met – he was telling me *he* had.

I have a son.

Through simple deduction and arithmetic I know who by, I know where and I know when. But I do not know him, not even his name, and there are insurmountable reasons why he will never – let's face it, *must* never – know me.

So how d'you like them apples?

I didn't want a child. Like that needs to be said. Hard to imagine fitting much in the way of family life around a busy schedule of assassination and wholesale slaughter. But discovering, knowing he's out there . . . oh Larry, you really stuck it to me, didn't you? He's loose in my head, toddling around, opening lids and doors and closets, and I seriously don't want him to see what's inside any of them.

That, in case you haven't guessed, *is* it. He's in there, and he's running the show, whether I like it or not.

I have in the past transformed myself, or at least

attempted to do so: cast off old trappings and emerged as what I imagined to be something new. But whether it was swapping my Queen records for Bauhaus or my Stratocaster for Semtex, the person inside never changed. Larry called that right. This, though, this truly feels like a transformation by some ancient power far beyond my control. This, as Freddie and the boys put it, is a kind of magic.

I'm forced to see the world through my son's eyes, as though new to me, my perspective involuntarily transferred. It's an attempt, if not to feel him, then at least to feel what it's like to *be* him. Then I see it once more through my own, and I feel a dread darker than anyone else could know; well, maybe not anyone else, but we'd be talking about a very short list. I feel a dread because I know what kind of men are sharing this world with my son.

Evil men. Men like me.

I'm feeling a new, alien emotion. Maybe it's not alien, maybe it's not even new. Maybe it's an instinct that's always been there, dormant, only recently activated. I feel a drive to protect, an anxious concern for this child of mine whose face I have never seen and whose name I do not even know.

I sense his vulnerability. That's something for which I've always had a facility: I sought out the undefended, probed for weakness, then gleefully exploited it. This vulnerability instead puts me on edge, compels me to vigilance. I consider the carnage I have strewn about me, and I am appalled to think of him getting caught up in something like that: collateral damage, among the gormless, faceless lemmings who just can't help but find themselves in the wrong place at the wrong time.

He is worth more than that, more than them. Far more. He is flesh of my flesh, my son, and the thought of someone harming him does not merely worry me – it offends me.

Deeply.

It is for this reason, therefore, as I sit here watching another father tend and protect his offspring, that I feel unexpectedly inclined to act upon certain information that has today become pressingly pertinent, but to which I would previously have been utterly indifferent.

A four-year-old English boy has gone missing from one of the big villas on the other side of the Old Port. It's all over the island this morning; everybody knows about it. That's why that father on the beach, like every other parent here, is staying that bit nearer to his precious child, watching that bit closer, grateful he has not been punished for lacking the same vigilance twenty-four hours ago. The kid's face is on the front of the local paper, and the police, plus dozens of volunteers, are combing the area. Divers will be brought in too, inevitably, but only if the parents are smart enough not to tell the cops about the ransom demand they are about to receive.

I know this because I know who has done it.

All life passes this bar, here in my sun-kissed purgatory, and it doesn't have to be wearing a bikini to catch my eye. It therefore failed to escape my attention on either of the occasions that Risto Balban and his moron brother, Miko, sauntered conspicuously along the boardwalk, having evidently travelled here in the past month with Club Thug. Risto used to be a big noise in the Kolichni separatist rebel movement, which employed his kidnapping and extortion skills to political and fundraising ends. Some of those funds ended up in my pocket for services rendered, which is why I know his face. But this was before his political convictions waned in the face of his realisation that he could get up to the same high jinks independently without having to hand over the resultant cash to any pompous ideologues in balaclavas.

It's common knowledge within certain less-than-exalted circles that he and Miko have been busying themselves around southern Europe ever since. They target the most upmarket holiday residences (not much ransom to be got out of the *Sun*-reading classes) and go for kids of four years and under because they don't tend to be much cop when it comes to giving the police descriptions. That's the ones whose parents keep it shut and pay up in time, of course. But despite their industry, you won't have heard about any of this, because the authorities in tourism-driven economies can bring rather a lot of pressure on the local plods regarding their after-the-fact interpretation of such events. Who's going to go down to Lunn Poly and book up for 'that resort where the wean got kidnapped last summer'? So the local kiddy-fiddler gets fitted up for murder, the 'isolated incident' is solved, and the Balbans move on. They've worked Greece, Turkey, the Black Sea, moving from island to island, coast to coast.

And now they're here. Risto: the brains of the operation, lithe, sharp-featured, canny, paranoid. Miko: tubby, thick, obedient and loyal, as proven by the metal holding his legs together since a mutually unsatisfactory interrogation at the hands of the Russian military. I knew what they were here for, I knew what they would do, and at the time it didn't seem to be of any import. I have always considered their activities vulgar, but none of my affair; indeed my principal concern when I saw them was whether my surgery would pass the eyeball test. However, now that they have actually done it, I find myself experiencing an unaccustomed outrage that I know I will not be able to contain. Besides, as I have said, I'm feeling a little different these days.

I sit in my jeep and watch the villa, easily identified by the police cars at the gate. I wait. I will give it an hour, I decide. This particular exercise is to ensure that my good deed goes unpunished, but there are other ways of doing that if an opportunity fails to present itself this morning. After twenty minutes, however, it does. I see the father walking out of the driveway with a pushchair, occupied by a tiny infant. He stops briefly to exchange words with one of the cops, gesticulating towards the buggy. He's telling them he's just taking the little one for a walk, but his other hand looks like it's the only thing holding his head on, so I know differently.

I get out of the car and pace myself to catch up with him out of sight of the police. He stops at a bench overlooking the water and sits down, offering the infant a bottle of water. The infant smiles at him and he smiles back, trying to hide how he's really feeling. I don't know whether the baby's buying it, but I'm certainly not.

I sit down next to him and speak facing out to sea.

'I know what you're thinking,' I tell him. 'And the answer is no. Don't tell the cops.'

'What did you say?'

'Ransom demand. Phone call. Voice-disguiser, right?'

He stares at me, standing up. I remain seated, still looking out to sea.

'Who are you? How do you know this?'

'If they even think you've told the cops, they'll kill the boy and move on. To them, it's not worth the risk; they can start again elsewhere tomorrow. You can't.'

'Listen, tell me who the hell . . .'

I turn to look at him, removing my shades so that he can see my eyes.

'I'm going to bring him back.'

'*You*'re going to . . .' Confusion and indignation give way to desperate hope. 'How?'

'That's my concern.'

'I don't understand. Who are you?'

'I'm in a position to help, that's all. I can't say any more.'

'And what's in it for you? What do you want, money? How do I know you're not part of this?'

'I'm not. And I don't want money. But I do need two things from you.'

'What?'

'First, that you follow my advice and don't tell the cops.'

'Christ, I haven't even told my wife yet.'

'And second, that when I return your son you forget I ever existed.'

'If you return my son, I'll remember you for the rest of my life.'

'No doubt, but you don't need to tell anyone, do you?'

*   *   *

In tracking kidnappers, knowing whodunit is far less crucial than knowing where they are, but if you know enough about the who, ascertaining the where is a straightforward – if sometimes necessarily messy – process. In this case, it is enough that I know the Balban brothers, not having much of a portfolio, prefer to invest their disposable income in concerns yielding a more immediate dividend: to wit, sex and charlie; or more accurately, hookers and charlie, given that the concept of Risto or Miko getting laid without paying for it is known in most cultures as rape. I know also that they are unlikely to be indulging in the former vice while they have a houseguest, so consumption of the latter is bound to increase by way of compensation.

I call several local suppliers, with whom I have, shall we say, a rapport, and run message-boy Miko's description by them. Arturo at the casino (where he is by far the busiest dealer) confirms a portly source of much recent custom. I make a business proposition and we arrange to meet within the hour. Upon my instruction, Arturo rings the mobile number Miko gave him and offers him the drugs equivalent of a fire-sale: he tells him he's having to get off the island in a hurry, and as he can't take his stash with him, the whole lot is available at a knock-down price, for a limited time only. Hurry, hurry, hurry. Miko goes for it with all the restrained dignity of a piranha, agreeing to meet early this evening. I pay Arturo the shortfall in the price arranged with Miko, plus a little more for his trouble, then head for a tool-hire outlet in the industrial area of town.

*   *   *

I watch Miko emerge from a BMW and approach the casino, walking as ever like a gorilla bursting for a shit. He's dressed in an evening suit in an attempt to look inconspicuously respectable, but given that primate gait and his mangled features, the jacket and tie in between look sufficiently incongruous that he might as well be wearing a T-shirt stating 'In-bred gangster trash'. I watch him enter the casino, then try his car door and find it unsurprisingly open. It's a common conceit among these criminal also-rans that people – especially their fellow crooks – are somehow aware of how *baaad* they are and would therefore never dare fuck with their person or their property. I lie down in the rear footwell and prepare to disabuse Miko of both presumptions.

He returns inside ten minutes, giggling like a kid who's raided the candy shop. I wait for him to place his prize in the glove compartment and reach for the ignition before spiking him in the neck with a hypodermic full of thiopentone. He reacts reflexively with a slap, thinking the jab is an insect bite, by which time the agent is already in his blood and my silencer in his face.

'Sweet dreams,' I tell him.

Miko awakes to find himself strapped securely to a steel table in a low-ceilinged, windowless room. We are in the cellar of my villa, in the hills overlooking the port, but Miko doesn't know this. Nor does he know that he's about to become nostalgic for the hospitality of those Russian soldiers.

He comes round slowly, groggily at first, but sharpens up very quickly as he takes in his surroundings and realises the circumstances. I remain behind him at the head end of the table. If he strains his neck muscles he can see me, but for now he is scanning the cold stone walls, bare but for cobwebs, and the ancient, dustbound workbench to his right. On it sit a rusted but serviceable vice, a power-drill, an electric paint-stripper, a hacksaw, a boombox and a feather duster. His breathing accelerates and his arms test the restraints. I'm guessing it's not the duster that's spooked him, but some people do have awfully ticklish feet. You never can tell.

Predictably, he asks who I am, trying it in French, English and Spanish.

'Let's save time and just lay our cards down on the table, Miko,' I say. 'I want to know where Risto is holding the boy.'

'How do you know my name?'

'I know a lot more than that. Most relevantly, I know that I would be insulting you to assume you'd give up your brother without first undergoing some quite unnecessary prolonged and excruciating pain. Equally, you would be insulting me if you thought I'd believe anything you said before that, so allow me to treat us both with all due respect.'

His eyes flit to the workbench again and he swallows, a look of determination fixing upon his features. Then I wheel the gas tanks from behind the table, into his line of sight, which is when he starts to squirm and whimper. I flip down the visor on my protective mask and press Play on the boombox. The sound insulation here is fine, but I find screaming to be very disconcerting while I'm trying to concentrate. I fire up the torch as the music starts. It's Neil Young and Crazy Horse live: not strictly my cup of tea, but I thought it appropriate, though I doubt Barry Sheene here gets the gag. The album is called *Weld*.

I stand back when I am done, waiting for Miko's hysterics to exhaust themselves. There is a strong smell of burnt meat filling the room. I've read medical staff distastefully describing the odour of charred flesh, and I imagine it must be pretty rank by the time you get it down to Casualty, but right now it's not a kick in the arse off barbecued chicken. The steel in the lower half of Miko's left leg is now fused with my table. It's not a very professional-looking job, and the table will never be the same again, but Miko is going to have a bugger of a time going anywhere without it.

'So, Miko. Bearing in mind that you have a lot more metal in those legs of yours, do you feel like telling me where Risto is holding the boy?'

He is hyperventilating wheezily, but I can tell he is summoning the breath to speak. I lean closer and he tells me the name of a villa outside Fornel, about forty minutes away on the road to the airport. I get him to repeat this then reach for a drawer under the table.

'Time for me to leave you, then,' I say. 'But before I do, one more thing. Don't take it personally, but it struck me that you just might be lying, you know, maybe to buy yourself time so that you could forge an escape. No pun intended.'

I produce two syringes and lay them on the workbench where he can see them: one containing clear fluid, the other a pale-blue liquid. I pick up the clear one and inject its contents into a bulging vein in his forearm.

'This is dihydromertile silicate,' I tell him. 'It's slow-acting, so you won't feel anything for a while, but it will stop your heart and your lungs completely in about two hours. I know you weren't paying much attention on the trip here, so I should let you know you're in an abandoned farmhouse in pretty much the middle of nowhere, and I'm afraid there's little chance of someone stumbling across you and coming to the rescue inside the time you've got left. However, on the upside, the blue syringe contains a neutralising antidote: monohydrate dosamide, and I'm going to leave it here. This is the deal: I go to Risto and, to avoid an unseemly squabble, I offer the location of this farmhouse in exchange for the kid. He saves you, I save the boy, and we're all happy. Unless, of course, you're lying, in which case *I* administer the antidote and we listen to Neil Young all night long.'

Miko closes his eyes, steadies his breathing, and in a broken whisper tells me where Risto really is.

The villa is set, rather picturesquely, in a sprawling vineyard, with high hedges thoroughly obscuring the building and its gardens from the road. As I turn into the vine-flanked avenue, the headlights of Miko's Beamie flash across a curtained window. Thus prewarned, Risto emerges impatiently from the front door just as I pull up, silenced Glock out of sight beneath my open window. I shoot him in both legs before he can speak, then step out of the car and kneel on top of his writhing body, patting him down for weapons. I find a nine-mill and a stiletto.

'Were you expecting someone else?' I say quietly to

him. 'Anxious times when family goes missing, aren't they? Where's the boy?'

He looks up at me, his eyes barely able to focus for the pain. 'Fuck you,' he manages to splutter.

'Don't worry, I'll find him myself. Can't expect you to help me with a bullet in your balls, can I?'

I let the remark register for a second. He pulls a single key from his trouser pocket and lets it drop on the flagstones.

'Thank you.'

I find the boy tied to a bed, gagged and urine-soaked. He flinches as I approach, and I remember I am carrying the Glock.

'It's OK. I've come to take you home.'

I remove his bonds. He looks uninjured but remains terrified. When he speaks, his voice is lower and more croaky than I expect, due to dehydration.

'What about the bad men?' he asks.

'They're very, very sorry. They won't be doing it again.'

'I want my mummy.'

I lift him up with my left arm, raising the gun again with my right.

'I'm sure they do too,' I say.

I carry him with his face rested on my shoulder, and tell him to keep his eyes closed until we are in the car. He complies, without question. I fasten his seatbelt and turn on the engine, then climb back out again.

'I'll just be a second. I'm going to get you a drink, OK?'

The boy nods, still trembling.

I drag Risto inside the house and out of sight. With the lights on in there, he is able to get a better look at me. The surgery is still making me hard to place, but I oblige him with a lingering stare into his eyes until he recognises mine.

'My God. You're . . . you're . . .'

'Not any more. I'm just a concerned parent.'

I put four bullets in his brain then head for the fridge and grab a Coke for the kid.

The boy obediently keeps his head down as we near the agreed rendezvous. I drive past the bench where we spoke this morning, then double back, checking the dimly lit sidestreets for any concealed cop cars ready to swoop in. It looks as though the father has been true to his word. He's sitting there, looking expectantly at the Beamie, as he will have done at every other car that has passed since he arrived.

He springs to his feet the moment his eyes meet mine. I stop the car but don't get out, merely reach back and undo the kid's seatbelt. The father opens the door and hugs his son, both of them crying. I look away.

'There must be something I can do for you,' he says.

'There is. I told you.'

When I get back to the villa, the first rays of sun are still loitering with intent behind the hills, the air pleasantly crisp before the heat starts to build once more. I drop Miko's bargain charlie in my safe then go down to the cellar to find the man himself. The scene does not disappoint. He is dead, face-down on the floor, an empty syringe lying discarded beside him. As I anticipated, he has freed himself from his restraints through brute-strength and desperation, but, with his leg welded to the table, was only able to reach the hacksaw, not the hypodermic. He has proceeded, therefore, to amputate his own foot, before injecting himself with weed-killer in a misinformed attempt to neutralise the harmless saline solution I gave him earlier.

It's uncool to laugh at your own jokes, but I can't help it. Maybe I'm getting whimsical now that I'm technically a generation older; and I know I wasn't around for the punchline, but you have to admit it was a belter.

I go back upstairs, grab myself a cold one and sit outside to watch the sunrise. It feels like a new beginning.

I think I'm going to enjoy being good.

ISLA DEWAR

Diva

T ILLY ALWAYS had a voice. And she was never shy
of using it. At family gatherings, and in her
young life there weren't many of these, she was never
shy of getting up to do a turn. Standing on a chair
singing her favourite Doris Day numbers – 'Secret
Love' and 'The Deadwood Stage' – was always a sure
way of gaining applause, which she loved, and six-
pences, which she loved even more.

She should have been in the school choir. Should
have sung the solo. But she was too much of a tear-
away. Too lippy. Too angry. But then Tilly's life was
awash with should-haves. She was bright, she should
have done well at school. Should have gone to university. But she didn't. And on Thursday afternoons,
she watched her two best friends, Babs Maguire and
Susan Curtis, go off to Miss Hayward's music room
for choir practice, whilst she, sighing and dragging her
feet, went to struggle, hopelessly, with maths.

Babs and Susan and Tilly had been best friends since
they were four, when they met at Sunday School. Babs
and Susan both lived in the bungalows that lined
Beeches Avenue. Tilly lived in a tenement in the long
canyoned Beeches Road that ran adjacent to the
avenue. And was out of bounds for most of the

bungalow children, including Babs and Susan, because the people who lived there were common, and their offspring wild, unmanageable. Keelies, they were called. Deeply hurt by this at the time, later Tilly would find it something to boast about. 'They were posh,' she'd tell strangers, pointing to her two friends. 'But I was a keelie. I was a wildly.' And she'd grin at the stupidity of all this. Whilst Babs and Susan would look slightly ashamed.

Their three lives were entwined all their childhood years. Though Babs and Susan were brought up properly by their parents, Tilly grew like a weed through the cracks in the paving stones. But a wonderful weed, strong, lustrous, beautiful.

Babs and Susan had rules to obey. They'd dutifully abandon their games of hopscotch or skipping at half-past twelve and five o'clock for lunch and tea. Though Susan was posher than Babs and had supper at seven. Tilly would hang about, sitting on their doorsteps waiting for them to return to the game.

'Don't you have a home to go to?' Susan's mother, who didn't like the sight of a somewhat grubby, underfed child sitting at her front door, would ask.

'No,' Tilly would reply. Though this wasn't true. She had a home, but nobody in it really bothered when she left it or returned to it.

'Hasn't your mummy got supper waiting for you?' Susan's mother would continue the interrogation. Hoping the child would take this as a hint, and go.

'No,' Tilly would reply. And this would be true.

But looking back on those years, Babs and Susan would remember themselves as polite, uptight, in pigtails and pretty frocks and white ankle socks. Tilly was always in her brother's cast-off jeans, and striped T-shirt. They'd cycle their red bicycles with neat little saddle bags at the back at a stately pace, single-file, along the road. Keeping close to the kerb as their mothers instructed. Tilly was always in their memories on a borrowed racing bike, tanking downhill, hair flying behind her, legs splayed out either side, grinning. Singing, as she whooshed by, 'The Deadwood Stage'. *Set 'em up, Joooooe.* Whenever they looked back on those times, Babs and Susan thought Tilly a wild child breezing through their youth. Tilly who did what she pleased. Tilly who sang songs in the street. Loudly. Tilly who pinched the icing from their mothers' cakes. And ate the soft insides from loaves fresh from the baker's oven. Tilly who got them into trouble.

'Do you have to play with that girl?' Susan's mother said. 'She's not very nice.'

Tilly who always had jam on her cheeks.

Neither Babs nor Susan had any idea of what they wanted to do when they left school. Though they both had notions of marrying someone rich and living in a big house with two bathrooms and a breakfast bar. Tilly, however, knew exactly what she wanted to do. One day in music Miss Hayward had played the class some opera. And Tilly had an epiphany. Maria Callas sang 'Casta Diva'. And Tilly cried. The rest of the class wriggled, giggled and rolled their eyes. What was this crap? They wanted Elvis. Or Jerry Lee Lewis. Or Del Shannon singing 'Runaway'. *Run. Run. Run. Run. Run. Run. Runaway.* That was great.

Unable to bear the noises around, whilst this exquisite singing was going on, Tilly got on her feet, turned to the class and roared, '*Will youse all shut up.*'

Stunned silence. And Tilly listened in rapture. And knew right then. Right there. That was what she wanted to do. Sing like that. Such depths. Such emotion.

'It just breaks me up,' she told Susan and Babs.

Three weeks later when the Careers Officer visited the school, Tilly had told her she wanted to be an opera star.

Mrs Jackson had laughed out loud.

'Tilly, your marks indicate you are hardly likely to pass an exam. You'll have to leave after this year and get a job. Learning classical singing is not an option. We like our opera stars to have studied music at a very high level. The way you're going it's the sweetie factory or work as a shop assistant for you, my girl.'

Tilly had shrugged.

'Well, you asked what I wanted to do. I want to be like Maria Callas.'

As she left she heard Mrs Jackson say, 'Opera. Maria Callas. I've heard some things in my time, but that takes the biscuit.'

News of Tilly's ambition spread round the staff room. How they laughed, Tilly Lambert, whose tie was always askew, shoes never polished, who didn't even own a proper gym kit, wiped her nose on her sleeve, never did her homework, bit her nails, chewed her pencils, had holes in the elbows of her school blazer – an opera star. Ha. Ha. Ha.

Tilly was teased. Children shrilled mock opera in charged falsetto voices when she passed.

In class teachers would say, 'Perhaps our little opera star will know the answer to this question. Tilly?'

And Tilly would squirm, look up from doodling on her jotter, and tell them that no, their little opera star didn't know nothing. She wished she'd kept her mouth shut.

When they were in their fourth year at school, their French teacher arranged a trip to Paris. Babs and Susan had to plead with their parents for permission to go. Tilly didn't. But whilst Babs and Susan eventually climbed into the bus that was to take them to Dover and then Calais, and finally, Paris, Tilly stood on the pavement and waved them goodbye. There was no way her mother, divorced from her father, and with four other children to feed and clothe, could raise the money to send her daughter abroad.

'Silly place anyway, France,' scoffed Tilly. 'They eat snails there. And don't even speak English. Who'd want to go?'

That night Tilly stole her mother's dark-green dress. It was tight-fitting, had a low, revealing neck. Pride of place in the wardrobe, it had cost £5 from C&A last Christmas. Tilly painted her lips with her mother's dark-cherry Revlon lipstick, put blue shadow on her eyes, coated her lashes with mascara. And took a number 16 bus uptown. She went to a new club that had opened, The Manhattan.

'How old are you?' the doorman asked.

'Twenty-one,' lied Tilly (she was sixteen), looking, she hoped, insulted to be asked.

'OK,' said the doorman.

And in she went. The place was dimly lit. A jazz band played a smooth version of 'Moanin''. Tilly was thrilled. She bought herself a Coke, that had ice and a slice of lemon floating in it. She thought herself sophisticated. Who needed to go to France? Stuff France.

She met Mike who said he was twenty-four. He was nineteen, and he too had lied about his age. He said he was studying art. He delivered milk. He wore a black polo-neck and spoke about a man Tilly had never heard of – Jack Kerouac – who was, according to Mike, cool.

And Tilly said she knew cos she'd got all his records.

He walked Tilly home. Two o'clock in the morning, the stars were out. The streets empty. Tilly was in heaven. This was magic. This was life. They kissed. Strange stirrings in Tilly's body. And at the corner of the road, where Beeches Avenue met Beeches Road, in the dark behind Lipton's grocery store, Tilly let Mike do what he had walked her home to do.

'It's all right,' he assured her. 'You won't get pregnant if you do it standing up.'

'Yeah,' said Tilly chewing her Wrigley's Spearmint Gum, and wanting to appear a woman of the world, 'everybody knows that.'

He said he'd phone her, and she wrote her number in Biro on the back of his hand.

Next day she hung about the house waiting for his call. It didn't come. Nor the next day, when, to the laughter and applause on *Sunday Night at the London Palladium*, she moved between the phone in the hall and the front door. Looking out at the landing, leaning over the banisters, staring down the stairwell, sure that she would see him coming to see her. To ask if she'd like to go for a walk. Surely, she thought, he wouldn't do *that* and not get in touch. But she never saw Mike again.

*   *   *

Nine months later when Tilly's mother was in the kitchen peeling potatoes, Tilly came into the room, doubled over in pain, clutching her stomach.

'Don't go looking for sympathy from me,' her mother said. 'Not after you stole my dress.'

Tilly had never been forgiven for that.

'I'm having a baby,' moaned Tilly.

And her mother dropped the potato peeler.

For months Tilly had kept her pregnancy secret. She bound her belly with crêpe bandages she'd bought from the chemist. She jumped from park benches hoping to dislodge the thing inside. She swallowed castor oil. At night, alone in her room, she bit her fingers, punched her pillow, fretting, worrying. What was going to happen to her?

Her mother called an ambulance. Sat on the bench across from Tilly as they were hurtled through town, berating her, calling her a stupid little slut.

At two in the morning Tilly gave birth to a boy. She held him to her, stroked his tiny head and fell truly in love.

'What are you going to call him?' the doctor asked.

'Dunno,' said Tilly. 'I thought it'd be a girl. I was going to call her Maria, after Maria Callas. What's the name of a man opera star?'

For the life of him, the doctor didn't know.

'Mario Lanza,' said the nurse. 'He's got a lovely voice. "Be My Love". They play it all the time on *Family Favourites*.'

'OK,' said Tilly. 'He's Mario. Mario Michael Lambert. And he's mine. And nobody's going to take him away from me.'

Monday to Friday at half-past ten during morning

break Babs and Susan would clutch the playground railings and gaze dumbfounded into Tilly's pram. A baby. So little. What did Tilly do with him? Did she feed him herself? Yuck. Did she change his nappies? Double yuck. But Tilly said having a baby was great, and they ought to do it, too. It was a lot better than boring old school.

Once, when Tilly was standing outside the playground talking to Babs and Susan, Miss Hayward, the music teacher passed.

'Tilly,' she said. 'How nice to see you. And this will be your little boy.' She leaned into the pram, lifted Mario's tiny hand. 'And aren't you just gorgeous? You're such a lovely little boy.' She beamed.

Tilly, Babs and Susan exchanged goodness-me glances.

Miss Hayward straightened up. Turned to Tilly. Smiled.

'Well, Tilly, I'm glad to see you happy. You've got a lovely baby.' She started along the street, turned, smiled once more. 'But I suppose this will have put paid to your plans to be an opera star.'

That was the only time Tilly cried.

A year later Babs went to university. Susan got a job at the local library. Tilly put Mario in a nursery and went to work at Evan's Creamery. She hoped she might see Mike. She'd tell him what happened. And he'd be sorry. And put his arm round her telling her everything would be all right. Then they'd get married. They'd move into a little house. They wouldn't have much money. But they'd have Mario. They'd be happy. But Mike wasn't there. He'd joined the army. Maybe when he'd heard that Tilly was coming to work at the creamery. Tilly didn't know.

Babs did two years of her degree before dropping out and running off to London with an art student who designed clothes. Susan passed her exams, and moved up through the library hierarchy.

Babs and her husband opened a small boutique, selling his designs. It took off. Soon their shop was getting mentions in the Sunday supplements. Famous models and pop stars shopped there. They started selling their designs by mail order. The clothes would come in an indigo-and-gold box, wrapped in tissue paper. They were declared to be fab. As were all objects of desire – human beings, cars, chairs – at the time. She had a daughter, Justine.

Susan became head librarian. She married Charles. They didn't have any children. But their house was large. Charles was an accountant. They were well off. They had two bathrooms.

Babs cut her hair in a severe style. Painted her nails outrageous colours, and spoke publicly on the importance of good design.

'There is no need for a spade or a toaster to be ugly. Everything has a right to be beautiful.'

It was, for a week or two, a famous quote. Her house was huge. She had four bathrooms.

Tilly married Gordon who drove a milk tanker. They had two children, Henry (it was to have been Enrico, after Caruso, but Gordon put his foot down), and, at last, Maria. They lived in a council house two streets from Beeches Road. Had one bathroom, that was, it seemed to Tilly, constantly occupied.

Tilly didn't go out to work any more. She cooked

for her family. She cleaned the house. She cultivated the little garden at the back with flowers – lupins, delphiniums, foxgloves – and herbs. At the front she put up window boxes and geraniums in pots. Every now and again, thieving children would steal them. Tilly would rush from the house after them. Tanking down the street in her pink slippers yelling, '*Put that bloody geranium down.*' She still had a voice. Though now she only used it to tell smaller, younger people what to do. Or, more often, what not to do. The geraniums were always abandoned in the middle of the pavement as the thieves scarpered. Tilly was a force to be reckoned with.

She still sang. But to herself. To her plants, leaning over them, trowelling in compost, whispering almost.

'It's lovely. It's from an opera by Bellini, *Norma*. I know all the words. But don't ask me what they mean. They were written by Felice Romani. And he had to do them eight times before old Vincenzo was happy with them.'

At night when the children were sleeping and Gordon was out at the pub, she'd put on Maria Callas, 'Casta Diva', and sigh.

She tried and tried to sing that song. But never could get it perfect. And she thought it deserved to be perfect. She always ran out of breath when there were words left to be sung, and had to heave air into her lungs, breaking the rhythm, to finish them.

'How does that Maria Callas do it?' she wondered. 'It's so controlled. So deep and wonderful. I mean with blues singers, they just let rip. Ray Charles, "Georgia", I love that. But you can hear how he lets go. Maria

never does. You'd think, then, there'd be no emotion.
But there is. Lots of it. I just don't know how she does
it.'

She was speaking to Mario, who was ten at the time.

He shrugged. 'Maybe it's magic.'

'Well,' said Tilly. 'It certainly is that.'

Tilly read. Every week she'd go to the library and
say to Susan, 'What have you got for me?'

Susan gave her romances, thinking they would be to
Tilly's liking. And Tilly put up with Susan's poor
judgement of her literary tastes, for a while.

But one day, she said, 'Give me something else. I'm
sick of all that love. All that weeping and longing. And
misunderstanding and breaking up and getting back
together again. Jack Kerouac, what's he like? I've
heard of him.'

She thought to say she had all his records. But then
she'd have to explain to Susan. Nah, she thought.
Some things are best kept to yourself.

Tilly read *On the Road*. Then *Big Sur*.

'What about women?' asked Tilly. 'Gimme something by a woman.'

Susan gave her Doris Lessing. Then Willa Cather.
Tilly enjoyed her. She read Antonia White and then
The Female Eunuch. Her family listened bewildered as
Tilly read and enthused, out loud. 'That's right.' And,
'Too true.' And, 'That's me. I felt that. I thought that.
You tell them, girl.' Banging her spoon on the table,
rather than supping her tomato soup.

Shyly, she joined a women's group. She thought it
would be full of educated women talking about things
she knew nothing about, using words she didn't know.

She quietly slipped into the room, which was above a pub, and apologised.

'I just thought I'd come along and see what it was like. I'm nobody much. I haven't been to university nor nothing.'

And they'd said, 'That's OK. Come in, take a seat. Everybody's welcome.'

On Thursday evenings, she'd pack her knitting into her big hessian bag and go along to say the things she'd bottled up for years. She met Mary Johnston who taught music at a private school, and took on pupils in her spare time. Knitting brought them together.

'I just love your colours,' said Mary, who was working on a blue jumper with a pattern of red apples across the front. 'Ochre and dark, dark red and black. I'd never have thought of that.'

'Just put them together in the shop,' said Tilly. 'And I thought that's a grand mix.'

Sometimes they went for a drink together, after the meeting. Mary drank pints. Tilly was shocked. She'd thought an educated woman like Mary would drink gin and tonic.

'Oh go on, try one,' said Mary. 'It's lovely. And if you only had a half you'd have to go back for another.'

So Tilly drank a pint of beer, and felt like a revolutionary.

'What do you do at these meetings?' asked Gordon one night.

'We talk,' Tilly told him.

Last week Tilly had talked. She'd told the group about Mike, about telling him she'd heard of Jack Kerouac and had all his records. And how it had been at the back of Lipton's, black and starry night, and her saying that of course she knew she couldn't get pregnant if she did it standing up. Everyone knew that.

They'd looked at her. A silence. The air in the room froze. Tilly knitted furiously. Click, click, click. It took her mind off her embarrassment. She shouldn't have told them. It was silly to tell them, they were all educated, sophisticated. She looked up.

'Well, we didn't have sex education in them days.'

Then Mary laughed. And Sandra laughed. And Irene laughed. And Amelia who was a professor of English at the university laughed. And Tilly laughed. They went to the pub and drank pints and laughed and laughed and laughed.

'I was a silly little bitch,' said Tilly, tears in her eyes. 'And I had on my mother's frock. Five pounds from C&A.'

Which suddenly seemed hilarious. Set them off laughing again. But for the first time in years she felt good about herself. She didn't tell them about wanting to be an opera star.

'And I knit, and Mary knits,' Tilly told Gordon.

'Knit!' he said. 'I thought you was wimmin libbers. Burn your bras. Equal pay for women. Knit?'

'Nobody's burnt their bra,' said Tilly. 'But we talk about equal opportunities. We talk about men dominating the workplace. And I knit. We talk about the importance of being a woman. Enjoying being a woman. Women's crafts. There's a kind of harmony.'

It was 1975. Henry was playing punk which thrummed from his bedroom above. Tilly thought it a din.

'You're not the same old Tilly,' said Gordon. 'You

never come down the pub for a rum and Coke. You used to like the singsong on a Saturday night.'

'I know,' said Tilly.

'There's someone else,' he said.

'I know,' said Tilly.

'Mandy,' he said.

'I know,' said Tilly. Then, looking at him long and hard, 'You might have picked someone who didn't live three doors down.' She breathed. Knitted. In, over, through and off. In, over, through and off. A soothing rhythm. 'You're not having the children. They're mine. And Mario is specially mine.'

The parting was amicable. Gordon moved where Tilly wouldn't see him every day – with Mandy and the baby Mandy was expecting – to Beeches Road.

When he'd gone Tilly sat her children at the kitchen table.

'That's it. We're on our own. Now, there's rules. You'll come home when I say. You'll be here for your lunches and teas. You'll eat good wholesome food. You'll not go about biting your nails with your ties askew. You'll not have folks laughing at you. If you want to do something daft or that nobody thinks you can do with your life, you'll bloody well do it.' Pointing a fierce finger at each of them in turn, she said, 'You will, none of you, turn out like me.'

'Oh Ma,' said Maria. 'Who'd want to be like you?'

Tilly gave her a mock slap on the wrist. Then a hug.

'That's my girl. And listen,' she said, glaring at them, 'we'll have no pregnancies. Pills, condoms, abstinence – that's my favourite for you all – whatever. Nobody's having a baby unless they ask me first.'

*   *   *

Fourteen years later, Babs came home. She'd divorced her husband. 'Golden Couple Split', the tabloids said.

'I'm going back to my roots,' Babs said.

She phoned Susan.

'It's been years,' she said. 'We must get together. We've got so much time we have to make up.'

They met at a wine bar. Babs wore Armani, made a point of switching off her mobile phone. Susan wore Marks and Spencer. She didn't see the point of a mobile. Who would she phone? Charles? He was at home watering the tomatoes. He'd retired last year.

'I'm dying to know,' said Babs. 'Whatever happened to Tilly?'

'Quite the feminist,' said Susan. 'Three children. Maria's a lawyer. Henry's a surveyor. And Mario, you know, the baby, he sings. Opera. He'd just done *Don Giovanni* at the Edinburgh Festival.'

She glowed with the importance of passing on this piece of gossip.

Babs put her hand to her mouth.

'My God. Who'd have thought it.'

Two days later Babs phoned Tilly.

'Guess who?' she said.

'I'm crap at guessing,' said Tilly.

'It's me. Babs. Remember? Babs.'

'No kidding,' said Tilly. 'How are you?'

They met at the same wine bar. Tilly wore Mario's cast-off jeans, baseball boots and a red roll-neck sweater. Babs said she looked wonderful, and meant it.

'You used to want to be an opera star,' said Babs.

'Still do,' said Tilly. 'What do you want to be when you grow up?'

Babs said she'd done a lot of things, but still had no idea what she wanted to do when she grew up.

'I think if there's something you really want to do, you should go out and do it.'

The words hung in Tilly's head for a fortnight before she phoned Mary. The women's group no longer met. But she and Mary kept in touch.

'Do me a favour,' said Tilly. 'Teach me to sing. Properly sing.'

And Mary said, 'Really. I'd love to.'

When Tilly first sang for Mary, in the small room where she still taught reluctant children to play the piano, Mary gasped. She looked at Tilly in amazement.

'My God, Tilly. You have a voice.'

For months Tilly went to Mary's room twice a week. She sat alongside petulant children who clutched their new music cases and swung their dangling legs that were too short to reach the floor. She listened to their slow painful scales dinning through Mary's house, waiting her turn. Tilly sang scales. She breathed. She learnt to sing from lower down, Mary poking her abdomen.

'Not the throat, Tilly. And breathe, Tilly, breathe.'

It was a small end-of-term recital. All the children's parents and grandparents were there, and Babs and Susan. Children thumped through Mozart, and Joplin rags and Debussy. Tilly sang. She was wrought with nerves.

'I can't do this, Mary. I can't. It's all people under seventeen. And me. I'm ancient. I don't belong here.'

'It's an end-of-term recital for *all* my pupils. I want people to hear you. You have an amazing voice.'

Shaking with nerves, throat dry, Tilly walked across the stage. Mary played the piano.

Ca . . . aaa . . . sta Di . . . iii . . . va.

Tilly's voice resounded across the room. She breathed. The abdomen, she thought. Not the throat. She clenched her fists, nails biting into her palms. She remembered how they'd laughed at Tilly the opera star. Mike, behind Lipton's, and his lies. And the nights lying in her room, sweating with fear. Loneliness. Nobody to talk to. Miss Hayward's words, '. . . this will have put paid to your plans . . .' She remembered Gordon, 'There's someone else.' She thought about her children, Henry the surveyor, so gentle now. And with a wife of his own, a baby girl, though he hadn't asked her permission first. Lovely Maria the lawyer, 'Who'd want to be like you, Ma?' And Mario, who sang. Like she'd wanted to do.

And when she'd finished, the applause was small, polite. Except for Babs and Susan, who stamped and cheered. Tilly bowed, and smiled the small weak smile of someone who knew they'd failed.

'I was crap,' she said to Babs and Susan afterwards. 'Too much emotion. Wrong emotion.'

They politely shook their heads.

'It was lovely,' they said. And didn't look her in the eye.

They had Chardonnay. Tilly was drinking a pint.

'Liars,' she said. 'Stuck-up, bungalow-brought-up liars.'

Two days later they drove in Babs's Jaguar to Southport for the day.

'It'll be fun,' said Babs. 'Us three again. Like the old days.'

They sang in the car, favourite songs from distant times, 'Catch a Falling Star', 'Unforgettable', 'It Had To Be You.' Then launched into songs from different times, 'Hey Jude', 'Satisfaction'. They shopped. They wore silly hats. Ate ice-cream and hot dogs. And laughed. They rolled up their trouser legs, paddled. Chill water running over their feet. Sun on their faces. They visited past times, swapped memories.

And said, 'Here's us. After all those years. My God, where did the time go? Look at us, we're three old ladies.'

Seven in the evening. That moment when tourists are eating, locals are preparing for their evening, they walked the empty pier. The sun sank, uncomplaining, down below the horizon. The sky turned pale, waiting for dark. A single seagull flew. Home, Tilly thought.

And she sang. She sang to the sea. She sang in praise of a fabulous day. When there was nobody but her old friends to hear. 'Casta Diva'. Like Callas had done, all those years ago in that sweaty classroom with children sighing, wriggling, whispering, giggling. And Tilly had been in heaven.

Her voice soared, crystalline. Note-perfect through the still. She did not think about her past. She didn't think about anything. She just opened her heart, and out it came. Like magic.

And when she'd done, an old couple sitting on a bench nearby clapped their hearts out.

'That was grand. You've made our day.'

Tilly turned to Babs and Susan who were standing nearby. 'I'd kill for a curry.'

'My God,' said Babs. 'You really can do it.'

'I know,' said Tilly. 'I can do it when I'm not

thinking about it. That's when the magic happens. When you let go and just let it. You have to believe.'

'But,' said Babs, 'it's not too late for you. All sorts of people are late-starters. You could . . .'

'What do you mean, I could,' said Tilly. 'I just did.' She looked at them. 'That was it. I just did it. I believed. Come on. Time for a curry. Last to Ally's Tandoori pays.'

And she took off up the pier, running, hair flying out, into the evening.

BEN OKRI

The Sign

To unveil the pentagram
Without speaking the magic
Upon which the folly of man
Rests, is to transform the tragic

And make of it the gold of Time.
The star of Merlin, the seal
Of Solomon; symbols rhyme
With dreams that are real.

Belief rests on what we know.
What we know rests
On that which we sow.
Truth endures all tests.

And so speak the star
And the circle that contains all.
Symbols are sent from afar.
We shan't fall further than our fall.

A NOTE ON THE CONTRIBUTORS

Andrea Ashworth's highly acclaimed memoir *Once in a House on Fire* is being made into a feature film. Formerly a Junior Research Fellow in English Literature at Jesus College, Oxford, Andrea is currently living in the USA, where she is at work on her first novel, set in New York City.

Kate Atkinson was born in York and now lives in Edinburgh. Her first novel *Behind the Scenes at the Museum* won the Whitbread First Novel Award, and was then chosen as the overall 1995 Whitbread Book of the Year. The paperback edition of her most recent novel, *Emotionally Weird*, was published in March 2001.

Celia Brayfield's last novel, *Heartswap*, has been optioned by Tom Cruise's production company for a film to star Nicole Kidman. Her next, *Mr Fabulous and Friends*, about five menopausal men in a rock band, is due from Little, Brown in January 2003. A single parent with one daughter, she is also a trustee of the National Council for One Parent Families. Celia thinks that a feminist without humour is like a bicycle without a fish.

Christopher Brookmyre was born in Glasgow in 1968, and has worked as a journalist in London, Los Angeles and Edinburgh. His novels include *Quite Ugly One Morning*, which won the First Blood Award for the best debut crime novel, *Boiling a Frog*, which won the 2000 Sherlock Award for Best Comic Detective, *One Fine Day in the Middle of the Night* and, most recently, *A Big Boy Did It and Ran Away*.

Lewis Davies was born in 1968 in Penrhiwtyn and now lives in Cardiff. Before becoming a full-time writer he worked for three years on a social programme to integrate the mentally handicapped into the community. He was the winner of the Rhys Davies Award for his short story 'Mr Roopratna's Chocolate'. His travel book *Freeways* was the winner of the John Morgan Writing Award in 1995.

Isla Dewar lives in Crail, a coastal village an hour's drive north of St Andrews. Her novels include *Keeping Up with Magda, Women Talking Dirty, Giving Up on Ordinary* and *It Could Happen to You*.

Emma Donoghue was born in Dublin in 1969 and now lives in Canada. She has been published as a literary historian and also writes drama for stage and for radio but is best known for her fiction, which includes *Stirfry, Hood, Kissing the Witch* and *Slammerkin*. Her latest book, *The Woman Who Gave Birth to Rabbits*, is a collection of historical short stories.

Maeve Haran is the author of *Having It All, Scenes from the Sex War, It Takes Two, A Family Affair, All That She Wants, Soft Touch, The Farmer Wants a*

Wife and *Baby Come Back*. A former TV producer, she now writes full-time and contributes to *The Times*, the *Daily Mail*, and various magazines. She is married with three children.

Joanne Harris was born in Yorkshire, of a French mother and an English father. She was a teacher of modern languages in a boys' grammar school for twelve years before becoming a full-time writer, and is the author of five novels, including *Chocolat, Blackberry Wine* and most recently *Five Quarters of the Orange*. She is married and still lives in Yorkshire with her husband and young daughter.

Jackie Kay was born and raised in Scotland. She is the author of one novel, *Trumpet*, and several collections of poetry including *Other Lovers* (which won a Somerset Maugham Award) and *Adoption Papers*. She lives in England.

John O'Farrell is the author of *The Best a Man Can Get, Global Village Idiot*, and the bestselling *Things Can Only Get Better: Eighteen Miserable Years in the Life of a Labour Supporter*. He has contributed to *Spitting Image* and *Have I Got News for You*, is a regular guest on Radio 4 and writes a weekly column for the *Guardian*. He lives in Clapham with his wife and two children.

Ben Okri was born in 1959 in Lagos, Nigeria. By the age of eighteen, he had completed his first novel, *Flowers and Shadows*, and moved to England where he still lives. He has won several prestigious awards, including the 1987 Commonwealth Writers Prize for Africa, and the 1991 Booker Prize for his acclaimed novel *The Famished Road*.

Michèle Roberts is the author of eleven novels, including *Fair Exchange* and *Daughters of the House*, which won the W.H. Smith Literary Award and was shortlisted for the Booker Prize. Half English and half French, she divides her time between London and Mayenne, France.

Meera Syal is a performer-writer, born in Wolverhampton after her parents emigrated from New Delhi. She studied English and drama at Manchester University. Her writing credits include the movie *Bhaji on the Beach* and the award-winning BBC series *Goodness Gracious Me* in which she also appeared. Her first novel, *Anita and Me*, won the Betty Trask award, was shortlisted for the *Guardian* Fiction prize, and will be a major motion picture next year. Her second novel, *Life Isn't All Ha Ha Hee Hee*, is being adapted for BBC2. She is currently writing the book of Andrew Lloyd Webber's new musical, *Bombay Dreams*, opening in June 2002.

Sue Townsend became a household name after *The Secret Diary of Adrian Mole* sold millions of copies around the world. In 1991 she wrote the bestseller *The Queen and I*, which has since been adapted for the stage. Her other ficton includes *Rebuilding Coventry* and *Ghost Children*.

Arabella Weir is a comedy writer and performer who appears regularly on television, most famously in *The*

Fast Show. She has written three novels, *Onwards and Upwards*, the bestselling *Does My Bum Look Big in This?* and *Stupid Cupid* to be published in spring 2002.

Fay Weldon was born in England and brought up in New Zealand. She studied at St Andrews University where she received her Master's degree in economics and psychology. She is the author of *The Bulgari Connection, Rhode Island Blues, Wicked Women, Splitting,* and *The Life and Loves of a She-Devil*, among many other novels, plays, and two books of non-fiction. Her autobiography is due for publication in May 2002.

A NOTE ON THE EDITORS

Sarah Brown is a Consultant at Brunswick Arts, a public relations company specialising in arts and cultural projects within the Brunswick Group. She also runs a non-profit venture, PiggyBankKids, which organises a range of voluntary projects for charities to support their fundraising efforts. She is married to Gordon Brown, Labour Member of Parliament for Dunfermline East and Chancellor of the Exchequer. They live in Fife and London. This is her first publishing venture.

Gil McNeil is the author of the bestselling *The Only Boy for Me* and is currently working on her second novel. Gil is a Consultant at Brunswick Arts, and works with Sarah Brown on PiggyBankKids projects. She lives in Kent with her son.

THE NATIONAL COUNCIL
FOR ONE PARENT FAMILIES

Today everybody knows someone who's a lone parent – a son or daughter, a sister, a best friend. With one quarter of all Britain's families now headed by a parent bringing up children alone (that's 1.7 million families, including around 3 million children), it's far from surprising. But the lone parents we all know are different from the usual stereotype – which typically portrays lone parents as irresponsible teenagers, who got pregnant to get their own flat, have several kids by different fathers and have no intention of finding a stable relationship.

The reality is rather different. Most lone parents are women – older women: the average age is thirty-five. Most have been married, and the majority of those who were not lived with the father of their children. On average they have smaller families than do parents in couples, and most never set out to bring children up alone. And as for teenage parents, who only make up 3 per cent of all lone parents in Britain, we know that their needs, and the needs of their children are often of the most acute kind, and yet their ambitions and determination to build a good life are strong. We believe that in a civilised culture, the response to these young families should be to provide them with the support they need to succeed, rather than pointlessly moralising after the event.

Every lone parent has a different personal history, but they do share one thing – the experience of public prejudice and of being portrayed as 'just a burden on the state'.

Lone parents do not choose to be poor, but they are the poorest group in society. Nearly half of all poor children live in one parent families. 50 per cent of one parent families live on gross incomes of less than £150 per week compared to just 4 per cent of married couples. This poverty means that many one parent families cannot afford to eat healthily. Many experience severe hardship, poor housing, health problems and debt.

The National Council for One Parent Families – a registered charity first established in 1918 (lone parenthood is far from being just a modern phenomenon) – exists to help tackle this poverty and disadvantage. Through our campaigning and lobbying work, our provision of advice and information services, including our national Freephone helpline, which takes over 16,000 calls a year, and through our development of new initiatives to help lone parents build a better future for themselves and for their children, we work to improve the prospects of what are all too often the most disadvantaged and excluded families. Through our high-profile campaigning work, we aim to tell the public and the politicians about what it really means to bring up children alone in Britain today, and to challenge the hurtful and unfair assumptions which are all too often made about lone parents.

But all this costs money! And we could help so many more lone parents – and their children – if we had greater resources to do so. Your generosity can help us to help more lone parents, who, like every parent, want the best possible life for their children.

Your support in buying this book is hugely appreciated. If you would like to know more about our work, or to support us further, or if you know a lone parent who might need our help, then we would like to hear from you. And thank you, for helping us to achieve our goal – to give every child, whatever their family circumstances, a fair start in life.

Contact the National Council for One Parent Families on freephone 0800 018 5026,
Internet:*www.oneparentfamilies.org.uk*
email: *info@oneparentfamilies.org.uk*

National Council for One Parent Families
255 Kentish Town Road
London NW5 2LX

The National Council for One Parent Families is a registered charity no. 230750 and a company limited by guarantee, registered in London no. 402748.

Kate Green, Director, National Council for One Parent Families